A NOVEL OF THE KRAKEN MC

CHARITY FOR NOTHING

The Virtues BOOK III

AJ Downey

Second Circle Press

Published 2016 by Second Circle Press
Book design by Lia Rees at Free Your Words
(www.freeyourwords.com)
Cover art and Virtues logo by Cover Your Dreams
(www.coveryourdreams.net)

Text copyright © 2016 AJ Downey

This is a work of fiction. Names, characters, businesses, places, events and incidents are either the products of the author's imagination or used in a fictitious manner. Any resemblance to actual persons, living or dead, or actual events is purely coincidental.

All Rights Reserved

ISBN: 978-1533423597

Author's Note

Being a spin-off, the events of this trilogy take place *after* the events of Damaged & Dangerous, The Sacred Hearts MC Book VI. If you have not read the SHMC series, references and events that are talked about in this book may not make sense to you. I highly suggest reading the SHMC series first, followed by Cutter's Hope, the first book in this trilogy.

Dedication

To all the paramedics who put in long hours to soothe our pain while empathizing and feeling it right along with us. You guys are over worked, under paid, and just frickin' amazing.

THE VIRTUES BOOKS IN ORDER

1. Cutter's Hope

2. Marlin's Faith

3. *Charity for Nothing*

Contents

Chapter 1	*1*
Chapter 2	*10*
Chapter 3	*12*
Chapter 4	*17*
Chapter 5	*21*
Chapter 6	*31*
Chapter 7	*40*
Chapter 8	*44*
Chapter 9	*49*
Chapter 10	*58*
Chapter 11	*62*
Chapter 12	*69*
Chapter 13	*72*
Chapter 14	*76*
Chapter 15	*80*
Chapter 16	*87*
Chapter 17	*91*
Chapter 18	*106*
Chapter 19	*111*
Chapter 20	*119*
Chapter 21	*123*
Chapter 22	*128*

Chapter 23	*132*
Chapter 24	*136*
Chapter 25	*143*
Chapter 26	*150*
Chapter 27	*153*
Chapter 28	*159*
Chapter 29	*166*
Chapter 30	*178*
Chapter 31	*187*
Chapter 32	*196*
Chapter 33	*200*
Chapter 34	*203*
Chapter 35	*210*
Chapter 36	*214*
Chapter 37	*218*
Chapter 38	*225*
Chapter 39	*232*
Chapter 40	*239*
Chapter 41	*242*
Chapter 42	*246*
Chapter 43	*250*
Chapter 44	*254*
Chapter 45	*261*
Epilogue	*265*
About the Author	

CHAPTER 1
Charity

It was hot, the sun beating down, and a wonderful change from the snowmageddon I'd just survived through up north. We were passing spring and heading into summer back up north where my university was located, but when I'd left, there were still patches of snow on the ground up under trees, combined with piles of dirty, melting snow in other places. Mother Earth was one pissed *off* mother and she was letting us know all about it, but according to most politicians, global warming wasn't a thing; go figure.

I was driving my white Jeep Wrangler, rag top rolled and strapped down, little trailer with all my worldly possessions bouncing along behind me, looking for this marina Hope had told me to find. She said I could park there and that they'd be right next to it on the beach.

Somehow, I expected this town to be bigger. I mean it was sunny Florida, and the rest of the state, from what I'd seen driving through, was as over developed as hell. Somehow, though, they'd missed this town. That or the people here still managed to hold their own somehow. I don't think there was a single building over three stories tall; it was great.

The main drag was a two way boulevard that ran along the water. It had decorative median strips down the center of it with old fashioned looking iron lamp posts. Strong, which I would guess you would need with hurricanes and the like. Speaking of which, there was supposed to be one building way off the coast, but a lot of these people were moving around unconcerned. I guess that was how things rolled around here.

Like so many things, once you got used to it, you just rolled with it… became complacent… like I had with the thought of never seeing Faith again. I felt a stab of some serious guilt over the fact that on the inside, I'd given up on my sister. Guilt that was seriously compounded by the fact that I hadn't skipped out on finishing up my degree and gotten my ass down here much sooner. Hope would have killed me, but I think what hurt more was Faith hadn't *wanted* me to come see her... at least not right away.

It wasn't like I didn't know what she was going through. As a part of my schooling, I'd been in an advanced work study program. I'd gotten my advanced nursing degree with a specialization in emergency medicine. That'd meant spending some time in the university hospital's emergency department over the last year. Technically it was post graduate work, but I'd still needed it to earn my degree, which sat in a glass frame, carefully bubble wrapped and just behind the locked doors of the trailer. It was going to be one of the first things to be unloaded so that I could celebrate my accomplishments with my sisters. I was so fucking excited to see them, I was going to die.

"*Your destination is on your left,*" blared out of my speakers, over the music; some Ashes & Embers. Faith had said they were her new favorite, so I'd downloaded everything and listened to them on the way down. It didn't hurt that they were all long haired, tattooed, and seriously built hot guys that were like *hello!* Instant lust. The lead singer sang oh-so-pretty, too.

"*Your destination is on your left. Arrived, 3221, Beachfront Boulevard, Fort Royal, Florida. Arrived!*"

"Thank you! I get it, you can totally shut up now." I cried at the GPS and rolled to a stop to let some girls in bikinis and boys in their board shorts cross the street in front of me. I hit my signal and waited with some serious impatience, bouncing in my seat, ready to scream at them to get their ass across already. I wanted to see my sisters damn it! I'd been good, I'd gotten through school, did everything I needed to do to set myself up for success and have prospects at a real fuckin' job when I got down here and now I just wanted to see my sisters, be a family, and set up shop.

It was time to have a life, a *real one*, again. A life that involved my family, helping people, and maybe meeting a guy or two. I was pretty sure I had a fling or two left in me, and according to Hope these bikers she and Faith were hooked up with were *hooooooot*. I'd told them to save one for me and Hope had laughed and had given me the 4-1-1 that if I were going to do the whole fling thing, that I'd want to stick with some of the beach body tourist boys. The men of The Kraken supposedly liked to play for keeps.

I whipped the Jeep into a left turn across the lane coming in my direction once it was clear of both pedestrians and traffic, and felt excitement bubble up in my chest. Hope had told me to park in one of the spots reserved for trucks and their boat trailers and to come down to the beach on the other side of the boat ramp. I pulled forward into one of the double long spots next to a big Ford pickup and killed the engine. A couple of decent looking, rugged guys were strapping a speed boat onto a trailer and they obviously checked me out as I refreshed my lip gloss in my rearview mirror.

I grabbed my purse and other items I didn't want stolen and locked them in the back of the trailer, leaving my Jeep empty. Not like I had anything to stop anyone with the hard top upside down in the back of the trailer with all my boxes of shit piled in it. Taking the time to roll the rag top back up wasn't going to really be any kind of deterrent against a box knife or anyone smart enough to operate some snaps and a zipper. I'd been equal parts prepared with weather reports and graced with good luck for the drive down. I'd had to keep the rag top on to cut the wind when I'd first started out, but I didn't regret my decision to leave the top off at the first chance I got for the rest of the trip. It was gorgeous down here, and I was a west coast California sun worshiping girl at the end of any day that ends in 'Y'. With the palm trees and sun, this almost felt like home... the difference? Holy god, the humidity!

I locked up the trailer, slung my beach bag over my shoulder, checked my hair one last time in my passenger side mirror before turning it and the driver's one in to keep them from getting busted off, and with nothing possibly left to do to stall from my sudden case of nerves, I headed for the beach. I walked across the blacktop, flip flops flapping, my heart in my throat, scared of what I might find in Faith. She was different, distant, and I was scared the sister that I remembered wasn't ever going to be the same again.

My steps slowed and I stood in the parking lot for a minute, the slight breeze ghosting over my skin, hot still, and I almost cried. It'd hurt so much that they'd wanted me to stay up north through all of it. That I wasn't wanted to come down and help, that it'd taken this long for me to get here, but at the same time I knew it was because they loved me and wanted me to finish school, which I'd done with full and the highest honors, because I was an overachiever and that's just how I rolled.

Once I set my mind to something, I did it and damn the consequences for the most part. It had gotten me in very little trouble, surprisingly enough, but then again, I was pretty good about making all the right choices. I'd learned from my mother's mistakes, and from my sister Hope's achievements. I'd never quite understood why my sister Faith felt the need to test Hope on everything, but then I realized, when it came to my closest sister, her heart beat wild and free, that she'd been at an honest loss as to what to do with herself and instead of helping… we just made it worse; me included by enabling her inertia.

I stopped to take one last minute to myself to get my shit together, and I made up my mind then and there, that I couldn't change the past, none of us could, so I might as well make a future that all three of us could be happy in. If that meant burying my butt-hurt over being left out of the gnarly shit, then that's what I would do. Resentment couldn't live here. I liked my heart light, wild, and as free as the ribcage it resided in would allow.

"Charity, right?"

I startled out of my reverie and looked to my right and *right into* a wall of muscular chest that was framed *very* nicely in black leather to either side. I let my eyes linger for a moment as I roamed the hills and valleys left by an absolutely superbly kept physique before my gaze slipped up over a shadowed jaw and came to rest on a pair of beautiful, deep gray eyes.

"Yeah, how did you know…" I left it open, voice dying off in hopes this handsome stranger would give me his name.

"Nothing."

"Nothing?" I asked confused and he smiled.

"My name, it's Nothing, and you look like Faith. Like a lot like Faith." That made me smile, a weight lifting off my chest just a bit. I don't know why I thought she'd look different. Probably because time and experience could change people irreparably and Faith had had both in abundance the last two years.

"Don't suppose you know where they are, do you?" I asked and he smiled. It looked really good on him, if a touch tragic; the ghost of something indefinable there.

"Yeah, they're this way," he held out an arm, gallantly, a really old fashioned gesture by today's standards and I smiled, taking it.

"Thank you, Nothing."

"Don't mention it."

I put my body in motion alongside Nothing's sleek, muscular, and taller frame. He looked to be in his early thirties, so not at all out of my price range; I liked them around ten years older.

Pretty quickly, my line of thought about the delicious number walking me towards my sisters vanished. My steps quickened and he let me go, the patter of my thongs on the asphalt of the parking lot giving way and taking me down the cement steps to the sand. I hadn't been able to keep myself from rushing forward at the rich, familiar laughter of my oldest sister. I stopped a few steps into the soft white sand, Nothing catching up and drawing even with me.

Hope was in the air, Cutter, her boyfriend, had her around the waist and they appeared to be play fighting. I grinned and thought to myself, *typical Hope*. Except in all the time I'd known her around boyfriends or even just occasional fuck buddies, I'd never seen her smile like this, nor had I ever seen them treat her like this guy did; like she wasn't dangerous to him. Dating Hope was like petting a pet panther in your lap. One minute it's a cute cuddly kitty, the next it was digging claws in and nomming your face off.

I stood back and scanned the beach for that familiar light blonde hair so like my own and I found it cuddled in the arms of a well-built man with shoulder length blond hair that was several shades darker than my sister's. He held Faith like she were a delicate thing, and she was. She smiled, but there was a tightness around her eyes and she was still thinner than I'd ever remembered her being. She looked like me in the body now, but from what Hope had sent me picture wise, she looked loads better than when she was at her worst. Her bones no longer stuck out so prominent against her skin and her cheeks had a healthy glow to them. Her hair still needed a trim, desperately, but I'd always been the one to do the homemade haircuts, at least after I'd turned sixteen.

I wondered briefly if Faith were waiting for me to do it for her and the thought instantly made me smile.

"Oh! Oh, holy shit! Put me down. Put me down now!" I turned my head just as Hope buried her elbow into her boyfriend's solar plexus. He 'oofed' and dropped my sister to her feet, doubling over grinning while also grimacing, which made me kind of laugh outright as my oldest sister barreled full tilt across the sand. I dropped my bag next to me and opened up my arms laughing and pretty soon, it was all three of us standing there hugging, laughing, and crying like idiots giving zero fucks about the spectacle we were making of ourselves.

"Oh my god, Blossom, we missed you!" Hope cried and sniffed, but Faith's tears had become something damn near inconsolable, and so had mine. We clung to each other, Hope getting her shit together first, as always, and looking on as Faith and I simply refused to let the other go.

"I missed you so much!" I cried brokenly.

"I missed you, too!"

"I love you," Faith cried and I answered with what we'd always said.

"I love you more!"

"Yeah, well I love you both most of all," Hope warbled before bursting into fresh tears and just like that... we were all home because home for a bunch of rag tag vagabonds like us wasn't a place. It never really had been moving up and down the California coast with our hippy dippy mother. No; home was the three of us, our mother's three virtues, all in the same place at the same time. It always had been and it always would be. Period.

"Okay, that's enough, that's enough! Jesus, you'd like to think y'all were at a funeral the way you're all carrying on."

"Shut it, Pyro." Hope grumbled against my neck.

I gave the finger in the general direction the voice had come from to a track of masculine laughter.

"Shit, is she like a mini-Hope?" Someone asked.

"All of the fearless sass you can handle," Faith said backing up and wiping tears off her face.

"Just a little less likely to cave your nuts in, she's got more patience than I do," Hope said, backing off and doing the same. I put my hands to my cheeks which were hot and tight from the salt of my tears and did my best to wipe them away.

"Well it's a party now!" Cutter crowed.

"It wasn't before?" a blonde tattooed woman asked.

"Not until the guest of honor arrived," he stated and threw open his arms at me. I laughed and gave him a hug, even though it felt awkward and a little weird. I wasn't used to strangers to me treating me so casually, or like I was family. That's exactly what these guys did though. Each one greeting me with an enthusiastic hug and a 'welcome home' or 'welcome to Ft. Royal.' There was a lot of laughing and greetings and *a lot* of really weird names that made me totally curious. Not nearly as curious as I was about Nothing though.

He stood on the fringe of the happy reunion, a sad little ghost of a smile on, what I found to be, some seriously sensual lips. It was like he set himself apart, but he was still one of them, and I found the dichotomy fascinating. It wasn't something I could study or explore, because all too quickly, my attention was ripped away, to greet yet more arrivals clad in the black leather vests with dirty but colorful patches on them.

Everyone was keen to stay on the beach, despite the leaden clouds on the horizon, stating they would have plenty of time to move the party to someplace they called The Plank before the rains reached us.

"Prospect!" Cutter called and a youngish looking man, maybe early to mid-twenties, perked up like a gopher out of a hole.

"Yes, Captain?"

"Get our guest's keys from her, would you? Take her Jeep and trailer to the house and unload it, then get your ass back here for food and beer aplenty on me," he ordered.

"Do what?" I asked.

Hope looked on bemused, "It's okay, Charity; give Trike your keys."

I handed them over to the eager young man and made a bit of a face for his benefit, "I'm sorry you have to do this," I uttered and he flashed a grin.

"I don't *have* to, I *want* to. It's all part of things and my pleasure serving a pretty girl like you."

"Aww," I laughed lightly and blushed, handing the keys over, "Thank you!" He nodded once, and trotted off in the direction of the parking lot. I noticed the big colorful patch in the center of his vest was missing and filed it away for later. I didn't know how any of this club stuff worked and usually the conversations with my sisters on the phone had been brief, either because of things on their end, or because of things on mine. Classes and studying had eaten my life whole, especially with taking the absolute maximum of classes allowable at any given time in order to graduate sooner.

I'd wanted to get down here and now here I was, and I was just so mentally and emotionally exhausted after such a harsh whirlwind of activity to get here, I didn't know where to start.

That was okay, apparently, according to the men and women of The Kraken, I would start by being introduced to every last one of them. A cold drink was shoved into one hand and pretty quickly, maybe midway through the introductions, a plate of food was shoved into the other. I sat down around a cold bonfire pit in the sand, back against a fallen piece of driftwood with Hope on one side and Faith on the other. Their men ranged out on the other side of their women. I listened to stories of my sisters and how they'd found their way to Ft. Royal.

Things grew a bit somber and quiet when they reached the part about finding and rescuing Faith, and I grew more than a little emotional. I looked to my older sister who looked back at me. We were very nearly a mirror of one another except for our eyes. Hers were a brilliant green-blue like the shallow waters just down the beach. Mine were just plain blue, and wet with tears as my throat closed on anything I could possibly say. Frustrating, that. All I had wanted was to drop everything and come down here and say so much and now, now I was here and couldn't say anything at all. What was there to say? Once again, when things had gone pear shaped, I had been coddled and relegated to the baby's table.

Except I wasn't a baby anymore. I was a twenty-four year old woman with world travel experience and a four year nursing degree under my belt. I looked over at Hope and Faith in turn and had to sigh inwardly. There were some things that would never change when it came to my little family of three… my being 'the baby' was likely one of those, no matter how hard I resisted the idiocy of it.

CHAPTER 2
Nothing

Only one time before had it happened; that feeling like I'd been punched in the gut, just from looking into a woman's eyes. The first time it'd been my wife Corrine's eyes. A strange shade of lavender as she'd beseeched me not to let her die. I scrubbed my face with my hands as I tried to banish the painful image of our first meeting out of my head before images of our last barged their way in.

Charity's eyes weren't lavender like Corrine's had been, so it wasn't that. I don't know what it was about them, other than being a startling, pale, shade of blue. Like shadows on ice, crisp and refreshing under the heat of the baking Florida sun. I'd led her to her sisters, but as soon as I was able to, I put a little distance between us, but my gaze hadn't exactly been sidelined from watching her.

Lightning dropped down next to me and knocked his shoulder into mine. "What 'cha looking at?" he asked and I tore my gaze away from Faith-lite.

"Not a damn thing," I grated.

"Bullshit," he said grinning, "She's single, according to Hope. You finally going to give it up and try something new?"

"Hadn't planned on it and still don't; I'm married."

"*Were* married," Radar said, dropping his ass into the sand on my other side. "At some point, man, you gotta give up carrying the torch for Corrine. She's gone, and it's been something like *three years*. You can't punish yourself for somethin' you didn't do for forever."

"What do you fuckin' know about it?" I demanded, and shoved some food in my face, chewing automatically.

"I know Corrine'd be pissed lookin' at you livin' like this, day in and day out. Hell, you aren't even living, you're just down here grinding it out. That ain't no way to be, my brother. That ain't no way to be."

"What would you fuckin' know about it?" I demanded again, and it sounded petulant, Like something Katy would have said which just drove the knife that much deeper.

"You ain't the only one to have dealt with loss, Nothing. Fuck you for suggesting otherwise." Radar said coldly and I wanted to punch myself in the face. He wasn't wrong.

"Sorry, man."

He got to his feet with his beer and his plate, "Get over yourself," he shot back over his shoulder and moved off to a different small grouping of us. I hung my head and gripped the back of my neck.

"Two points," Lightning said coolly.

"Yeah, batting a thousand," I groused.

"That's on you, Man," he said getting to his feet.

I swore softly under my breath... *and then there was one.* Just me, all alone, which is pretty much all I fucking deserved in this life.

I rolled my neck and shoulders and finished my food and beer, figuring I could go help Trike with the girl's stuff. It'd give me something productive to do without having to be around the rest of the guys in my fouled mood. They didn't deserve it, and I wasn't entirely sure I could rein it in. So what if I had the ulterior motive of digging into what kind of person she was?

Charity had knocked me off balance with one look and that scared me some. No one had ever been able to do that before. No one except Corrine, and I didn't want to go down that road again. I really didn't. It ended on a lonely stretch of highway over near the glades. It ended with a lot of screaming, broken glass and loads of pain.

It ended with two dead bodies and left me behind with no way to pick up the pieces or to stitch the wound left by my guilt.

It left me what I was.

Nothing.

CHAPTER 3

Charity

The party moved down to a little bar in the leading edge of town called, not surprisingly, The Plank. I had to laugh at the sign above the door; it read *The Plank* in burnt in big block letters and below that, *it's beachy, it's manly, it's made of hard wood,* in a gilded script.

"Who came up with *that*?" I'd asked and someone had launched into the story of Mac, the bar's previous owner and the club's old president.

We, and by 'we' I meant Faith and I, had been driven there in an old, beat up, green Subaru wagon full of paint in the back. Marlin had done the driving and it'd been nice to watch him hold my sister's hand as he'd taken the two or three turns, refusing to let go, compensating for his lack of grip by using his knee to hold the wheel while he repositioned his one hand to follow through. He really loved her, and it showed.

The bar on the outside was unassuming, even nice to look at, fitting with the rest of the town with its white clapboard sides and royal blue trim. It didn't have *windows* in the traditional sense, but rather old, reclaimed portholes edged in bronze, and really rather huge, were set into the building's side. The glass was thick and discolored with age, and one of them was cracked, appearing to have taken a B.B... or bullet.

Neon beer signs glowed from within one or two of them and when we went through the door into the loud, dimly but warmly lit interior, it was to the rain just beginning to patter down outside. Marlin led us into the back, past a front room filled with tables and chairs, and off to one side, pool tables and dart boards. The alcove he led us back through opened up into a smaller room, a raised dais directly across from the opening against the back wall, similarly set with portholes to the outside.

On the raised little stage was an electric chair, and on the electric chair, Cutter held court, my sister Hope in his lap. I blinked at the near absurdity of it all. The portholes to either side of the chair lit up blue, the thunder crashing in time with the lightning and I jumped. Laughter ensued at my expense and I couldn't help but laugh nervously in turn.

Marlin took a seat at a four person table to the right of Cutter's oddball throne, and tugged Faith, similarly, into his lap. He curved his arms protectively around her and she smiled, resting her forehead against Marlin's, murmuring something only he was likely to hear over the jukebox.

I sank into the seat beside Marlin's where I could see everything going on, and it wasn't lost on me that every male in this back part of the bar and *at* the bar were in Kraken colors. The prospect from earlier jogged out from behind the bar and up to me, asking "What'll you have?" with a warm smile. I smiled back and bit my bottom lip.

"Jack and Coke?" I asked.

"Seriously?" he sounded surprised. I nodded and he smiled even bigger, "Coming right up!"

Radar dropped into the seat across from mine and asked, "What'd you order?"

"A Jack & Coke."

"Nice!" The prospect came jogging over and Radar held up a hand, "Cough it up buddy."

"Ahhh!" He made a mock noise of being severely put out, but his smile never faltered. He reached into his back pocket and slapped some money into Radar's palm before returning to the bar.

"You guys bet on what I'd be drinking?" I asked amused.

"Yep. Trike there thought you'd go for something girly, I said, Nah. You're a girl that likes the basics." He grinned at me and wrinkled his nose and I had to laugh.

"Think you have me all figured out, huh?"

His mouth downturned in that way that said he wasn't trying to be impressive even though he was trying to be impressive and I fought down the urge to laugh at him. He gave a one shouldered shrug and didn't commit to an answer one way or the other, I raised my eyebrows and took a sip of my drink which was good and stiff. I wasn't going to let him off the hook that easy.

"More or less," he said breaking into an even broader grin.

"Uh huh," I said dubiously. "Coffee or tea?"

"Are you kidding? You're just coming out of grad school, coffee."

"That was an easy one," I leaned back in my seat and tried again. "Fine, okay, dog or cat?"

"Cat."

"Reasoning?"

"Self-sufficient creatures, a lot like you!" Hope called and I frowned at her.

"You stay out of this!"

There was laughter and a shadow fell over me, a droplet of water splashing onto my arm, I whipped around and looked up. Nothing stood by my seat and held out the keys to my Jeep to me.

"I put the soft top on, it's out front," he said and I blinked.

"Then how'd you get so wet?"

"Walking to the door," he said with a shrug and sniffed. Water streamed down his face, and plastered his hair to his forehead and cheeks.

I took the keys and said, "Thank you, is it really coming down out there, or what?"

"Or what," he said and with a shrug, turned and walked away. I stared at his back and felt myself frown.

"What's his deal?" I asked the empty air and no one in particular.

Radar answered me, "That fucking guy," he said shaking his head, "Doesn't know when to quit."

"Quit what?"

"Grieving," Marlin said simply, but before I could ask, a new song hit the jukebox, pulse pounding and *loud*. Radar laughed, jammed for a second on an imaginary air guitar, bounded to his feet and dragged me up by the hand to the little patch of cement floor left bare for dancing. I laughed and obliged him; he seemed nice enough for all that he wasn't my type in the looks department, being around even with my height and rather compact. I preferred my men taller than me but that was neither here nor there when it came to the men of the club. I'd taken Hope's warning to heart that these guys liked to play for keeps and to get my kicks somewhere else… but honestly, my mind kept drifting back Nothing's way.

Something about him was nagging at every instinct I had to heal, fix, and protect and Marlin's little admission had the gears turning in my head. What was it Nothing had to grieve? By the sounds of it, it was an old and deep wound. I should leave well enough alone but I had to ask…

"What did Marlin mean?"

Radar grinned, "Got a thing for our boy, Nothing?"

I blushed; I couldn't help myself, "Just curious more than anything."

Radar spun me out and then back, when we came back together, he said, rather somberly, "I'd give any ideas about flirting or whatever the boot right now. Nothing ain't over his wife and kid."

"Oh…"

"He should be, it happened forever and a fuckin' day ago. I lost my Ol' Lady to cancer something like two years ago. I can't imagine living like it was only yesterday that she died for almost *four years*." He shook his head, adding, "That shit just ain't right."

"Oh my god…" I uttered, "His wife *died*?" I felt horrible, and more than ever wanted to fix it.

"And his kid," Radar said. "It was a stupid fucking accident. Anyways, best just to steer clear, he's pretty much turned into a lost cause. We all fuckin' love Nothing like a brother from another mother, but he ain't gonna change. He just ain't got it in him."

"Is that why you call him Nothing?" I asked.

"No, he calls *himself* Nothing. The road name we gave him, he pitched after it happened."

"I got the impression you were stuck with whatever was given to you, so is that even allowed?"

"Yeah, not so much, but we made an exception. He wasn't gonna let it go." Radar grinned and spun me one more time and back in, the song ending. Other couples around us broke apart applauding and I smiled.

"Thanks for the dance," I said and almost immediately regretted it, because Radar winked at me.

"Sure, no problem," he said, before melting through the archway and sidling up to the bar. I cursed myself and went back to my seat and my now watered down drink, taking a strong sip. I really hoped he didn't think I was interested or up for anything more. It was a knee jerk reaction from spending the last four years in a college town with entitled trust fund douche bags who took a smile as 'pursue me.'

I was truthfully also a little disappointed, I'd been hoping Radar would finish the story, but oh well. It wasn't like I was going anywhere and Nothing either. I was sure there would be plenty of time to learn more.

The rest of the night was spent dancing, because apparently Radar was a trendsetter and *everybody* had to get their time in with the new girl. I was beginning to get the picture that as far as semi-permanent or permanent residents went, Ft. Royal was as small town as they came and there wasn't a whole lot to choose from out of the native stock.

Lucky me? Oh well, I'd always been raised to make the best out of every situation thanks to Hope.

CHAPTER 4
Nothing

She was dancing with Stoker. I sat at the end of the bar and watched her, curious about this woman, this girl, who made me feel something after so long. Of course, it shouldn't have surprised me. Her older sister, Hope, had made my dick stir back in New Orleans, even if making out with her had been in the line of duty, so to speak. Still, Charity had accomplished something only Corrine had ever been able to do before. She'd stopped me in my tracks with one look. My heart stuttering in my chest like I was some teenaged fucking nerd boy who's crush had spoken to him for the first time.

I didn't know what bothered me more, *that*, or the fact that unpacking her things, I'd found nothing but evidence of a loving, driven, loyal and all around sweetheart of a young woman. The first thing I'd encountered was the carefully bubble wrapped framed diploma she'd received on graduation. I'd hung it for her, right over the bed, the first thing you saw when you walked into the room she would be calling home for the foreseeable future.

Helping Trike unload her shit was probably the creepy as fuck way to go about it, but that's what I'd done. I'd learned a lot moving her boxes from the trailer into the Captain's house. One, she was organized, every box neatly labeled in her clear, precise, handwriting. Two, she was a fucking minimalist. Three boxes of clothes, a couple of books, and a damn few of those judging by the weight. She had only one box of toiletries and one box labeled 'personal items' and that was it.

I hadn't split anything marked 'personal' open, at least not on purpose, but the bottom had dropped out of the personal items box. Picture albums, a jewelry box that must have been something she'd had since she was a little girl, and a few other items of no consequence. The pictures that were framed, a few of the glass plates had broken, and the jewelry box had spilled out onto the bed where I'd gone to set it when the bottom of the box had given way. I'd cleaned up the glass and busted out the vacuum, careful to get it all while Trike had gone to work putting the top onto her Jeep before the rain could set in.

The hard top we'd stashed against the side of the house, and the paperwork for the little U-Haul trailer we'd found on the passenger seat of her rig. I'd had Trike it back to the closest one while I'd carefully put away Charity's things for her. It was like once that box had split giving me a deeper glimpse into her life, I'd needed to know more. Before I knew it, over half the boxes contents were put where they belonged. Clothes hanging, and useless bedding relegated to the linen closet. I'd taken the time to run out and get her some useable bedding before heading to The Plank. She had a thing for the color blue, like light blue, so I'd gotten her sheets that would match her eyes.

She was all moved in, completely set, and I had some really mixed feelings about it. I turned on my bar stool and rapped my knuckles on the scarred wood surface of the bar. Trike loaded my glass with another double and I took a decent slug of it. I was way past the burning sensation and in that territory where the buzz was beginning to blur into a haze. Radar, slapped me on the back, hanging on me for a second before dropping onto the stool next to me. I only halfheartedly shrugged him off and he stared at me with that shit eating grin of his that screamed 'I know something you don't know.'

He kept right on staring, knowing that it'd eventually get under my skin, until finally, exasperated, I growled out, "What?"

"She likes you. Don't ask me why; I mean, you're an ugly fucker, but she started asking all kinds of questions. I think she's *the one*, Nothing my man."

"One what?" I growled and finished off my double. Fuck me, but I wanted to drink tonight.

"Come *on*, man. You should hit it. I mean *look at her*," I shrugged him off of me as he tried to wrench me around on my bar stool to look in her direction. Except I didn't want to look at her. I felt guilty as fuck that I'd almost let Corrine's memory slip from my mind the last few hours.

"Seriously, bro?"

"Seriously, leave it the fuck alone tonight, Radar. I'm not into it."

Radar shook his head, "Man, you can't keep *doing* this to yourself."

"I can, and I will. It's what I deserve." I slid off my stool by way of emphasis and made for the door. Fuck it. I'd walk home. I was in no shape to drive and Marlin would need the Subie to take his woman home, out of the rain. I'd given him my spare key to it when it was apparent Faith was a permanent fixture. She couldn't ride all the time, not in the wet, and I couldn't paint houses in the rain.

I pushed my way out the front door and into the downpour, tipping my head back to let the warm wet wash some of my guilt away. Not like it mattered, though. There was always plenty more where it came from.

"Don't let him get to you."

I whirled and looked at Hope; she was tucked back into the alcove next to the front door out of the water streaming from The Plank's eaves. I'd walked right by her. She raised her glass and took a sip, raising an eyebrow at me over the rim. She'd quit smoking long before she'd ever hit Ft. Royal, but sometimes we'd catch her slipping out and standing where the smokers could be found. A 'fresh air' break, she called it, but really, I think it was because she would get overwhelmed in close quarters; she was just too much of a badass to admit it.

"I don't," I said.

She smirked, "Liar."

"Whatever you say, Hope." I started up the street, turning from her look of surprise. I'd never spoken to her like that, and I guess it was a mark of how far under my skin Radar had gotten.

Or was it really Radar at all? The little voice in the back of my head asked me. I told it to shut the fuck up and kept pounding pavement. About twenty minutes into my walk, and about ten minutes from home I cursed myself out hard.

Radar damn sure wasn't the reason I'd noped right the fuck out of there. It was all Charity. It was all that fucking *look* in her eyes in the marina parking lot. I'd seen her hesitate, seen the dismay on her face, and when she'd looked up at me, it'd nailed my ass to the asphalt. I couldn't tell you exactly what it was. Truthfully, I didn't know if it had a name, but it was damn sure a look I remembered. One that Corrine and I had both shared once upon a time... back in the beginning.

I was past soaked to the skin by the time I reached my door and let myself in to my lonely house far too big for just one. It'd been perfect for my little family of three, back before I'd let everything be taken away from us. I went straight to the kitchen and cracked the seal on the bottle of Canadian whiskey on the counter.

I wasn't numb enough for this. I wasn't numb enough for tonight, and the storm, and everything that came along with the lightning and the rain. I closed my eyes so I wouldn't have to see and hit the switch on the stereo on the kitchen counter filling my house with Stoker's band's angry fucking music. Something between hard rock and death metal blared from the speakers and I sank into it, grateful. I knelt down by my bike in the middle of my kitchen floor and wiped stray water off my face before picking up a socket wrench.

She needed maintenance, and I may not be able to fix my broken, but I could at least keep her in fine running order. At least until I needed sleep. I wanted sleep, but tired as I was, if I fell into bed before full exhaustion set in, I would have to relive it. I needed a sleep away from nightmares tonight; so I worked on my bike instead. I may be nothing, but at least with my bike and my club I *had something.*

CHAPTER 5
Charity

I laughed and dodged into the house off the front step, Faith, Hope, Marlin, and finally Cutter, dodging in right after me. The rain was coming down in *sheets* out there and I'd been grateful that Nothing had seen to it to put the top on my Jeep. We all stood dripping on the hardwood, just inside the entry way for a moment looking at each other, waiting awkwardly for someone to suggest a 'what's next.' Cutter saved the day.

"You should probably get settled in, Trouble," he said to me and I grinned.

"Thank you," I said simply, kind of at a loss to say anything else. I mean, I was this weird mix of shy without being shy. I didn't really know how to be around these two men that meant so much to my sisters, but the rest of the lot of them, I felt like I could just be myself.

"Come on, Blossom, c'mon, Bubbles... you boys are on your own for a minute," Hope declared. She linked her arms with mine and Faith's and led us to the stairwell to the left as you came through the door. We followed her upstairs and she took us to, what was presumably, my room.

"Oh!" My diploma was the first thing to see when you came through the door. Right smack in the middle of the white expanse of wall over the bed which was covered in a light comforter, a beautiful gradient sand to aqua fading into a deep blue at the bottom that reminded me of the beach dropping off into the waters out at the shore. The sheets a light, cool blue to match.

"Wow," Hope commented and her mouth turned down impressed. That was my first clue something was amiss. My second was the boxes that were stacked against one wall; there weren't enough. I could tell just by looking at what was there.

I frowned and went to the closet and slid open the door on its track. "Well that's both sweet and a little bit creepy," I commented under my breath.

"What?" Faith asked curiously.

I stepped aside and showed her, "They put my clothes away for me."

"*Nothing* put your clothes away for you. I don't see Trike thinking about the details," Hope flopped down on the queen sized bed on her stomach and looked at me, "You must have made an impression."

"I didn't think so," I said drawing my mouth down on either side and sliding the doors back shut. I shrugged, "Thank you for the bedding, all my stuff was twin from the dorm bed."

"Wasn't me," Faith said with a shrug. I looked at Hope.

"Wasn't me either, if I had to place even money, I'd say Nothing again."

"What can you tell me about him?"

"Later, I want to hear about *you*. Tell me about school. Who'd you hook up with? Anyone good?"

I rolled my eyes, "A couple, they just weren't for me. Nursing programs, sad to say, don't have a lot of guys in them. Mine was no exception. Had a girl on girl hookup for a minute, but she was definitely the exception and not the rule. I don't know, there was just something about *her* specifically…" I looked to Faith and winced, I didn't know if I should ask or not if this was bothering her. Sometimes just by asking it could set a person off.

It was one of those being double teamed by a rock and a hard place moments, but my sister quickly let me off the hook by smiling and saying softly, "I'm fine."

We stayed up late, and it was like a million other times we'd done it when Faith and I had been just teenagers, when we went a long time without seeing Hope, because of her schedule and because of deployment. Finally, I kicked my sisters out of the room and they went down to where their men, presumably, waited for them downstairs.

I sighed, suddenly exhausted, and slid open the closet door again. I pulled one of my oversized tees off a hanger and changed into it. I went through one or two of the boxes and bit my lip between my teeth when I didn't find them right away. I turned and opened up the nightstand's drawer, remembering what Hope had said about the details, and there they were... minus their glass, a note perched on top.

Bottom of the box dropped out. Will get you some new frames or at least some new glass tomorrow. Forgot them when I was at the store. Sorry.

N.

"Huh," I muttered to myself. Well that was interesting.

I pulled back the blankets and sheets on the queen sized bed and they held the stiffness of new fabric. They certainly weren't the bedding from my old dorm twin bed and I frowned. I looked around and found the room's little wastebasket. A bag from a big box store was crumpled in the bottom of a wadded up bag.

"I owe Nothing seventy-three dollars and eighty-six cents," I mused aloud. Why call yourself Nothing when you had a perfectly good name like 'Shepard/Dominic,' by the looks of the receipt? I instinctually knew it was Nothing's real name, but I didn't know why he would do all of this for a stranger. He was a strange guy; *that* was for sure. I'd caught him more than once, watching as I'd danced with some of the other members of his club. I'd secretly wished he would cut in or come up and ask me, but he hadn't, and I was vaguely bothered by the fact that maybe it was because I wasn't pretty enough, or that maybe I looked too much like Faith, after all she'd been through.

I switched out the light and got into bed, listening for a long time, to the rain pounding against the eaves of the house. I couldn't help but think about him, and the odd little extras he'd done for me. *He'd just met me, why would he go to all the trouble?* It was a question that kept turning over and over in my mind.

After such a long and exhausting drive, followed by the flurry of social activity, I couldn't fight off sleep for too long to ruminate over it, so I slept. My dreams of a hard body and the most sorrowful set of grey eyes I'd ever seen.

* * *

The next morning I was jolted awake by both my sisters jumping onto me squealing like a couple of teenagers. I sat up, laughing with them and asked, "What's all the excitement about?"

"Oh my god! We have so much to *show* you!" Faith cried and it was as animated as I had seen or heard her to be since she'd been brought back to us.

"Okay! Where are we starting?"

"Well, I figured we could start with a good workout," Hope said dryly and the look on Faith's face sent us both into hysterical fits of laughter.

"Oh my god, you should see your face!" Hope cried, wiping tears.

"Not funny!" Faith yelled and ripped my pillow out from behind me, hitting Hope square in the face with it.

"Oh, shit! It's on!" Hope cried and no joke, it was a full on pillow fight between the three of us.

"Fucking Christ, I think I've died and gone to heaven. Seriously, pinch me, Cap."

The three of us turned to the bedroom doorway, where Cutter, Marlin, and Cutter's self-described best friend Pyro all stood, watching us. Cutter took a drink out of his coffee mug, eyes fixed on Hope in such a way you could almost see the distortion from the heat between them shimmer in the air.

"I want a guy to look at me like that," I said flatly.

"Mm, mm, mm, if I were single I would totally volunteer," Pyro said and I raised an eyebrow.

"Trouble in paradise?" I asked and he frowned.

"What? No!"

Cutter laughed, "Can't bullshit a bullshitter my man."

"What the fuck's that supposed to mean?" Pyro said, on the defensive.

"It means, dumbass, that if you were happy with your girl, you wouldn't be making comments like that about my sister." Hope lobbed a pillow at Pyro and he caught it.

"Just a rough patch is all," he said unhappily, and Marlin snorted. He was looking at Faith like she were his own personal angel and it warmed me down to my toes to see it. I wanted a man to look at me like that, too.

"Right, fine, adventure awaits! How am I dressing for this?" I asked.

"Comfy," Hope said, "We're headed out on the water. If you got sunscreen, bring it."

"Okay, then." I sucked in a deep breath and let it out.

As good as promised, we spent the day on the water with Cutter and Pyro. Marlin had gone off to his fishing boat with Faith, while Hope and I diverted to the *Reclaimer* which was Cutter and Pyro's state of the art maritime salvage boat.

"Doesn't look like much, but she's one of the fastest and surest out here," Cutter had remarked.

Hope let me in on just how much money the guys had put up to not only get Faith out of trouble, but her as well. Apparently lawyers in New Orleans, like anywhere else, don't come cheap. As much as everyone wanted to take time off and just hang with me and get to know me, the club's coffers were running on the dry side and work needed to be done to fill them.

"So, what are we doing?" I asked.

"Got a call to tow in a partially submerged yacht. Should be worth a cool eight grand, but we need to move it," Pyro had said.

"You girls just sit tight and catch up," Cutter had chimed in, and so we did.

"So, what do you think so far?" my sister asked me.

"I can see why you like them," I said.

"Anyone stand out to you?" she asked.

"I listened to what you told me, Buttercup. No need to fish so you can reiterate it, and to answer your question, yes. One of them has my curiosity."

"Which one?"

"Which one is Dominic Shepard?" I asked.

Cutter turned his head, "We don't go by civilian names, Darlin', why would you ask that?"

"Because whoever he is, I owe him some money. He bought the sheets and blankets on the bed. Mine were for a twin not a queen."

"Ah, well you can consider it a gift from the club. It all comes out in the wash anyways."

"Seriously," I said and he looked back at me over his shoulder from where he was coiling line. "It was Nothing, wasn't it?"

Cutter gave me a crooked grin and shot back, "I will neither confirm nor deny."

"I think you just did." I didn't know why it was so important to me to have confirmation, but it was. I think that was as good as I was going to get, though which was just going to have to be good enough.

"Well," Cutter said, drawing out the word. "Ain't you just a bunch of trouble wrapped up in pretty packaging?" he asked.

"I will neither confirm nor deny the possibility," I said with a wink. He laughed outright.

Hope knocked her knee into mine, "Be careful when it comes to Nothing, Char."

"Why, what's up?" I asked.

"Nothing's wife died and he still has a lot of feelings about it," she told me.

I frowned, "Radar said something about it last night, and I think it's awful, the poor guy."

"It was, when it happened, over three years ago," Pyro said catching on to the conversation.

"What happened?"

"Accident," was all he said before moving off. The engines rumbled to life and Cutter steered us out towards the open water.

"How do you know about it?" I asked.

Hope shrugged, "We were at this strip joint in New Orleans, hot on Faith's trail. Nothing and I had to pretend to be a couple. We had to make out to make it look good. He was a wreck, kept going on about what his wife would think. I told him I was sure she'd understand and he told me she was dead. I didn't pry, it was none of my business."

"Oh."

"Yeah."

I mulled it over while the conversation meandered over several other topics. It was a long, fun day. Full of interesting new things enough to keep my rapt attention. Pyro was hilarious, and it was fun to watch him and Cutter move so efficiently and quickly, performing their respective duties with such practiced precision.

"What 'cha thinkin' baby sister?" Hope asked me at one point.

"I was just hoping that when I start work as a nurse, for real, that I can provide care for my patients so quickly and effortlessly precise. It'd be awesome, you know?"

"Sweetie, you're going to be a great nurse. As badass as everything else you've ever taken on, but you gotta remember… you're going to be treating people. It's different than towing a boat or fixing a car. Don't let the technical shit get in the way of what you're really good at."

I looked at Hope curiously, "And what do you think I'm really good at?"

"Being human. Relating to people on their level no matter what that level is." She sighed, "I fucked up a lot of things with Faith. I just hope I didn't fuck you up, too."

I felt my shoulders drop as my sister's eyes welled up with tears and the guilt came pouring out her eyes. Was it true that she and Faith had always had a fundamental difference in opinion and lifestyle choices? Yes. Did that mean Hope came down harder on Faith than she did me? Also yes. What it didn't mean was that she 'fucked up,' as she so eloquently put it.

We talked, and I'd like to think that by the end of that talk she felt better, but Hope was the best out of the three of us when it came to hiding behind her walls. If she didn't want you to know how she was feeling, you didn't know. It was a bitch of a disconnect between her and Faith and yes, even me, when it came to the whole abuse thing with our dad. I felt a certain amount of guilt over that now. Never in a million years did Faith or I want to believe that he'd done what Hope had said. It wasn't until my final year in college, and my rotations through the ER, that the blinders had really been peeled back.

There was a lot of soul searching and honest talk between me and my sister, and it was needed. The day ended up going long in some respects and I think that when both me and Hope disembarked back at the marina, we both felt equal parts better and emotionally wrung out. At least I know *I* felt wrung out.

We had a low key dinner on the back patio of Cutter's house, the three of us and their two men and I honestly called it a night early. The sunlight still peeking over the horizon despite the fact the sun had gone. I showered and dried my hair, taking the time to straighten it before going to bed. I clicked off the bedside light to the low rumble of thunder in the distance, sighing out into the night.

A long day, but a good one…

***

An exasperated sigh, "Son of a bitch," a masculine voice, the words slurred around the edges. I sat up and listened to the rattle of glass and metal, somewhere close, right beside the bed.

A flash of blue light illuminated a crown of dark hair, lank with the rainwater that lashed the window.

"Nothing?" I asked softly and he looked up, in my direction, squinting in the dark. Thunder boomed and I jumped with a little girly yip, slapping my hand over my mouth. I reached over and clicked on the light. He put a hand up to shield his eyes and I took in the scene in front of me.

The drawer on the bedside table was open in front of me, my pictures in their broken frames in a neat pile on the floor. Nothing sat cross legged in the middle of the cream carpet, a plastic grocery sack open next to him. He was fumbling with the back of a new frame, trying to slide the little clips aside and open the back.

"Nothing, what are you doing?" I asked softly and pulled back the blankets, swinging my legs over the edge of the bed.

"I broke it, I need to fix it," he mumbled, or some iteration thereof. I knelt down beside him and could smell the alcohol.

"Please tell me you didn't drive here…"

"Bike's broke, Marlin has my cage, so I walked." At least that was clear enough.

"Can I help you?" I asked softly, putting my hands lightly over his, stilling his fumbling.

He looked at me, his soft gray eyes meeting mine, filled with such sorrow, such pain, and he uttered clearly, "No one can help me."

It hit me in the center of the chest, and if it'd been a physical blow, it would have knocked the air clean out of me. I sighed out gently and tried my best to smile under the weight of his sadness.

"Can I try?"

He let me take the frames from his hands, one drifting up and cupping the side of my neck, thumb grazing gently along my jaw. He made eye contact with me and his eyes held so much.

"Those eyes get me every time," he murmured. "Can't stop thinking about them. Like shadows on ice, not like hers, but the same. The same deal, same effect, you know?"

"I don't, I'm sorry," his hand dropped away and he squeezed his eyes shut, pressing the heels of his hands deep into the sockets.

"Hey, here, don't do that. You were going to help me, remember?" I drew his hands away from his face with mine and he stared at them, my hands in his, his hands in mine.

"I broke them, I fix them."

I smiled, "You don't have to."

"Yes, I do."

"Okay, okay then; let me help you."

We sat on the floor of the bedroom, in the close, golden glow of the lamplight, the rain thrashing outside and re-framed my pictures. He'd chosen simple black frames and I liked them. I was never a fan of overly fancy things, preferring a less was more approach most of the time.

"There, all fixed," I said solemnly.

Nothing nodded and I was almost afraid of just how inebriated he was. He staggered to his feet and I rose with him.

"I broke them," he said and the pain was raw on his face.

"You fixed them," I said and smiled and he looked down at the pictures in my hand. He shook his head back and forth.

"I broke them, and you can't fix people when they're broken that badly," he said cryptically.

"Nothing, what do you mean?" I asked, a knot of fear taking up residence in the center of my chest.

"What is it about you? Why are you different?" he asked abruptly.

I was taken aback, "I... I don't know." We stood for several long drawn out moments, him blinking owlishly at me through his haze of drunk.

"Sleep good, Charity," he said abruptly and hooked a hand behind my head, I stiffened but he leaned forward when I wouldn't bend and pressed a kiss to the top of my head, his hand a steel band around the back of my neck. Not hurting, just firm.

"Nothing," I started but he was gone, my bedroom door swinging wide. I stood, frozen and a moment later the front door gently opened, the roar of the beating rain growing louder before growing muffled again. I went to the window and watched Nothing stagger down the driveway and felt powerless.

I wanted to do something to heal that raw, naked, hurt in his eyes but I didn't know how. I wanted to stop him from leaving, but I didn't know how to do that either.

I looked down at the photo of my two sisters and my mom, smiling on the distant California shore, the Pacific behind us and wanted so badly to fix some of Nothing's broken. I think I decided that I would do just that, I just needed to figure out how.

CHAPTER 6
Nothing

The pounding in my head was made way heavier than it needed to be by the pounding on my front door.

"Nothing!" someone shouted, "C'mon man, it's almost noon! Open the fuckin' door!"

I rolled off my couch onto all fours and shook my head before pushing up onto my feet. I staggered for the front door and shouted, "Alright; alright, alright!" in a vain attempt to get the fucking renewed pounding to stop.

I threw open the door and squinted into the blinding light, throwing up a hand to ward off the bright.

"Jesus Christ, man. What the fuck?" Marlin pushed past me and into my entry way.

"The fuck do you want?" I mumbled.

"Some respect for one, I ain't fuckin' Radar, I'm your VP," Marlin glowered at me and shoved me into the wall. I slid down it onto my ass and put my head into my hands.

"Sorry," I grumbled.

"Yeah, well, you gotta get up. We gotta start battening down the hatches. Storm switched track, it's comin' this way and should make landfall in five to seven days. We're operating on the whole 'five' to be safe. Some of the boys and me are here to help board your house first since you never leave it."

"Shouldn't you be yanking your boats out of the water?"

"Captain has that arranged, the Scarlett Ann's in his hands. I agreed to take land based action. Supplies, that sort of thing."

"Why you starting here, again?"

"Because I fuckin' said so, now get your hungover ass up off the floor and let's do this." He kicked my booted foot which rattled all the way up into my brainpan and I suppressed a groan.

"Fuckin' great," I grumbled, but I hauled my ass up.

"Girls are spending time together, so I want to get this done before they are so I can be there with *my* girl."

"Fuck man, Charity's been here a whole day and we're getting ready for a hurricane? Welcome to Florida," I groused. Marlin gave me a bizarre look, like I was out of my fucking mind.

"What?" I demanded.

"You been in here pickling your fuckin' self," he shook his head, "Get in the fucking shower."

"What?" I demanded again, frowning, and he gave me a shove in the direction of my bedroom.

"Charity's been here more 'n two fuckin' days, bro. You've just been too fuckin' drunk to notice or answer your fuckin' phone. What gives, brother?"

More than two days?

"Nothin', I'll get changed."

"*Shower!*" Marlin practically bellowed at my back and I raised a hand, waving him off back over my shoulder. I ached from head to toe and no wonder, after a however many day fucking bender.

I stayed under the spray until the water started to run cold before I got out, and when I did, it was to tapping and banging out front and the rattle and clink of bottles and cans in my kitchen. I threw on some jeans and a faded tee shirt and stepped into the main living area, rubbing a towel over my hair.

"Man, you didn't fuckin' drive like this did you?" Trike asked from my kitchen and I simply stopped and stared at him. He stared back at me until the light went off behind his eyes and he said, "Ah! Yeah, sorry man..."

"Couldn't fuckin' drive anyways if I wanted to. Marlin has my fuckin' car *and* my keys."

"Good thing, too. Still don't know how the hell you got into the Captain's house."

"What?" I asked, blinking at him blearily.

"Charity said she woke up to your drunk ass fixing her picture frames, told her sister, Hope about it. We aren't supposed to know, but Hope is more 'n a little pissed about it."

"You serious?" I asked. I didn't remember doing it.

"When she heard I was heading over she said to give you this, she's acting like nothin's weird like she's afraid we'd whoop your ass for being both a creep and a dumbass and she's not wrong. If it wouldn't get Hope busted we probably would go toe to toe. Man, what the fuck were you thinking!?" he held out a wad of bills to me and I frowned.

"I wasn't, I was drunk as fuck and don't remember a fuckin' thing about it; I swear it. What's that for?" I asked jerking my chin in the direction of the bills in his hand and immediately regretting the decision to do so.

"The bedding and the replacement frames, she insisted."

"Fuck that, I get the frames but how'd she know about the rest?" I looked at Trike, "I told you not to say shit, man!"

"I didn't!" he exclaimed and Marlin, who'd come in from outside, smirked.

"You're the only Dominic Shepard the fuckin' club's got. Next time, take the receipt with you. The girl's smarter 'n Hope. Captain's already named her 'Trouble.'" Marlin took the money from Trike and stuffed it in the front pocket on my tee shirt; I glowered at him.

"I need fucking coffee for this shit," I grumbled.

"You need a hell of a lot more than that."

I scrubbed my face and groaned, "Okay fine, tell me, tell me what I need oh great one," I bit sarcastically in his direction.

"Well, since you asked oh so nice, for one, you need to admit Char's struck a chord with you somehow."

"She hasn't," I denied.

"Right, that's why you're fuckin' putting away her crap and buying her things like a Grade A number one stalker head case."

"Dude, I was drunk as fuck, I don't remember –"

"Exactly my point," he cut me off, "You know what they say about drunks and the truth."

I shut my damn mouth. Marlin sighed, "I think I've picked on you enough for one day, brother. Let's get your house buttoned up, get your supplies, and get on over to Hossler's next."

"She weathering the storm at her place?" I asked a little surprised.

"Her power goes out, she says she bags up all them snakes and sleeps with 'em to keep 'em warm."

"Oh, fuck that shit! You serious?" Trike asked dropping an empty bottle into the garbage sack he was quickly filling, wandering around my kitchen.

"You got a better incubator idea?" I asked.

"That's fucked up," he said and looked a little green. He hefted a full garbage sack over his shoulder and went out the front door. The window above the kitchen sink went dark as a thick ass chunk of plywood went over it.

"Today, Nothing… we want to get the houses kitted out as fast as possible, you know once it comes to the bigger boats coming out of the water it's gonna be all hands on deck."

"Yeah, man, sorry, let me get my boots on…"

We spent the better part of the day both cleaning and boarding up my place only to head out and do it all again over at Hossler's. The Captain's house is typically where everyone weathered the bad storms, but his place was easy. He had state of the art rolling storm shutters that just needed padlocking to the ground and to heavily bolted in strips at the bottom of the second floor windows.

The boats went into dry dock at a facility nearby the marina. They'd take the live-aboard boats first, The Scarlett Ann and the Mysteria Avenge. Then they would spend a couple of days getting the Reclaimer, Cutter's salvage boat, out of the water. That was all them. It was my duty, along with whatever prospects we had, and Lightning, to get our bikes to safety in a stout, cinderblock, storage unit about a half hour away.

My bike wouldn't be going. I had discovered a significant enough oil leak that required practically a full engine tear down, so that was the plan for me during the storm. I wanted to get it fixed as soon as possible, so I figured I'd drive the crash truck and the guys back from the storage facility. That would be tomorrow or the next day's project.

With such a full day, of boarding up and supplying two houses today, I was surprised to find that we wrapped it up while there was still sun in the sky. The plan, as I heard it for tomorrow, was for the The Locker to come out of the water, so I was off the hook. That was all Marlin, the Captain, and Pyro. Some of the other guys with more maritime experience were expected to pitch in; I would be on hand here in town in case of any accidents.

With nothing better to do for the rest of the afternoon, I found myself on the beach, sitting in the sand and staring out over the water, some wraparound, dark sunglasses covering my eyes to bring my light sensitive hangover down to a dull roar. Movement on my left had me flinching just as Faith sat down beside me, except it wasn't Faith, it was Faith-lite… Charity.

"Hey," she smiled at me and shaded those light blue eyes from the glare of the sun.

"You should get a pair of sunglasses."

She laughed a little, the sound light and soothing, carried away on the wind into the crashing surf, "I had a pair, they broke."

I pulled her money out of my shirt pocket and held it out to her, "Here, go buy a new pair."

"I can't let you pay for my bedding, or for the picture frames, or for my sunglasses. Thank you, though." She closed delicate fingers over my own and pushed my hand back towards me.

"They were a 'welcome to Ft. Royal' gift, and 'you break, you cry, I break, I buy' on the picture frames. Take it, or you might hurt my feelings… all one of 'em that's left." I said and tried a smile to soften the harshness of my tone. I was angry, but not at her, just at myself for being so messed up.

She nodded silently and took the money from my fingertips, tucking the bills into her white bikini top. It took a second to register I was staring, but I think the glasses hid it. To be fair on my end, it'd been a long time, and she was something else in just her white bikini and long, gauzy, see through, blue and aqua wrap that sat low on her hips.

"Thanks," she said, voice low and careful, and I could almost detect a faint blush on her cheeks. I propped the glasses up on my head, and sure enough, there it was. I couldn't explain the tight feeling in my chest that the sight caused.

"Don't mention it."

We sat in silence for a time, and she sighed, "You want to talk about it?" she asked.

"Talk about what?"

"I kind of figured you wouldn't remember," she said and she sounded a bit chagrined.

"Remember what?" I asked, careful not to let on that the boys had told me full well of my asinine behavior.

"I woke up and you were on my bedroom floor, trying to put my pictures into unbroken frames night before last, you don't remember?"

"Fuck, you serious?" I asked and tried to sound surprised. Her face held no lie, "Shit, I'm sorry." The embarrassment I felt now I didn't bother to hide.

"So, where you been?" she asked, changing the subject for me so I didn't have to.

"Stuck around the house, working on my bike. The boys showed up this morning to help me board up and get ready for the storm."

"I see, is it really that serious?"

"The hurricane coming? Yeah," I shrugged, "It's a hurricane."

"We don't have storms like that in California."

"Yeah, I guess not… What're you doing out here?" I asked, changing the subject again when the silence went too long.

"Needed to go for a walk. Hope and Faith opted for an afternoon nap, but I was feeling a little restless."

I got up, probably a little abruptly, but this feeling I had buzzing through my veins… I just wanted it to quit. I covered up my eyes with my glasses and held a hand down to her. She smiled up at me and grasped my hand and I hauled her lightly to her feet. She dusted off her shapely ass and I forced myself to look away from her and out to the water. I'd intended to walk with her some, but that's when I saw it and the emergency medical professional in me leapt out to the surface.

"Oh, god!" I heard Charity exclaim and she was right on my heels as we ran full tilt down the beach and onto the wet sand. A woman was struggling onto the shore with her child in her arms, limp... arms and legs flopping, likely not breathing.

Fucking shit.

Charity didn't miss a beat as I snatched the little boy from the screaming and crying lady and laid him out on the sand. She knelt by him, ear to his chest, and shook her head.

"Begin chest compressions," I snapped out and she assumed the trademark position and began her count. Bones and cartilage crackled and popped beneath her hands as they worked to pump life back through the kid's veins. This shit was real, and nothing at all like in the movies, but Charity the nurse was in the house and I was suitably impressed.

"Breathe!" she called and I bent, sealing my mouth over the boy's. Tilting his head back and pinching his nose.

"Again," I said and she began her count. We were a team, the two of us melded into a working unit and I was surprised at how seamlessly. She'd had some good training, and me? I'd kept up with my certifications, mostly for the club and for the odd emergency like this one.

The kid coughed and choked, my mouth filling with sea water and I sat up, spitting it off to the side. Charity rolled the kid into the recovery position and helped him choke it all up. His color started to return from the sickly blue purple he'd come out of the water with, and he started to cry.

"Somebody call an ambulance!?" I called out and was met with a random 'yeah' out of the crowd. I didn't see where it'd come from, because my eyes were on Charity who was all about her patient right now. *Fuck that's hot...* I thought to myself and instantly, the guilt slammed into my chest at the same time my respect for her rose more than a few notches. *Fuck my misplaced attraction for her.* I struggled with it. *Corrine doesn't deserve it.* I chastised myself, but for the first time, maybe *ever*, a tiny voice flitted out from the back of my mind and whispered, *Corrine is gone, maybe you've punished yourself enough?*

Sirens, medics, she and I helped carry the kid across the sand on a backboard, his mother thanking us over and over again profusely.

"Good thing you were here, Shepard."

I shook my head at O'Reilly, one of the medics I'd used to work with and told him, "It was mostly her," inclining my head towards Charity who was consoling the mother.

"Man, wish you'd never given it up. Any thoughts on coming back?" he asked me, eyeing Charity critically, as if taking her measure.

"Nope."

"Then why you keep up with all the certs? Saw your name on the re-cert course at the community college last round. Perfect score and putting us all to shame, per usual."

"Reasons, O'Reilly. I got my reasons."

O'Reilly shook his head and sighed, "So who is she? Where she come from? You know?" he asked.

"Up north, just graduated with a nursing degree. She's my club captain's girl's sister."

"A nurse? Well fuck, there goes that idea."

"What idea?" I tore my gaze away from Charity's which was locked on mine and looked up at O'Reilly who was a tall bastard at six foot eight. He rubbed a hand over his close buzz cut and shook his head.

"We lost Phillips to a heart attack last month," he said and I bowed and shook my head. Phillips had been one of the older medics to show me the ropes when I'd first gotten down to Ft. Royal with Corrine.

"Man, I hadn't heard."

"You were out of town." O'Reilly kept talking, "Anyways, Phillips went, and Marty retired. A couple of the young bucks quit on us; couldn't handle it. We're hurting, we're hurting *bad* for personnel. Will you at least think about it?"

"You know what this job cost me..."

O'Reilly sighed, "I know what you *think* it cost you, but Shep," he put his hand on my shoulder, "You know deep down there was nothing you could'a —" I shook the hand off and started walking away to O'Reilly's sharp exhalation of breath and muttered curse.

I didn't feel like it. I really fucking didn't. It was selfish as fuck, but I'd been having a good day as far as days went. I didn't want to think about it too much, which was hard as is, with the date coming up. Charity eyed me curiously and helped the woman into the back of the ambulance with her son. O'Reilly climbed in after her while his partner, a guy I didn't know, got in to drive.

Charity waved and rapped twice on the back of the cab and the bus pulled away from the curb, lights going up and siren wailing, piercing through my receding hangover like a marlin spike to the temple.

I needed a fucking drink, so I took the opportunity to disappear into the crowd before Charity turned back, making long strides down the boulevard heading for The Plank, and the familiar taste of oblivion that was Crown Royal before the ugly memories splattered themselves up on the inside of my skull in horrifying, living color.

CHAPTER 7
Charity

I saved a life. I stood at the curb, watching the ambulance drive away and felt lighter than air, but at the same time, full of an effervescing energy. *Wow.* I'd *saved a life,* what's more, I'd saved a life *with Nothing.* Who knew we had medical training in common? I turned to him and said, "I didn't know you were a med-" but the words died on my lips. He was gone, and I couldn't see through the throng of people in which direction he'd travelled.

"Son of a bitch," I whispered.

"Hey!" I turned and an attractive man stood on the curb, hands buried in his cargo shorts, button down shirt open at the collar, sleeves turned up casually to the elbow.

"Yes?"

"Not going to lie, that was pretty spectacular. Let me buy you a drink?"

I smiled, "And you are?"

He grinned, an award winning smile, and held out his hand, "Greg Hanson, what's your name?"

"Charity," I took his hand and shook, his grip light, but firm.

"Nice to meet you, Charity. Can I interest you in that victory drink?"

I smiled, "Some other time, maybe? I've got to get going. There's a hurricane coming don't you know?"

"Ah, yeah, I'm in town on business. Bad timing yeah?"

"At least you can *leave*," I said laughing, "I just moved here."

"Is that right?" he smiled and flashed perfect white teeth. He was attractive, as far as men go, probably no older than his late twenties, but he didn't have that general dark mystique that I was finding so attractive in Nothing.

"Yeah, moved here to be with my sisters."

"You know, I really do hope you'll take me up on that offer of a drink. If I ever see you again."

"It's a small town, so yeah, likely as not, we'll run into each other again."

He grinned broader and winked at me, "I'll be sure to keep an eye out, but then again, a woman as beautiful as you, you *do* stand out in a crowd."

I laughed outright and started up the sidewalk, looking back over my shoulder I proclaimed, "Flattery will get you everywhere!"

"I'll keep that in mind!"

I went down the boulevard, back in the direction of Cutter's house where everyone was supposed to meet anyways at the end of the day for some grilling and drinks. It was a fifty-fifty shot that Nothing had already gone that direction.

I wondered about him as I walked, he'd looked awful drawn and when he'd moved his glasses, he had been clearly hungover. After spending four years in college, it was hard not to recognize a night, or several, of binge drinking. I was surprised to find I was worried about him. It was probably just the natural caregiver in me... I was well aware that I couldn't save the world but it didn't stop me from trying.

My thoughts drifted back to the boy and to the medic climbing into the back of the ambulance, the taller one, he'd said to me, *"If you could get Shep to come back, you'd be doing this area a bigger service than you could imagine..."* It made me wonder about the man called Nothing. Why had he stopped in the first place? Clearly he had the training and was a phenomenal medic... why just stop?

"Hey! Here comes Trouble." I looked up and smiled, surprised at how far I'd come in so little time.

"What're you doing out here?" I asked and Cutter shrugged, opening up the mailbox.

"Can't a man check his mail?" he asked. "You look thoughtful, wanna tell me what's up?"

"Yeah, I think I just saved a life. Well, Nothing and I did."

"No shit? What happened?"

I told him as we ambled up the driveway at a sedate pace and he listened, thoughtfully. Finally, he nodded.

"Well I'll be damned, good on you, Darlin'!"

"Thanks," I said and smiled, "I've been meaning to ask you something."

"Yeah, what's that?"

I stopped and looked up at him, "Why do you call Faith 'Firefly?'"

He smiled, that easy, lazy grin of his that I could totally see why Hope got all twitterpated over it. "Because," he said, "Your sister has a fire inside that's been dulled by some really shitty circumstances, but when she doesn't let all that get in the way, and she remembers to do it, boy can she ever let that light of hers shine!"

I smiled broadly and looped my arm through his, giving his arm a hug, "I am so glad someone sees it."

"Oh, I ain't the only one. Marlin sees it clear as day."

"I'm glad she has him."

Cutter nodded, but said nothing. I looked up at him, "So why you call me 'Trouble' then?" I asked.

"Oh because you are. You're trouble that's just waiting to happen."

I laughed and he let us into the front door of the house, Hope was sitting on the couch, Faith on the floor in front of her while my eldest sister brushed my older sister's hair.

"You need a trim," I observed.

"That mean the salon is open?" Hope asked.

"I'll run up and get my scissors," I said and breathed out a sigh of contentment. It'd been a good day. A jumpstart to my heart, but so far, a good day… even with Nothing's peculiar behavior. The mystery had deepened, and my curiosity was definitely piqued. I was wrestling with myself a bit on if I wanted to learn more or if I should just take the brush offs he'd been giving me to heart.

I went and got my scissors and trimmed both Faith and Hope's hair, all the while listening to Faith prattle on about some man named Bobby and his orange grove. I smiled, and I was happy for my sisters, both of them, but I couldn't help but have my thoughts pulled regularly back to a pair of solemn gray eyes.

Damnit, I think Dominic Shepard AKA Nothing had gotten under my skin. There was something different about that. I'd never had anyone make me so curious after a couple of nonchalant, scratch that, a couple of nonchalant, one creepy, and one *intense* meeting. I think I'd decided then and there, that I would make an effort to get to know him which made me make a wry smile... I could be persistent if need be, and I think I'd figured out where my new nickname was going to come into play. Cutter was an insightful bugger.

Trouble indeed.

CHAPTER 8

Nothing

Shit. Charity dropped onto the barstool beside mine and dropped her keys on the scarred wood surface of The Plank's bar. She raised an eyebrow at me.

"What?" I asked.

"It's raining again, figured I could offer you a ride home, seeing as your bike is in the shop and Marlin has your car."

"I'm good," I said and downed the shot of Crown in front of me. Lightning took the shot glass off the bar and sighed.

"You're done, bro. I ain't going to watch you do this to yourself all over again."

Fuck.

"Let me take you home?" she asked gently. I shook my head and ran a hand over my hair.

"I'm not ready to go home."

"Okay, fine. Then I'll sit right here until you are."

"Fuck, really? Go find someone else to take care of," she flinched at my tone but I didn't apologize or back down. I was bad news; she didn't need any of what I had to offer. She was a nice girl... Corrine had been a nice girl, too. Corrine and I had made the sweetest little girl together... *Fuck. Fuck, fuck, fuck, fuck,* fuck.

"It's the time of year, Honey. It's not you," Hossler said at my elbow.

"Fuck, Hoss, stay out of it!"

"You're drunk and acting like an asshole; Charity's a guest. Take your sorry ass home, Nothing. People are sick of your fucking pity party for one."

I stood up abruptly and staggered, definitely unsteady on my feet. Charity reached out and put a hand on my arm but I jerked away from her.

"Just fucking stay out of it, all of you!" I barked and headed for the door.

I saw Radar get up out of the corner of my eye and I didn't want to deal with him, or anyone, so before he could get to me I went out the door and into the pouring rain outside. He caught up to me, grabbed my elbow and I was in the mood to force the issue. I turned and raised my fist but was cold cocked by Charity's glacial stare before I could swing.

"The fuck?" I asked.

"I could ask you the same thing, except I'm done asking. Get your ass in the Jeep."

I blinked and opened my mouth to reject the notion but before I could, she was speaking again, tone full of consternation.

"You can either, get your ass in the Jeep and let me drive you home, or I can tell your leader how you almost cold cocked his woman's sister in the face." She arched a light brow, her face set in stone and I shut my gob and looked this way and that, striking out in the direction of her white Jeep Wrangler.

"Thank you," she said, chirping the alarm, the locks unbolting themselves. I got in on the passenger side and she climbed in to drive. She started the engine and turned to me calmly, water dripping off the end of her nose.

"Where did you go?" she asked softly.

"Nowhere," I said looking hard out the window.

"Well you went *somewhere*. I turned around after loading Thomas into the ambulance and you were just gone. One minute you were talking to the tall paramedic, the next you just vanished. What happened?"

"Nothing," I lied.

"Nothing is your *name*, not what happened back there. I didn't know you had medical training, why didn't you say something? You know I just graduated with a nursing degree."

"I'm not a medic, not anymore... I just paint houses for a living."

"What, why?" she asked and I could hear that I'd startled her. I couldn't resist, I refocused my gaze from outside the dark window glass to her reflection in it. Her mouth hung open, her blue eyes livid with surprise.

"Doesn't fucking matter, I'm not that guy anymore."

She shut her mouth, "I call bullshit," she said and I turned to look at her, "If you weren't that man anymore you wouldn't have seen them, you wouldn't have gone running down the beach to help them."

She had me there, and it irritated me, I didn't want to answer anymore of her questions, didn't need her peeling back any more layers. "Just take me home," I grated and stared her down for a long time. The silence growing long and uncomfortable between us.

"Fine, where am I going?" she asked.

"Hit the boulevard, go right on Everglade Road."

She put the Jeep in gear, did her checks, and pulled into a smooth u-turn, following my directions.

"I don't get you," she said after a moment.

"What's not to get?" I muttered.

"You, your behavior, help me out here. You do nice things for me, but any time I try to talk to you, you get yourself drunk as fuck and are an ass about it. What gives?"

"It's for your own good."

"Excuse me?"

"Don't pretend like you didn't hear me – ow!" She'd punched me in the arm and pulled the Jeep to a stop right there in the middle of the road.

"This isn't fucking kindergarten, you ass! You don't get to pull my hair and be a bully as a way to tell me you like me. All you're doing is pissing me off."

I shook my head and slicked my hair back off my face with one hand, "That's not it," I said shaking my head, laughing at myself in self-deprecation. I couldn't argue her point, it was kind of what it looked like.

"Then what is? What gives, Nothing? What are you running from?"

She put the Jeep back in motion, headlights in her rearview cut a swath of light across her eyes and I was mesmerized until they were cast in shadow again.

"Nothing... nothing gives, I'm not running from anything."

"If God went around hugging liars, he'd break every bone in your body," she uttered disgustedly.

She made the turn onto Everglade and I blew out a breath, "Take the next right. It's the third house on the left."

She pulled into the driveway of my sad, lonely, boarded up house and killed the engine.

"Can we just start over?" she asked.

I eyed her warily, "Like how?"

"Like, 'Hi my name is Charity, you know my sister, Hope.'" She stuck out her hand and waited, while I eyed it like it was going to snap out and bite me, like one of Hossler's snakes.

"Nothing," I said, reluctantly, I took her hand in mine and shook it. Her skin was so soft and smooth against mine. Some of the hardness I'd tried to put up around my soul melted a little bit, softening up.

"Pleasure to meet you, Nothing," she said and I snorted. Her face crumbled into a frown and I reached out without thinking, moving a lank piece of her hair out of her eyes, tucking it behind her ear.

Silence stretched between us, until finally, she said softly, "I don't understand you."

"That makes two of us," I murmured. More silence, filled only by the sound of the driving rain pattering against the hard top on her Jeep. Someone must have put it on for her. I would have done it... but I didn't know *why*. Why did I want to do things for this girl? Why did she do the things she did to me? Why couldn't I be a better husband when I was around her? *Because you're tired of being a miserable fuck and she's a breath of fresh air*, that damn internal voice spat out of the dark corners of my mind. It was true, only problem was I didn't deserve to be happy, and she didn't deserve me making her miserable. Fuck. *Why did this have to be so complicated?*

"Good night, Charity," I said and she drew a breath to protest but it was too late. I'd opened the door and was out into the wet. I let myself through my front door and leaned against it. It was probably a full two minutes before I heard her Jeep start back up and back down the drive. It was the longest two minutes of my life.

Damn, but I fucked that one up good. It was probably for the best for her though. I turned and looked at the photographs on the walls of my smiling wife and our beautiful little girl.

No probably about it, it *was* for the best.

CHAPTER 9
Charity

"Okay, spill. What's Nothing's deal?" I stood just behind the couch, dripping on the hardwood floor of Cutter's entryway. Hope leaned her head way back over Cutter's thigh so she could see me, while Cutter just nonchalantly turned his head my direction. They were cute together, her lying out on the couch, head in his lap, but right now; there was no way I was going to admit it out loud.

"Well, if I had to hazard a guess," Cutter drawled, "I'd say you struck a nerve in our boy, and given his feelings over his late wife and the like, I don't imagine he quite knows how to handle that."

"Charming," I said, and felt my shoulders drop, "What happened anyways? All anyone will say is that it was some kind of accident."

"Well that's just not my place to tell, Darlin'. You'll have to get that from the horse's mouth."

I looked to Hope for help and she snorted, shrugging her shoulders indelicately where she lay across Cutter's lap, "Don't look at me, I know as much about it as you do. Some things are just Nothing's story to tell; it's how it works with these guys. Can't say I didn't warn you about that."

I looked at the ground and closed my eyes, placing the palm of my hand on the back of my neck and pulling to ease the tension from it.

"I'd like to help him if I can," I admitted, "There's something about him."

"Well, see, that there's your problem, Darlin'. There ain't no one that can help Nothing but Nothing. You can't help someone who isn't willin' to help themselves and he just ain't there yet."

I nodded, and thought about it, "Right, thanks... I'm going to bed."

"So early?" Hope asked, searching my face.
"Yeah, I'm beat."
"Okay, g'night Blossom."

I went upstairs and changed out of my wet clothes and into dry, pulling down a towel from the top of my closet to dry my hair. It would turn into the soft waves that Faith's hair held when it dried. I needed to straight iron my hair to keep it flat. I didn't see a whole lot of keeping it straight if it rained all the time like this. Or with as much swimming as I planned to do when the sun finally came out to play for longer than an hour or two at a time. I plugged my phone in on the bedside table and sighed, picking up the picture frame Nothing had drunkenly fixed with my help.

"I miss you, Mom," I murmured and kissed my fingertips, placing them over her image behind the glass.

I thought for a long time about Nothing and his odd behavior since I'd rolled into town and came up with zero conclusions, because truthfully? What could I conclude? I was missing pieces of the puzzle and couldn't yet tell the whole picture from the pieces I had. The only thing I could do was wait for Nothing to hand the missing pieces over.

I blew out an explosive breath and crashed, only when I got up the next morning, instead of sunshine, it was just more of the steady pounding rain with the odd gust of wind. Apparently the storm was moving in for real now.

I got dressed and went downstairs and found Hope in the kitchen looking miserable, waiting for the coffee to brew; I laughed.

"Shut up," she grumbled at me.

"Where is everyone?"

"Storm's moving in quicker than anticipated, some of the guys are getting the *Reclaimer* out of the water and the rest are moving the bikes to a storage place sturdy enough to withstand the beating coming our way.

"Shouldn't this place be boarded up?" My sister shook her head.

"It has rolling shutters."

I jumped and let out a yip at the unexpected voice behind me, I turned around to see Faith wide eyed and jumpy just as much as I was at the dining room table. I laughed and she laughed with me, both of us nervous.

"I had no idea you were there," I said.

"Sorry, we were expected to be seen and not heard, I guess I'm still working on some things."

I frowned and shook my head, "Don't be sorry, it's not like Rome was built in a day."

Faith smiled and I smiled back, going to my sister and hugging her tight when she got up to meet me. A strong gust of wind startled us and we turned just in time to see the sliding glass doors bow inwards with the force of it, the glass flexing in the frames.

"Holy shit," I murmured.

"And on *that* note," Hope said and went to a closet door at the far end of the dining room. She opened it up to a small electrical closet and turned a key in a panel. A light lit up green and she pressed a button holding it down. Metal storm doors slid down out of rolls that had been disguised by a trick of the architecture. I blinked noticing that the back patio had sandbags piled high at the top steps, even with the waist high rock walls surrounding the stone deck. The table, chairs, and barbecue had all been moved. Stashed away somewhere.

"Wow, this is really serious isn't it?" I asked. Faith looked solemn… afraid. Hope just shrugged.

"We'll see, won't we?"

"How many people are supposed to come here?" I asked as we lost the daylight, the shutters closing everything off.

"Cutter, Marlin, Lightning, Pyro and his girl, Radar and his family typically weather storms here, I don't know who all else."

"Trike," Faith supplied. I nodded, and hoped that Nothing would show; I was hoping to talk to him some more.

"What now?" I asked.

"The shitty part," Hope said and Faith made a face. I raised my eyebrows and Faith twisted her lips into a look that was classically mom's 'I disapprove' look.

"We wait."

Lovely.

"They boys are cavemen at heart, Cutter wouldn't even let *me* go out with them, not that I really wanted to head out in this." Hope sighed.

"Fun, anybody got a Monopoly board or something?" I asked. We all exchanged a look and started laughing in the dim kitchen.

"Hit the light would you? I'm gonna die if I don't get some caffeine," Hope said.

"They'll probably be hungry when they get in," Faith murmured as the harsh overhead light filled the kitchen.

"Probably," Hope conceded.

"Well alright then, something to do, at last!"

We set about fixing sandwiches and some soup for when the guys got back. I worked on a couple of salads while Faith crafted a platter stacked high with fruit slices. Hope had it easy; the soup was premade in a bag and from the freezer. She made sure sodas were within easy reach and when the front door blew open an hour or two in, it was to the boisterous noise of a bunch of the guys hurrying their way in.

"Go dry off and get in here! Food's ready!" Hope called.

I went around the corner and stood in the hall, gaze roaming over face after familiar face but missing the face I was looking for. No dark hair, no gray eyes… no Nothing.

"Where's Nothing?" I asked Lightning quietly.

"Riding it out at his place," he said and he didn't look happy about it.

"Alone?"

"Yeah."

I nodded and went back to serving some of the guys up as they came down in drier sweats toweling their hair.

"Where's Cutter?" Hope called.

"Locking down the shutters with Pyro, Radar, and Marlin," Stoker called. I handed him a plate and he smiled, inclining his head once in thanks.

A little bit later Marlin, followed by Cutter, Pyro, and Radar came through the front door dripping in Gordon's Fisherman yellow rain slickers and hats.

"Fuck, its bad out there!" Cutter declared, "Radar, go do your thing."

Radar nodded, "Soon as I dry off I'm on it. Hey Charity, mind fixing me a plate?"

"Sure," I murmured and went to do just that.

Eventually people were settled around the huge dining table eating, Radar set up at one end on three laptops scrolling and clicking through screens.

"What's the word?" Cutter asked.

"Not as bad as it's gonna get, Cap. It's still early."

I felt bad for Nothing, weathering the storm all by himself. It wasn't a time to be alone so I made a decision. I quietly went about packing up some Tupperware and while everyone was gathered around Radar and his laptops looking at what he was pointing out on the three screens, I ghosted upstairs with my haul and brought out one of my extra bags. I packed up dry clothes, a couple of towels and the food and slung it over my shoulder. I tucked my phone into one of the side pockets, made sure my room was neat and presentable and with a nod, took up my keys. My heart fluttered erratically in my chest. It really *was* bad out there and I didn't exactly want to drive in it, but I couldn't fathom Nothing being all alone. It just didn't sit well with me. It didn't feel right.

I slipped out the front door in my Keds and shut it firmly behind me. My summer dress was plastered to me in the matter of half a second. Undeterred, I bolted across the driveway and flung open the door of my Jeep, throwing in my bag and diving inside. A gust of wind battered my vehicle, rocking it mercilessly and I gasped. I thought to myself maybe this is a bad idea, even as my hand turned the key and my baby fired up into life.

"Bad idea or not, you're in it to win it now, Charity." I told myself. I pressed down on the clutch and shifted it into gear, and with the wipers going full bore, I eased around the circular driveway and hung a right onto the street.

It was a freaking nightmare out here. Wind battered and buffeted my Jeep so hard I thought it would topple over. No one was out here, the streetlights, what few the town had, all seemed to be hanging on by a thread. I squinted through the flying leaves and debris and eased my way through the sheets of rain looking for Everglade to make my turn; crowing in triumph when I spotted it.

I laughed at myself for using my signal. Ft. Royal was a ghost town, there wasn't really a reason to. I inched down Everglade and made the next turn, driving around a fallen palm tree, having to go up onto the sidewalk to make it. This was bad, and I'd like to say that pulling into Nothing's driveway in front of his closed garage door was enough to ease the knot of anxiety in my chest, but it wasn't. I still had to make it to his front door and hope that he could hear me knocking above the howling and the raging of the growing storm.

I killed the engine and slung my bag over my shoulder, taking a deep breath. Another gust of wind shoved my Jeep from behind and nudged it forward a couple of inches even with the parking brake set. I shuddered and climbed over the center console into the passenger seat which was closer to the house's front door. I waited for the next crazy gust and when it petered out, leapt out the door and was drenched again before I could slam it shut. I ran, head ducked, for the small front porch and knocked loudly at the front door, huddled in on myself, the thin fabric of my summer dress clinging wetly to my body.

The door opened and Nothing stared down at me, stunned. He grabbed me by the arm and hauled me across the threshold before slamming the door shut behind me and latching it.

"What the fuck are you *doing* here?" he demanded and I looked up, startled.

"I didn't think you should be alone…"

The anger in his gray eyes softened marginally before he rallied and it came back full force.

"How did you get here?" he demanded.

"I drove, why?"

He put his hands to his head and gripped his hair like he was ready to tear it out, "Why!? It's a goddamn fucking *hurricane* going on out there, Charity! You could have been hurt, or killed! What in the absolute fuck? Don't you California girls have any fucking sense?"

"I'm sorry," I hugged myself and shivered, feeling like a child well and truly admonished.

"Where's your Jeep?"

"In the driveway."

"Fuck, give me your keys," he ordered and held out his hand, waving his long fingers towards him twice. I dropped them in his palm. "Come this way," he ordered and set off past the living room, hanging a left just before his kitchen and opening the first door in the hall on the left. He went down a couple of steps.

"When I say 'go' press that button," he demanded, pointing to the garage door button next to my head. I nodded and tried not to think about him being shirtless now that my butthurt from being yelled at was wearing off.

"Go," he ordered and I hit the switch. I wondered vaguely what he'd been waiting for, as the door trundled up and the rain and wind swept in. I bit my lower lip as some things blew off a shelf and out the door. I think I heard Nothing curse as he ran out into the storm and got into my Jeep, pulling it into the garage.

"Shut it!" he yelled and I hit the button, the garage door trundling down, settling into place just as the next big gust knocked into it with a shuddering bang. He got out of my Jeep, shirtless, wet, and dripping; bare feet slapping the smooth concrete of the garage floor. He shook some of his midnight dark hair out of his eyes and burned me with a look.

"I can't fucking believe you, I can't fucking believe the guys let you leave like that," he grated.

"Don't be mad at them, they don't know I did."

"You fucking serious!?"

I swallowed hard, "I'm sorry," I repeated and hated the feeling that came with the apology. I had apparently fucked up big time, but I hadn't seen the harm, I mean the storm was just getting started, right?

He pushed past me and I closed my eyes, he was *really* angry, and I guess it was more serious out there than I'd thought. I followed him to the kitchen and stopped, in the middle of his kitchen floor his bike leaned over scattered newspapers. Oil spots dotted the newsprint and the engine was in various stages of pieces under the harsh overhead fluorescent light.

"You work on your motorcycle in your kitchen?" I asked.

"More comfortable than in the garage and it's not like Corrine is here to bitch at me," he said irritably, scooping up his phone off the kitchen counter.

"Corrine… is that your late wife?" I asked.

He turned his head to look at me over his shoulder and glared at me. I bit my lips together and hung back in the doorway as he swiped his thumb across the screen in whatever obscure pattern to unlock his phone. I couldn't see who he was calling, but truthfully, I was distracted by a bead of moisture rolling down his spine.

"Yeah, Cutter. Yeah, I know, she's here. She fuckin' drove here, in a hurricane," he paused, "She's safe. No, it's way too bad out there. No, it's cool man; I got it. Want to talk to her? Doubt it. Yeah. Sure, thing. See you when it's over." He hung up and let the phone clatter onto the Formica countertop.

I set down my bag and automatically went to him, hugging him around the waist, resting my head against his back as we both dripped rainwater onto his kitchen floor.

"Please, don't be mad at me," I breathed. He put his hand over mine and stood stalk still for a really long time, struggling with some invisible force and I simply stood there, tense. I didn't want him to be mad at me. I just *really* didn't want him to be all alone, either. I think he'd had enough of being alone.

He let out a pent up breath slowly, and as he did, grew less ridged beneath my touch, but only by a little. He turned in the circle of my arms and looked down at me. His hands found my hips and he turned me gently, hauling me up so I sat on the empty counter.

"What were you thinking?" he asked, gray eyes tumultuous.

"I didn't think, I guess," I gripped the edge of the counter to either side of my hips and trembled as much from his proximity as from cold. The air conditioning had kicked on and swirled through his kitchen, raising goosebumps on my skin.

He touched the side of my face and I held my breath, *please kiss me*, my mind plead and I think it may have filled my eyes. He frowned, and the anger and frustration swirled behind his eyes.

"I'll ask you again, *why did you come here?*" he demanded and I felt the tension I hadn't realized I'd been holding ease out of my shoulders.

"I didn't think you should be alone anymore, not with this," I raised a hand and waved ineffectually to take in the howling wind and raging rains pattering against the house. It was that and the electric hum of the house's AC unit and nothing more that hung between us. I could see the war on his face, feel it in the tightly coiled energy of his body, raised just above his skin. He shifted forward and back on his arms, his hands planted firmly on the counter's edge.

It was like he needed that final little push, to take that leap of faith, except I didn't know what to do or say to make him comfortable enough to make it. His indecision rose on the air, making it thick, making it hard to breathe; making me hold so very still, like he was a predator in my midst. I swallowed hard and his eyes snapped to my throat, watching the motion. He closed his eyes and bowed his head and I couldn't resist. I raised a hand slowly and smoothed back his glossy dark hair. His head snapped up, and there must have been something in my eyes because before I knew it, his mouth was on mine and it was everything I had imagined it would be.

CHAPTER 10
Nothing

I couldn't believe it. I couldn't believe *her*. Driving through a fucking hurricane so I wouldn't be lonely? She had to be out of her fucking mind… and I know for sure it drove me out of mine. *She could have been hurt, she could have been killed, all because of you…* my mind whispered and I, just for once, wanted it to *shut up*.

She tasted so damn *good*, so soft, sweet like whatever she'd last eaten or drunk. My hands found her hips and pulled her hard to the edge of the counter even as I let my tongue delve further into her mouth, taking a reprieve from just… *everything*. Her arms snaked around my shoulders, her fingers burying in the back of my hair as I drew her hard up against my hard on.

Wet jeans and an erection this fierce did *not* get along. I was about to tear my mouth from hers to ask if this was something she wanted, when she answered me wordlessly before I got the chance, her ankles hitting the backs of my knees and pulling me tighter against her body. I groaned into her mouth, and ripped it away.

"Are we doing this?" I managed to spit out and she nodded, her hands smoothing my hair, gone too long between cuts, out of my eyes.

"Yes," she moaned and it was all I needed. I pulled her off the counter and her flats slapped against my kitchen floor. I spun her around and she fetched up hard against the counter. I winced, but I was too busy moving her wet hair off her shoulders, around to the other side to pay much more notice. I attacked that sweet spot where her neck met her shoulder with lips and teeth, sucking and lightly biting.

"Oh, god!" she moaned and went languid in my arms. I pressed her body against the counter with my own and gripped her dress in my fists to either side, raising the wet material in increments, bunching it in my hands and cursing how it clung wetly to Charity's soft skin.

You shouldn't do this, let her go, let her go now and you won't have been unfaithful. I shoved the thoughts aside. I wasn't being unfaithful; you can't be unfaithful to someone three years and more gone. I knew that in the front of my head, but my heart and the back of my mind begged to differ. Right now, though? Right now I could only concentrate on the woman in my arms. I wanted her, I wanted the warmth and soft solace she'd been offering me and now she was here and we were alone and my weak ass couldn't hold out anymore.

I craved her; I craved everything about her, from those soft blue eyes, to her gentle touch, to the sweet understanding she'd displayed every time we'd encountered each other so far. I wanted desperately to warm my frozen soul against the fire she had inside, and *fuck* those soft little moans of pleasure she was making. Jesus Christ, they were stripping my control, my last vestiges of sanity away from me with each and every last sweet soft sound out of her lips that were swollen from my kiss.

She's not Corrine, she's different; she's not fragile like your wife...

It was true, and I let myself go, let myself be different with her. She deserved that much, but so too was I afraid of hurting her.

"Tell me to stop if I get too rough," I said and she damn near broke me with her breathy response.

"Don't stop, don't you *dare* stop."

I raised her skirt up onto her lower back and smoothed my hands over her ass, backing up to admire it. God she was wet, pussy swollen and glittering at her entrance. It didn't even occur to me that she wasn't wearing any panties, too involved was I with getting my button fly undone.

Victory!

My cock sprang free of its prison of wet denim; head damn near fuckin' purple with how hard it was. I ached something fierce with the need to be inside her and I didn't waste any time.

Oh, fuck.

Her body was hot, tight, and so wet, ready for me as I sank into her inch by inch. I pressed her flat to the counter, and dug fingers into her hips, surging forward powerfully, squeezing my eyes shut and bowing my head, just giving myself over to the sensation of her. She pressed her hands flat to the counter and arched her back, driving herself back onto my dick with every forward thrust. I was sure her hipbones were cracking into the counter with every thrust, and I was sure that it wasn't pleasant but she paid it no never mind and with the way her body was squeezing down on my cock? I couldn't bring myself to stop or adjust to a different position.

"*Nothing!*" she cried out, and it was so sweet, so perfect hearing her call out my chosen name I very nearly came right then and there.

"Not yet, Baby, just a little bit more," I urged, voice tight, controlled the way my thoughts and emotions would never be. I felt like a total basket case, thoughts, fears, anger – not at her but myself, all swirling into a dark miasma that was blown clear away by the fire of my orgasm. I came hard, driving into her. Pulling her back onto me by her shoulders, back stiff and my body taut as I shot jet after jet of my cum inside her.

"Fuck," I uttered and she went limp against the counter.

"What?" she gasped out after a few unsteady breaths.

"I didn't use a condom."

"IUD," she said.

"Doesn't protect against STD's, Baby."

"I'm clean," she murmured, her head to the side, cheek pressed against the counter as she rested.

I didn't like that. I didn't like that at all, she needed to be more careful than that, period, so I said, "And you're so sure *I* am?"

She froze and I pulled out of her slowly. Watching a white spill of my sperm slip out of her after my removal was such a dirty fucking turn on I was nearly hard again instantly. Instead, I tucked it back in my pants and buttoned up while she stood slowly, her dress falling to cover her, as she turned and leaned her shapely butt against the counter.

"Are you?" she asked nervous.

"Maybe I am, maybe I'm not. That's why you should always use a condom." I wanted her to be safe, at the same time I was angry with myself for letting this happen, for losing control like that. Some sadistic part of me was enjoying her discomfort so I didn't fess up right away about the status of my sexual health.

"Are you?" she repeated and swallowed hard.

I simply stared back, neither confirming nor denying for the moment.

"You can be a real dick, you know that?" she asked and I neither confirmed nor denied that either.

She cursed and drifted past me and my bike sitting forlorn in pieces in the middle of my kitchen floor. She snatched up her bag and made for the hallway and I broke.

"Charity…"

"Save it, Nothing; just save it," she said, voice wavering with tears. A moment later I heard a door shut and the bath start to run in the guest bath. A moment or two later and the shower kicked on, right about the same time I started kicking myself.

She was right, that was a real dick thing to fuck around about. I bowed my head and pulled on the back of my neck to ease the tension knotting me up between the shoulder blades. Finally with a sigh, I took a seat on the overturned five gallon bucket, picking up a socket wrench and got back to work. It was hard to concentrate. The feeling of her soft skin on mine a sense memory, a ghost of feeling I hoped hung around a while.

God I was a fucking mess.

CHAPTER 11
Charity

I shut the bathroom door and started the bath to let it get warm before switching it to the shower. I sat for a minute on the closed lid of the toilet and shook. Sex with him had clearly been a really, really bad idea but it'd felt so amazing at the same time. I buried my face in my hands and scrubbed at it furiously to wipe the tears away.

Why would he do that? What could he possibly have to gain by saying those things to me?

I stood up and tossed my wet clothes in the sink. My bag was still really damp on the outside, but inside everything was dry. I pulled out the towels and set them on the toilet next to the bathtub and got into the shower. The hot water soothed any residual chills out of me, except for the one that ran through my blood at what he'd said to me...

"Maybe I am, maybe I'm not..."

Who fucking *does* that?

I showered and pulled myself together. For better or worse, I was stuck here until at least the storm was over and who knew how long hurricanes lasted, I hadn't thought to ask. I stepped out of the shower onto the thick bathmat and wrapped my hair in one towel and my body in the other. I took the time to brush and braid my hair and dressed quickly. Bra, panties, denim short shorts and a pink tank top. I dressed for the Florida heat, and not the way I really wanted to after his comments which was as covered as possible.

When we'd been having sex, I was all for it. It'd felt amazing, wonderful, and had been totally erotic and hot in a desperate down and dirty kind of way. After what he'd implied after, though? Now I was just left feeling dirty and on uncertain ground. I hated mind fucks like the one he'd given me. How was I ever supposed to trust or believe anything he ever said again? I don't think guys realized what kind of damage they did with those kinds of head games, you know?

I tried to put on a front that looked braver than I felt before going back out to that kitchen to face the music. I was half hoping he would be standing there feeling guilty about what he'd said; hoping he would start immediately apologizing... no such luck. He was seated on a dirty, white, overturned bucket, turning a socket wrench with that familiar ratcheting sound. When I'd been a little girl, before my dad had been kicked out by my mom for what he'd done to Hope, I used to sit on the grass next to the driveway while he worked on his truck.

I closed my eyes now and tried to pretend it was the sun on my face, a book in my hands. I tried to let the sound take me back to that time and place when I'd still had both parents. When I'd felt safe and loved and everything was still bright and shiny with a future full of endless possibilities.

"What are you doing?"

His gruff voice pulled me right out of my fleeting daydream and I sighed. He may not be able to tell the truth, but I would never be that person.

"Pretending I was back home in California, my dad working on his truck in the driveway."

He squinted at me, hands still working at his bike, "Why would you do that?"

"Because right now, anywhere else would be better than here," I said softly and he sighed, hanging his head with a soft curse.

"Look, I'm clean, I don't know why I said that..."

"Because you're an asshole. Only assholes say things like that to girls they just banged against their kitchen counter."

"Fair enough, I deserve that."

"I brought you some food," I set down the Tupperware containers full of what I'd pilfered from Cutter's house on the edge of the nearest countertop – the one, thankfully, we hadn't just fucked against.

"Look, Charity –"

"Save it, Nothing. I don't want to hear it," I told him and walked away.

He cursed again and there was a sharp bang and clack followed by what I imagined was his socket wrench skidding across the kitchen floor. I'd left my bag and wet things in his bathroom, but right now, I just wanted to be surrounded by something that was mine. I didn't want to go wandering through his space, so I went back out to the garage and huddled in the driver's seat of my Jeep. I cried some more, and I think, eventually, I fell asleep. Had to be better than awake.

God, I was such a stupid girl.

* * *

I woke up somewhere that wasn't my brightly colored bed in Cutter's house. It took me a minute to realize it wasn't my Jeep, either. I pushed back the black comforter and sat up. The dresser at the foot of the strange bed was made of dark wood, an antique mirror against the wall was attached to it, the silvered glass spotted at one edge where it was either flawed or flaking in the back.

Pictures were tucked into the edges of the mirror, surrounded by the same dark wood as the dresser and foot board of the bed. The storm sounded like it was still going strong out there, and I realized that the light that illuminated the room wasn't from a nightlight, it was the blue-white light of a battery operated camping lantern.

I threw back the blankets and picked up the lantern from the bedside table, which matched the bed and dresser. I glanced through the doorway beside the bed and noted the small master bath through it, but the pictures around the mirror were like a siren's call. I couldn't resist.

The pictures were of a pretty auburn haired woman with blue eyes that held just a hint of lavender to them. She held a smiling girl about four or five and they were laughing at the man behind the camera, sitting in the back of an ambulance's open bay doors. Tucked behind the picture were two EKG readout strips, one had pen in the upper right hand corner in blocky letters that read 'Katy.'

The other, when I edged Katy's out of the way, read 'Mommy.'

There was another picture above the one with the EKG strips, this one had the ambulance in profile, and standing in front of it, was a younger looking Nothing, the smiling woman tucked against him in the crook of one arm, the little girl sitting on her father's shoulder, an arm tight over her lap, her arms raised in the air in triumph.

A happy family. N*othing's* happy family... except now he was all alone.

I let my eyes roam from picture to picture, settling on a close up of Nothing's wife. She had pale white scars along the side of her neck, her hair in the first and second picture had hidden them away, but this picture she was coming up out of a swimming pool, her hair slicked back behind her, showing them against her pale, freckled skin. The scars on the side of her throat drew the eye down to the heavy patch of scarring on her chest and so intent was I on the images I didn't hear the door open, or see Nothing standing there, shoulder against the door jamb until he cleared his throat, scaring the ever living crap out of me. I jumped and put my hands to my chest, startling hard with a short bleated shout.

"I put you in here so you'd be more comfortable than sleeping in your car, not so you could snoop through my shit."

"I hardly think looking at some photographs in plain view constitutes snooping," I snapped.

He pushed off the doorframe with a snort, "Whatever. I was coming to see if you wanted something to eat."

"The power gone out?" I asked.

Nothing raised his eyebrows, "What do you think?"

"I think you're behaving like a real cocksucker, that's what I think," I muttered dispassionately.

He bowed his head, and let it bounce a couple of times before grabbing the back of his neck and pulling to ease the tension between his shoulders. I knew it for what it was, I did the same thing.

"Fair point, well made," he conceded.

"What I can't exactly figure out is why?"

He gave a Gallic shrug, "Maybe that's just the kind of guy I am."

It was my turn to raise my eyebrows, "Really? The same guy that carried me from my Jeep to his bed so I'd feel more comfortable?" I asked.

He smiled, and it changed his whole face into something different, something beautiful, like an angel that'd fell to earth… or a devil. Wasn't Lucifer an angel once?

"Fair enough. Hungry?" he asked.

"Is there coffee involved?"

"Power's out, but I've got some energy drinks in the fridge, still cold I think."

I made a face, "Those are so crap for you."

"And coffee isn't?"

I gave him a look that said clearly, 'don't be stupid' and he laughed this time. I hugged myself and went towards him, he reached out and I just automatically shied back. I still felt gross and I think he knew it. His face fell and he nodded, I hoped an apology was coming but no dice.

He just gave me the next best thing instead, "I'm clean, for real. Guess I just felt the need to teach you a lesson."

"What, to never, ever trust a guy again? Lesson learned."

A stormy look crossed his face, a scowl, but I don't think it was aimed at me. He stepped aside and gestured, saying "After you."

I stepped past him and padded barefoot down the hall to the kitchen. I must have been asleep longer than I'd thought because the motorcycle seemed to be mostly back together, fewer pieces littering the newspaper, which also seemed to have been picked up and refreshed, new lying on the ground.

"What was wrong with it?" I asked.

"Critical leak, needed to replace some gaskets, it's almost done."

"How long was I out?"

"Long enough. Can I ask you?" I turned to look at him and waited patiently for the question. "Why'd you crash in your car? You could have just asked me…" I cut him off.

"What, like I asked if you were clean?" He had the decency to look at least halfway chagrinned.

"Right," he said instead and held out a plate of food to me, a sandwich, but not like the ones I'd brought with me. Something he'd likely crafted.

"An apology come with this?" I asked softly and my gaze flicked up to his. His gray eyes were shuttered tight, his walls high and impenetrable.

"Nope."

"Fucking great," I muttered taking the plate.

"You need to be more careful," he intoned gravely.

"Thanks, Mom."

"I'm not your mother, Charity. I'm not your daddy either," he said when I opened my mouth to be flippant. I shut it resolutely.

"You're an asshole," I said finally and he nodded, but there was no smile attached to the movement.

"I won't disagree with you there," he said and it was the last bit of talking that we did. He went back to working on his bike and I hoisted myself up to sit on one of the kitchen counters and eat my sandwich. A bite or two in, he rose and wiped off his hands with a rag. He turned opening up the fridge beside me, and wordlessly handed me an energy drink. I eyed him warily and took it, cracking it open. It was cool, but not cold, which I could live with.

I finished the sandwich and sat and watched him work for a while before working up the nerve to ask him, "When does it look like I can leave?"

He paused, his sexy as hell shoulders dropping minutely before he asked, "Can't wait to get away from me?"

"Do you blame me?"

"No, I guess not… and the hurricane made landfall a couple of hours ago."

I frowned, "I don't understand, didn't it make landfall before I even arrived?"

"That's a fallacy, Baby."

"Don't call me Baby," I said stopping him, he sat there, mouth hung open mid-response before closing it and nodding once.

"Okay. As I was saying, landfall isn't when the hurricane starts tearing shit up, it's when the eye reaches land and passes over."

"Oh."

"Yeah, we're over halfway through at this point."

"That's good," I murmured.

He nodded, and went back to work and I watched him, hating myself at how I couldn't tear my eyes from the muscles moving beneath his skin. I'd close my eyes to block it out but all *that* did was take me back to the feel of him moving inside me. I hadn't tipped over the edge, hadn't come from his relentless fucking, but it had felt phenomenal just the same.

I sighed and leaned my head back against the cabinet, and the sound caused him to look over his shoulder at me, he paused and his mouth thinned down into a grim line.

"Don't worry, Char. Pretty soon the rain will end, the sun will come out, and you'll be free to go."

"Yeah..." I said, thinking to myself, *not soon enough*.

CHAPTER 12
Nothing

I'd hurt her, and I was surprised to find that the knowledge hurt *me*. Still, I needed to stick to my guns here. She was better off without me. I couldn't give her enough of me. I wasn't the man for that. Too much of me still belonged to Corrine and to Katy, and they were gone, *and it was all my fault*.

I worked on my bike, her accusatory glare boring holes in my back, which I deserved, so I let it fly. I still couldn't figure out why I'd found her asleep in her car, and I was grateful she was a heavy sleeper. It made moving her a lot easier. I'd watched her for a while, asleep in my bed, and couldn't help but think she looked good there.

She was the first woman I'd done anything with since Corrine and I felt guilty, not about what we'd done… no, I felt guilty about the fact that I *didn't* feel guilty. I felt guilty for playing the mind fuck I did on her, but I had been really mindful up 'til this point about not apologizing. She needed to stay away from me. Now more than ever, now that I realized this attraction went both ways. I couldn't afford this to be a fatal attraction for a girl like her. She had too much to offer the world to have everything cut short.

I turned the wrench, tightening down a bolt, and it slipped. I busted a knuckle against the frame and dropped my tool with a clatter and a curse, sticking the offending joint in my mouth. Suddenly she was there, hands gentle around my own pulling it free of my face to have a look.

"Oh, we're going to ice this," she said soothingly, and I had to bet it was her nurse's voice. The one she reserved for patients. I went to take my hand back but she'd already let go, and was at the freezer pulling out the ice tray.

"Melted?" I asked and she shook her head.

"Just a little around the edges, but not too bad, if the electricity comes on soon, you might be able to save what's in there."

"It won't and I won't, but that's what the post-storm cookout is for."

"Post storm cookout?" she asked, brow raised as she emptied the ice tray into a gallon freezer bag.

"Yeah, everyone brings their frozen food that didn't make it and we cook it all into a one big 'I survived' kind of a feast. The whole town does, as far as I know. This is only my second hurricane and the first one wasn't nearly as bad. It's been about ten years since Florida's been hit. We've been lucky."

I was rambling, I knew I was rambling, but her hands were around mine again, gently laying the ice across my fingers, skin soft against my own and I couldn't help but close my eyes. My cock stirred to life, wanting a round two, but I couldn't, and wouldn't, let that happen. Once was enough. It had to be enough.

"I don't get you," she said softly.

"You don't want to."

"That's the problem, Nothing. I do, too. I really do."

Fuck. I didn't know what to say so I remained silent, and eventually with a defeated sigh, she moved back to her place on the counter. Eventually she started yawning, and the yawns became more frequent, until finally I looked up and said, "You're welcome to go lay back down."

She held on for about twenty minutes more before sliding off the Formica and onto her bare feet.

"Thanks," she said shortly and padded off, back in the direction of my room. The room I didn't sleep in anymore. The room I tended to avoid because of the memories on the mirror. I slept on the couch most of the time, but she didn't need to know that.

I went back to work on the bike, and listened to the storm gradually grow less until the rain petered out and stopped. I checked out the front door. Still windy, the streets littered with debris, but for all intents and purposes, clear for her to go. I nodded, satisfied she'd be safe, and pointedly ignoring the empty pit the thought of her leaving caused in my stomach.

"You can't have your cake and eat it, too," I murmured to myself, shutting the front door. I sighed and went to my bedroom doorway.

She looked like an angel when she slept, the lines of her face smoothed out and peaceful while she dreamed. There was something more open, more fragile, about her but stronger at the same time, too.

She was beautiful. Ethereal in the blue white light cause by the storm lantern. It was so late at night as to be early morning. An hour or two more and the sun would start coming up over the houses. I guess her departure could wait until it was light out. It'd make it safer for her, so instead of waking her, I watched.

Who was lying to who now?

CHAPTER 13
Charity

I pulled into Cutter's driveway, tires on the Jeep sloughing through leaves and palm fronds. I braked to a stop in front of the doors, and shut it off, throwing it into gear and applying the emergency brake. Slinging my bag of belongings over my shoulder I got out, the front door opening before I reached the top step. Hope looked pissed, and I guess she had a right to be, but my breaking down into tears on sight threw her for a loop.

Her face changed from anger to fear and her arms went up and out immediately. I fell into them and bawled against my oldest sister, and it was one seriously ugly cry.

"Charity, what happened?" Hope cried, and hugged me tight, smoothing down my hair. I heard masculine echoes around us.

"She alright?"

"What happened?"

"Is she gonna be okay?"

Hope gave an exasperated sigh and turned us, my bag was lifted off my shoulder and I blindly gave it up to whoever was trying to take it.

"Move! Out of the way, guys," Hope said in her Corporal Badass voice and it was like the parting of the red sea, or in this case, the black sea for all the black leather vests.

Hope took me upstairs, Faith floating behind us like a ghost, and my sisters shut me safely in my bedroom, which was just as I'd left it.

Hope dropped us onto the edge of the bed, and Faith sat down on my other side, taking up my hand and squeezing it. I cried it all out in bitter, broken sobs against my sister and spilled the whole story.

Hope had gone wooden by the time I'd finished and asked, "He apologize for any of this?"

"No," I moaned.

"That *mother*fucker," she said low and with feeling. "Where the fuck does he get off using my baby sister like that? Getting you all worked up and for what?"

"I don't know," I moaned, "He's an asshole."

"Yeah he is," Faith agreed, but she sounded uncertain, confused.

A knock at the door, and Hope got up, passing me into a hug from Faith. She opened the door and I caught a glimpse of Cutter and Marlin on the other side.

"Hey, she alright?" Marlin asked, and both he and Cutter wore mirrored expressions of concern.

"Let's just say Nothing *really* took the prize this time, if the prize is King of the Assbags."

"What'd he do?"

Hope glanced back at me and I sniffed, nodding. I looked away, humiliated, but she'd explained to me that the law with these men, was different. That they handled things differently and lived by a different code than the rest of the outside world, than your average… what had she called it? Civilian? No, that wasn't right, no she had said *citizen*, only the way she'd said it made it sound like something less, like what dog was to human. With the same sort of affection a human would refer to a dog. Nice, cute, fluffy, and great to have around, but dumber than a box of rocks.

"They had sex, and it kind of escaped them both to use protection," she raised a hand, before the guys could go there. "She's on birth control, but when they finished, Nothing implied that he wasn't clean in a bid to freak her the hell out. Pulled a real mind game on her and now she's upset."

"Fuck yeah, I'd be upset, too!" Cutter said, bewildered. He exchanged a look with Marlin and Marlin nodded.

"We'll take care of it," Marlin said, and didn't sound at all happy about it.

"What does that mean?" I asked and Cutter looked up sharply from Hope's face, to my tearstained one.

"Club business, Trouble. I can't say, but whatever happens won't be your fault. Nothing brought this on himself. That was disrespect, plain and true, and you're not a woman to be disrespected in such a way. There're plenty of 'em that come through this town, but not you. I'm sorry he did that."

"You don't get to apologize for him, but thank you for doing it all the same," I said quietly and his face fell just a touch.

"Marlin," he said.

"Oh, I'm on it, Captain," the big blonde man said and he disappeared down the stairs.

"Don't you worry your pretty head, Trouble. We've got this, and you'll be gettin' your apology, straight from the horse's mouth."

I was scared of Cutter in that moment, the cold radiating from his usually warm brown eyes. Hope murmured something to him along the lines of Nothing should be grateful it was one of the brothers going to deliver the message; that it wasn't her heading over there. Cutter looked down at her and his gaze visibly thawed. He cupped her cheek, thumb grazing across her jaw before giving her a nod. He looked up and gave Faith and I a nod of our own before disappearing back down the stairs.

I looked at Hope and sniffed, "They aren't going to hurt him are they?" I asked and she raised her eyebrows.

"Probably not as much as I think he deserves," she said.

I bit my lower lip and shook my head, "Don't hate him, please? I think there's something going on with him."

"Oh there's a lot going on with Nothing, baby sister, but nothing that he gets to treat you like that. That's how you treat a club whore, that's *not* how you treat either of my girls. He needs to know that."

I looked at Faith and she looked at me, her lips pressed into a thin line of disappointment mixed with distaste. She nodded her agreement and I think my mouth fell open in surprise.

"You agree, of all people?" I asked and she nodded emphatically.

"The pacifist was burned out of me a long time ago, Char," she said and shuddered. I hugged her and she hugged me tight.

"It's so nuts," I whispered.

"What is?" Hope asked.

"The fact that even though he was such a dick, I still really like him," I said.

"Hence why he needs to learn his lesson now."

I looked at her, "Because there's no way I'm going to let you invest yourself in a man who treats you like that, so I'd better fix him now before you do, because when you put your mind to something, we all know you're going to do whatever it is anyways. You're just like Faith that way."

Faith laughed, and I looked from her to a smiling Hope and back again. I couldn't help but smile, too.

"I love you, guys."

"We love you, too, Blossom," they said practically in unison and I felt better.

A rap came at the door, "Yo, Charity! It's Radar, can I borrow your keys, Sweetie?"

Hope held out her hand and with a sigh I pulled them from my hip pocket, handing them over, a tiny knot of dread taking up residence in the center of my chest that grew with the guilt I fed into it.

Hope opened the bedroom door and slapped the keys into Radar's hand, "Do what you need to do," she said and Radar gave a curt nod before backing out of view.

"Don't hurt him!" I called out before Hope shut the door.

I prayed silently, *please don't hurt him*, and found myself praying that it would be enough.

CHAPTER 14
Nothing

I finished tightening the last bolt down on my bike, just as a hard knock came at my front door. Sounded like the guys were out and moving around. This was probably my call to the town clean up. I wiped off my hands with a rag and went for the front door, just as the next, more impatient knock landed.

I opened the front door to Radar's fist in my gut.

"Oof!" I doubled over and hit the hardwood on my knees hard, trying like hell to suck air into my lungs thanks to my collapsed solar plexus.

Shit. Charity.

"She alright?" I wheezed and Lightning got behind me, putting his hands under my arms and hauling me onto my feet.

"What do you care?" he asked.

"I care," I said.

"Yeah, I call bullshit," Radar said and clocked me one in the side of the face.

I deserved this. I'd hurt her. She'd gone back to the Captain's house and whatever'd happened, had sent my brother's over here to teach me a lesson. One I richly deserved.

"Captain sent us over here to school you, Nothing. It ain't personal," Lightning said, and he held me up for Radar to deliver another blow. I did what I was supposed to. I stood there and took it.

"The fuck it ain't personal," Radar said. "That girl is *Hope's sister*. She's one of us; she ain't a random piece of ass passing through town. What the fuck were you thinking doing her like that?" Radar demanded. He hit me again and I saw stars.

"That's the problem, I wasn't thinking," I groaned.

"No, you weren't," he agreed. "Club voted, you're going to take this ass whoppin', then you're going to help with clean up, and *then*, you're going to go apologize to Charity. You get me?" he demanded and lifted my head by the front of my hair so I could look him in the eye. I nodded feebly and took my schooling well, and to heart.

He was right. Charity was one of us, and she hadn't deserved what I'd done. She deserved better than me. She deserved one of my brothers to love her and protect her from the shit I'd delivered... Why the fuck was it, that the thought of her with one of them hurt worse than the whoopin' Radar put on me?

He rained blows into my midsection, but avoided the face for the most part after only one or two blows to it. Probably because my thick skull hurt his hands and he needed his hands for what he did as a bail bondsman. Not only for all of the typing he had to do, but for the take downs and arrests. Hard to manipulate handcuffs with your hand in a cast or fingers in a splint.

"Let him go," Radar said with some disgust, and Lightning dropped me like a sack of potatoes onto my living room floor.

"Get your shit together, Nothing. Way I see it, that girl is a gift from god when it comes to you. Lightning, let's go."

Lightning stepped over me and went out past Radar, a grim look on his face. He hadn't enjoyed kicking my ass. Neither had Radar, but Radar could shut that part of himself off. Divorce his feelings from anything he did. It's what made him a good Sgt. at Arms.

"You got an hour to get cleaned up and find the rest of us in town on clean up. I'd get moving if I were you."

I coughed and pushed myself up into a sitting position. Radar spit on the ground and with a final disgusted noise that hollowed out the pit of my stomach, marched across the debris field in my yard and climbed into the driver's seat of Charity's white Wrangler. He leaned across Lightning and called out the passenger window, "For the record, she asked us not to hurt you! Not sure why that girl thinks you deserve mercy after the shit you said, but she does."

He fired up the Jeep, put it in reverse, and backed out of my driveway. I sat for a few minutes and took stock of myself from a professional standpoint. I was going to be sore as fuck for a day or two, bruised enough to give it a good show, at least in my face, but all told, Radar had gone easy on me.

I got up and got a shower, pushed my bike, with difficulty, back out into the garage and filled her with fluids. Moment of truth, I fired her up, and she fired true. Well at least one thing had gone right.

I had fifteen minutes to get where I was going, which in a town this small? That was easy. I shot a text to Radar and asked where they were at. A second later he pinged back with '@ the Capt,' so I headed there first, a knot of dread in my chest. I didn't like pulling displays of humility after fucking up. No one did; but I was due one.

I rode carefully around and over debris, and pulled into the Captain's circular drive. Several of the guys were standing around planning cleanup, briefing on where to start. I kicked palm fronds out of my way until I had a patch of bare paver to lean my kickstand on. Tipping the bike gently, I leaned her over onto her stand and shut her off.

"We get the bikes?" Trike asked frowning.

"No, I just finished rebuilding my engine, she weathered the storm with me."

"Oh," he said and Stoker smacked him in the shoulder, talking down to him all the while giving me a harsh glare.

Guess no one would be talking to me until I made that apology. I'll give my brother's one thing... they were good at keeping a wayward man in line when he strayed off the path that was right by the club and his brothers. Seemed to me that Charity may have charmed the pants off of more than just me, I just seemed to be the only man here she'd done it to, *literally* rather than figuratively. I went up the steps, straightening my cut over my weathered Red Hot Chili Peppers band tee and with a sigh, stepped over the threshold of my Captain's open front door.

It took a second for my eyes to adjust, even after raising my wraparounds to the top of my head. I blinked and glanced at Cutter, Marlin, and Pyro who wore triplicate grim expressions set in stone and I nodded.

"Anyone know where Charity is?" I asked.

"Right here," she said softly and I turned. She was standing practically beside me at the bottom of the staircase.

"Hi," I said, startled. She was dressed different. A peach, fitted tee replacing the pink tank, but the shorts were the same. She had on socks and what looked like hiking boots, a pair of work gloves sticking out of her back pocket. She'd straightened her hair and had it up in a high ponytail, and her makeup was done, light but there.

I wanted to ask her 'who does their makeup to clean up a town' but I didn't. Instead I did what I came here to do. I got down on one knee and looked up at her and said, "I apologize, I was an ass and there's no excuse for it. I'm sorry I scared you, I'm sorry I hurt your feelings, and I'm sorry that I made you cry." I swallowed hard, the seconds ticking by one by one and added, "That's not me, that's never been me, and I don't know what my fucking problem is."

I waited with baited breath for her to say something, anything…

CHAPTER 15
Charity

I came down the stairs, slowing when I saw Nothing standing at the bottom, sunglasses perched on his head, a fresh bruise on his cheek up near his eye. The bottom of my heart dropped out and I felt a swirl of guilt which I tried valiantly to beat back down with my quickly evaporating anger.

I had a problem staying angry at someone when they were hurt. All I wanted to do when I saw hurt was fix it, so that it didn't hurt anymore. I'm sure some psychologist would have a field day with me and my fucked up family issues and drawing inference on just why I became a nurse in the first place, but I didn't have time for all of that.

"Anyone know where Charity is?" Nothing asked, and my heart gave a leap for a totally different reason. I swallowed hard, and licked suddenly dry lips even as Cutter raised his eyebrows at me.

"Right here," I forced out and hated how soft and fragile it sounded. I felt like a rabbit that'd been caught by human arms; its little heart going a mile a minute, trapped in place when all it wanted to do was run.

He turned, those solemn gray eyes taking me in from my feet, all the way to the top of my head as I forced my feet to move down the last couple of steps to stand on the final, cream carpeted riser, before I met him even on the golden hardwood.

He turned and approached me, going down on his knees and looking up; I think my heart froze solid in my chest, skipping a beat, when his eyes met mine. Then he started to speak:

"I apologize, I was an ass and there's no excuse for it. I'm sorry I scared you, I'm sorry I hurt your feelings, and I'm sorry that I made you cry." He swallowed and added almost as an afterthought,

"That's not me, that's never been me, and I don't know what my fucking problem is."

I let out the breath I'd been holding and the part of me that wished to remain angry with him snapped that this was all well and good, but it was obvious his club *made* him apologize… still, the softer, more forgiving side of me chimed in with, *yes, but the words were all his.*

I touched the side of his face gently, and he let me, palpitating around the bruise and swelling with the pad of my thumb. He winced, and flinched and I sighed.

"Come into the kitchen with me, we'd best get some ice on this before it swells much worse," I murmured. If he read between the lines, then he would know I'd just accepted his apology, but the part of me that was entirely Hope's little sister couldn't let him slide through completely unscathed. Let's see how he liked having his head fooled with on something important.

He did something entirely unexpected then. He palmed my hand that I'd been about to take back and turned his face, planting gentle lips against my fingertips. Well damn, guess he knew he'd been forgiven and I was a little bit perturbed with myself that I'd let him get away with it that easy.

"Sure, ladies first," he said and got up onto his booted feet, moving aside for me to go past him. He trailed me into the kitchen and sat down at the large, glass, dining room table. I went to the refrigerator which was still working. Cutter, in addition to state of the art storm shutters, had backup generators to run the house when the power went down.

I put ice into a kitchen towel and brought it to him, he accepted it with a grateful nod, and put it against his face. While he did that, I captured the hand I'd done this for only hours ago and looked at the knuckle. He'd lost a gash of skin and it was bruised, but the swelling had gone down considerably.

"You'll live," I said, releasing his hand and he looked up at me, palming my hip and giving it a squeeze, a strangely casual touch given all that'd occurred in such a short amount of time.

"Thanks," he said.

"You're welcome," I murmured and moved away from him and back out to the foyer. Cutter and Marlin looked at me quizzically and I nodded carefully.

"I'd like, very much, to just forget it if we could?"

"Don't blame you one bit, Trouble," Cutter said kindly.

"What can I do to help?" I asked.

"Well, we was just talking about that actually," Marlin said and heaved a big, Husky black and yellow tool box up and over the couch. It was the plastic kind, with something similar to a suitcase's arm and wheels.

"We was hoping that you could man the first aid kit and station, while we put Nothing to work this time."

I nodded, "Of course."

"We get all sorts of minor cuts, scrapes, slivers and thorns. It's not glamorous, but it keeps everyone working."

"Sounds good," I said and smiled.

"Alright then, let's get out there."

I was surprised to find that Cutter and the men of The Kraken didn't start with Cutter's house or the Plank. Instead, we walked down the street, by about four houses. The men all had various tools. Shovels, rakes, bolt cutters, pruning shears, tree pruning sticks, chainsaws, hand saws, utility belts with hammers and nails... we looked like a leather clad construction crew walking down Sand Dollar Lane.

They went up the drive of a smaller home and Cutter knocked on the door. An elderly man and woman, stooped with age answered it after what felt like forever.

"Mr. and Mrs. Pilchuck, we're here to clean up your yard and we've brought a nurse with us to check y'all's health. You two do okay?" he asked.

"Oh my, yes!" the woman called and the man nodded, the couple was all smiles and before Cutter had even finished talking, the men had scattered throughout the yard and had begun dragging fallen limbs and detritus off of the spongy grass and into the drive.

"Charity is a nurse and she's going to check y'all over make sure everything is running great, okay?"

"Oh, you don't have to do that, Anders!" the man cried.

"I know, Mitch, but better safe than sorry, yeah? Charity, why don't you follow Mr. and Mrs. Pilchuk into their kitchen and give 'em a once over."

"Yes of course," I said smiling and hefted the first aid kid from hell up the two steps of their front wrap around porch. They led me carefully back to their kitchen and Mr. Pilchuck sat at the table while I took stock of what was what in the big rolling kit, smiling at the stethoscope, oxygen meter, and blood pressure cuff.

"Can I see your finger?" I asked Mr. Pilchuck and he chuckled and held out his left hand. "You gonna put a ring on it? 'Cause I'm already married!" I blushed and laughed and clipped the O2 meter to his ring finger.

"Just relax and breathe normally," I assured him. "Are you taking any medications?" I asked and so began the basic health rundown that every nurse was trained to do.

Mr. and Mrs. Pilchuck, for both being in their early eighties, were in remarkable health. Mr. Pilchuck's blood pressure was a little high, but considering his prescription for it and all the excitement, it was within normal parameters. Even so, I relegated him and Mrs. Pilchuck to the front porch swing to merely watch the goings on around their home versus any actual participation. Well, aside from Mrs. Pilchuck and me making lemonade and sandwiches for the boys and my sisters.

Hope was wrestling tree limbs and hacking at things alongside Cutter, just like one of the boys while Faith was doing more fetch and carry. I treated Trike for a deep, nasty sliver, digging it out carefully with more of the plethora of supplies in the kit, handing him my work gloves and sending him back into the fray at one point.

I was surprised the clean up only took around two hours at the Pilchucks before Cutter gave a shout, and all was packed in to move to the next stop. I bid the elderly couple a goodbye and hefted my kit back down to the street and followed along to the next house, which, surprisingly, wasn't anywhere near the first.

"How do you pick them?" I asked, walking alongside Cutter and Hope, my eyes on Nothing's back.

It seemed I wasn't the only one to forgive him, the rest of the club had gone back to literally acting like, well; nothing had ever happened... no pun intended.

"We go by age, disability, and need. Same way we do it buttoning up houses," he said.

"For a rough bunch, you do a lot of good then?" I asked.

Cutter grinned, "You don't see the town's boys in blue out here do you?" he asked and Hope shot him a dirty look.

I laughed, "No, why?"

"When I first got here, I accused Cutter and his men of having the town in their pocket from fear," she explained. "It's how a lot of MC's work. Protection rackets and the like," she said.

"Why use fear when kindness goes a lot further?" Cutter asked.

"So the town's businesses don't pay you guys to keep order then?" I asked.

"That's club business, Trouble," he said with a wink.

"Uh huh, that's what I thought. So Hope, you were half right," I said.

"I didn't say that, now did I?" Cutter asked.

"No you did not," I conceded, "But sometimes it isn't what you say."

"Smart girl," he mused and we amassed in another front yard.

Again, I checked on the woman inside. She was disabled, a diabetic on oxygen, and her sugars had climbed dangerously high. I treated her with some of her own insulin and we got her comfortable and back down to manageable levels.

The men worked hard and tirelessly, and when it grew dark, they put lights on their heads attached to headbands and kept working. When it started to rain, Cutter called it a day and we went back to the house for much needed showers. We'd done five houses today and tomorrow he was hoping to do even more. Hossler's being the first on the list. Power had yet to be restored to the town, and at one point Cutter approached me with Nothing.

"I need you two to take your Jeep over to Ms. Julia's house." The diabetic on oxygen.

"Why what's wrong?" I asked alarmed.

"Nothing yet, but she called to let me know she's gonna be in a fair bit of trouble if the tank she's on runs out. She ain't got no power and she's getting' low on oxygen. Called the power company and they ain't got no designs on heading this way until at least tomorrow, maybe the next day."

"Right, what do you need me to do?" I asked.

"Go to her house, have Nothing load up her empty travel tanks, and get on over to the Hospital, it's about forty-five minutes up the highway."

"Okay, then what?"

"I have a contact there," Nothing said, "I can get the tanks switched out, and maybe one or two extra, enough to hold her until they get crews out here to restore power.

"Yeah, sure. Sound's good. Let's leave now," I suggested.

Cutter pulled me into a hug, "That's my girl's girl. Thanks for takin' care of my town."

I smiled, "Taking care of people," I glanced at Nothing, "It's what I do."

I drove us, and it was in utter silence, I kept glancing sideways at him, but Nothing was lost in his own little world, eyes glassy and fixed, far away and lost in thought. Finally, about midway to the hospital by the glowing clock in my dash, he shuddered and took a deep breath, like a man coming up out of the water for air. He turned and looked at me and his expression was both eerie and unreadable.

"I really am sorry I hurt you," he said and I jumped when his hand wrapped around mine where it rested on the shifter.

I turned back to the highway, to pay attention and breathed out, and in, out and in, to steady my sudden case of nerves. His fingers found the spaces between mine and I hazarded another long look. He was fixated on my hand and his, and his expression was troubled, like he was at war with himself.

"Nothing, please, just *talk* to me," I urged.

"I can't talk about it, I just can't... I just need you to know that I liked it. I liked being with you like that... a lot... and I just don't know what to do with that, you know? You're the first person I've been with since…" he swallowed hard and I gasped quietly.

"Seriously?" I asked and he nodded, looking so vulnerable it tugged at my heartstrings. Well, crap; that explained a few things now didn't it?

"You're beautiful, you're sweet, you're kind and gentle and you put up with shit that no woman deserves. Why the hell, out of everyone in the club did you set your sights on me?" he asked.

"Maybe it's the healer in me," I suggested, "Or maybe you just look really, *really*, hot without a shirt on."

He laughed and the heavy atmosphere in the Jeep lightened some before he grew somber again.

"Pick someone else, Charity. You deserve a lot better."

I couldn't disagree when it came to the treatment so far, but… "I don't know, Nothing, you gave it to me awfully good," I said and his eyes widened in surprise. I smiled, "Think we can just forget about all that for now, and just try to be friends?" I asked.

"How many do overs are you going to give me?" he asked.

As many as it takes, I thought to myself, but out loud I said "Oh, I think I have one or two more in me."

We finished the ride to the hospital in silence, save for the odd direction or two Nothing had to give me to navigate this new and strange part of the country I was in. The atmosphere around and between us had fallen into a fragile truce, and for that I was grateful.

CHAPTER 16
Nothing

I met my contact, traded out the travel tanks and collected a couple of extra down in one of the deeper parts of the parking garage, money traded hands out of Charity's sight, and we were off, headed back down the freeway towards Ft. Royal.

She yawned just before getting back into the Jeep and asked, "You want to drive?" I closed my eyes as a set of headlights swept us, and pushed back the sounds, the screaming the broken glass and crumpling metal, the white hot agony in my leg and took a deep breath.

"No," I uttered and got in on the passenger side.

"Okay," Charity said a little bewildered, and she drove us back to Ms. Julia's. We made quick work of unloading and getting her hooked up, just in the nick of time, really. Charity took her O2 stats when we got to the house and she was in the low 70's. Her tank had run out only something like a half hour ago. It wasn't good.

We stuck around, watched her oxygen levels come back up into the 90's, and headed back to the Captain's house just as one of Florida's typical thundershowers started up. My bike was right where I left it, but a little rain wasn't going to hurt it aside from requiring I give her a wash in the coming days. Charity looked beat, which was funny because I was the one who'd gotten the beat down and had worked my ass off all day. I knew what it was though; it took a different kind of energy right out of you to treat patients all day. It could be exhausting all the same. A mental and emotional exhaustion that once you depleted your reserves past a certain point manifested in a very real, very physical, kind of tired.

"Come on, let's get you to bed," I said and she nodded.

I opened the front door to the Captain's house for her. Stoker, Radar, and Lightning looked up and over the back of the couch where they sat lounging, open beers in hand, a movie on the screen.

"Ms. Julia all good?" Radar asked.

"She's fine," Charity answered, "O2 stats were in the low nineties when we left her."

"Good," Radar said, but he was looking me over with cool appraisal.

"C'mon, Charity. You need sleep, tomorrow's going to be a whole 'nother day of taking care of people." I said and she nodded, half dead on her feet.

"Need a hand?" Stoker asked, eyeing Charity and I scowled.

"I got it."

Radar scoffed and turned back to the television, taking a slug off his beer, Lightning giving me a dirty look before doing the same. Stoker didn't look thrilled but he minded his own business as I gestured for Charity to precede me up the stairs.

"Where is everyone?" she asked tiredly.

"Getting the *Reclaimer* back in the water before any of the other salvage companies do. Storms are a prime time for the Captain and Pyro to make some fucking bank. They need it, and the club needs it," Stoker said.

"Oh," Charity said and nodded. She sighed and moved to the stairs. I hesitated at the bottom, but followed her up. I just wanted to see if she was alright.

Yeah... and pigs fly.

Truthfully, I hadn't liked the way Stoker had eyed her, but it wasn't like I had a right or a claim. I'd made that abundantly clear, right?

Charity stopped just inside the bedroom door and turned abruptly, her arms going around me, hugging me tight. Her head fit perfectly under my chin and I couldn't stop myself. I let my arms go around her and rested my lips on her hair. She smelled good, her shampoo something tropical and fruity.

"I know they made you do it, but thank you anyways," her voice was muffled against my chest, her breath warm through the thin fabric of my tee.

"For what?"

"For apologizing."

I chuckled lightly, "They didn't have to make me; I would have done it anyways eventually. What I did was wrong and I'm sorrier than you could know. I really am, Charity."

She looked up abruptly and our lips just sort of naturally met, I didn't think it was on purpose, but even if it was – oh hell. I stopped for once. I just stopped trying to pick it apart and kissed her back. It felt so damned good, her lips silken and warm against my own. The attraction raced like fire along gasoline, over and through me, setting me ablaze until I had to force myself to let her go. It was a hell of a battle to do it.

When I opened my eyes, it was to her beautiful face, flushed pink from the contact. She opened up those icy blue eyes of hers and pinned me to the spot.

"I'm sorry," she breathed.

"Don't be," I murmured.

"I'm the one who suggested we just try at friends and friends just don't kiss each other like that."

"I kissed you back, Baby. Friends don't kiss back, do they?"

"I don't know."

"That makes two of us," I breathed bowing my head and pulling on the back of my neck with one hand to ease the sudden tension taking up residence between my shoulders. Anxiety trembled down every nerve ending, my heart picking up pace as the confusion set in.

"What is it?" she asked.

"I… my wife…" I said and she nodded a little sadly, and stepped away. I suddenly felt cold and bereft.

"I'm sorry, I shouldn't have done that," she murmured and looked genuinely upset.

"No, I'm just as much to – look, can we start over?" I asked and she laughed lightly.

"Sure," she agreed.

"I'll see you tomorrow, Charity, my friend."

She nodded, "I'll see you tomorrow, Nothing, my friend."

I backed out of her doorway and gave a little wave like a lame jackass and beat a hasty retreat down the stairs, adjusting my cock where it strained, uncomfortably, against my zipper.

Friends, yeah right. I thought and slipped out the front door into the rain, tipping my face up to the splish and patter, letting it cool my lips which burned with the memory of hers on them.

Christ. I had it bad, but just like a moth to flame, I would be back in the morning for some more of her presence. It was becoming a sweet kind of torture, really. A whole new kind of punishment for myself. *Look but don't touch.*

Christ, I was one seriously fucked up motherfucker. I went home, riding slowly in the rain, dodging some of the debris still left behind. The able bodied townsfolk had mostly looked after their shit, but my place was still a wreck. So were the streets. That was the last thing that The Kraken got around to doing things like we did. Weak and disabled town folk had their places looked after first, both cleaned up and repaired, then the boats went back in the water, then we focused on our own places, and finally, if it hadn't been looked to by municipal or county crews by then, we cleaned up the streets.

I pulled into my driveway and walked the bike carefully into the open maw of the garage, locking things down tight behind me. I spent a long minute in the shower and when I got out, I braved my bedroom. The bedding still lay folded back, the sheets rumpled from where she'd slept and creepy motherfucker that I was acting like, I laid down where she'd been and breathed deep. I didn't mean to, but I ended up passing right the fuck out.

CHAPTER 17
Charity

The rich aroma of coffee dragged me the rest of the way up out of sleep. I opened my eyes to a paper cup being wafted under my nose next to a denim clad thigh.

"Peace offering," Nothing said, holding out the cup to me.

"What is it?" I asked.

"Didn't know what you liked, so I chanced it and got you my usual."

"Which is?"

"Sugar free vanilla latte."

"Gimme the real thing next time and you're golden," I said sitting up and taking the cup, sipping. "Although for no sugar, this ain't half bad. What're you doing in here?"

"Like I said, peace offering. That and the guys are already up and moving for another fun filled day of storm clean up. You ready?"

I groaned, "Let me finish caffeinating and figure out clothes and then I should be."

He lowered his own cup from his mouth and swallowed, "Kay."

"Charity, you okay?" Hope asked from the door, scowling at Nothing.

"He brought me coffee, it's okay, he's one of us," I said in an attempt to diffuse any ugliness about to go down.

"He brought *you* coffee, but did he bring *me* any coffee? I'm the one he needs to be afraid of."

"It was hard enough bringing two on the bike, and she's technically the wronged party, so if you can hold off on the ire, I solemnly swear the next time I have access to my fucking cage I'll spot you."

Hope narrowed her eyes and pursed her mouth in her mock

angry look, "I'll let you get away with it this time," she said and breezed down the stairs. Nothing shook his head.

"A real ball buster that one," he muttered and I raised my eyebrows.

"Yeah, try being raised by her."

He smiled and, oh my god, he was gorgeous when he did that. Deep smile lines appearing, miraculously, out of nowhere, etching themselves to either side of his lush mouth and framing it to perfection. I suddenly, very much so, had to resist the urge to grab him and pull that mouth to mine.

His smile faltered, "What is it?" he asked, and I felt myself blush deeply.

"Nothing, Nothing. Now why don't you let a girl get dressed, and I'll meet you and everyone else downstairs."

"Okay," he got up and leaned over, hesitating at first, before planting a swift, chaste, kiss on my lips. I blinked and he was gone. I looked down at the cooling coffee in my hands and drank some more of it before kicking the blankets off my legs and going for clothes. We had another long day ahead of us.

I ended up driving the first aid kit and like four of the guys across town to Hossler's place. When we got there, she had a big square of the front lawn, all bright with sunlight, cleared of debris she'd pushed off to the side and was bringing canvas sacks out of her house, laying them out on the bare patch.

"Aw, hell no!" Trike cried from the back seat.

"Shut up, Prospect, and try not to be such a puss." Stoker said laughing beside me. I looked over at him.

"What are they?"

"Snakes," he answered and got out of my Jeep. The passenger seat was thrown forward and Trike, followed by Lightning and Gator, got out.

"I'm with Trike," I muttered and got out too.

Hossler's roof ended up needing repair. Nothing and Radar ended up spending most of the day up there fixing it, while I helped Hossler clean rat cages. It wasn't glamorous work, but it was honest and with as many kids as Hossler had hanging around, both hers and the neighbors, she was appreciative of my assistance. Besides, the rats, unlike the snakes, were cute. I could handle one snake at a time, they *were* cool to look at, but Hoss had something like sixty or seventy. That was more than a bit much for me.

After Hossler's and some talk, it was decided that was all there was room for, for that day and that the town cookout needed to happen to use the freezer food for the homes without generators before it went bad.

To the beach we went with a good three or four hours to go before sunset. I drove the guys to a storage unit around a half hour away so that they could get their motorcycles out and listened with a smile at their joyous sounds. Nothing had ridden, and he stood by smiling as the rest of the guys were reunited with their bikes. Hope went up to hers and hugged it. She'd ridden with Marlin, Faith, Cutter, and Pyro in Nothing's beat up old Subaru wagon. Cutter and Pyro had been picked up at the marina, their work with and on the *Reclaimer* having been done for the day.

"You sure?" Marlin was asking Faith and she scoffed.

"I'm sure, I remember how to drive an automatic! I'll be right behind you."

I smiled at them as he kissed her fiercely.

"Let's mount up!" Cutter called. Judging by everyone's wide grins and animated talking, I think it was safe to surmise they'd all had a good day.

We went back to the marina, Faith in front of me in Nothing's wagon, and in front of her, the long, double line of motorcycles, Hope just behind and to the left of Cutter, Marlin beside her.

It was both fun and a little strange to watch the hero's welcome the guys got. Townspeople running to the curbs, waving and cheering, clapping at our arrival as we turned into the marina's parking lot. People came forward to shake hands and welcome Cutter and the rest of the guys like we hadn't just been gone an hour or so.

The edges of the marina's lot were piled with temporary tables and barbecue grills. A bunch of the restaurant and bar owners manning them like the professionals they were, cooking up everything from chicken, to pork, to beef and even fish in some cases, to order. Salvaging what they could from defunct freezers.

Pyro had told me just about every place along the boulevard, and the town's bed and breakfasts all had generators to power them through, but it was likely a fuel run would have to be put together for tomorrow if the power wasn't restored tonight. Really it was the poorer and elderly folks of Ft. Royal that suffered when storms big enough to knock out power blew through.

I stood watching everything, smiling because I couldn't help it, and wishing that the rest of America would get on board and start behaving like this one little Florida town. Even if just a neighborhood banded together like this in some of the bigger cities, what a difference could be made.

Someone tapped me on my shoulder and I turned to look on my right side, a laugh from my left drew me back around.

"Ah! You're still here!"

"I am! I see you weathered the storm just fine, too," Greg said.

I nodded, "It's been interesting; that's for sure."

"You uh, here with anybody?" he asked, looking around at the mingling bikers and townspeople.

"No, not really. My sisters are with them, I just moved here to be with Hope and Faith."

"I see, think I could maybe interest you in that drink?" he asked, and his expression was steeled for rejection.

I laughed, "I still feel like I'm 'on duty' so to speak, so would sharing a bit of food do?"

He smiled like he'd won the lottery, "Perfect! What's your poison?" he asked.

"God there's just so much to choose from! I don't know," he stuck out his arm gallantly and I looped mine through it.

Greg was funny, and light hearted, taking me on a tour of everything there was to eat with a faux French accent like he was some sort of snooty maître d'. We chose our food and he asked me, "So what have you been doing the last couple of days? Where'd you weather the storm?"

I didn't quite know how to answer so I fudged it just a little,

"Um, well, the guys have been working on some of the older folks' homes, taking care of the disabled around Ft. Royal first, and I've been going along. I just graduated the advanced nursing program so I've been kind of putting the skills to good use, checking up on people. You know, the usual, blood pressure, oxygen stats, that sort of thing. Treating minor cuts and bumps, a sliver or two." I bobbed my head in a nod, blushing furiously, feeling like I was rambling.

"No, that's great! That's fascinating, really. Congratulations on graduating. You out looking for a job?"

"Yeah, I've got some applications in at some of the area hospitals and doctors' offices. I put a bunch in before I left to come down here. No call backs yet, but with everyone getting ready for the storm, and now cleaning up? I'm not really surprised. I'm sure I'll start hearing back soon."

"I'm sure you will," he agreed with a dazzling smile.

It was nice talking to Greg. Easy in a way that wasn't with Nothing. Things were so thick between Nothing and I, it made small talk awkward for the most part. Greg and I continued to make small talk until I spotted Nothing watching us, his gray eyes unreadable behind his wraparound Oakley's. Radar said something to him and he turned, a scowl deepening his features and I felt bad. It seemed Radar and Nothing were having a fundamental difference of opinion with one another lately, and rather than finding resolution, they were just antagonizing each other. I sighed and smiled at whatever Greg was saying, even though I hadn't heard a word.

"You haven't heard a word I've said for the last couple of minutes, have you?" he asked and I felt my shoulders drop.

Busted.

"I'm so sorry, my mind is just wandering something terrible," I said and sighed.

"No, no! Hey, it's okay I get it. You've just moved here, big storm, now you're helping put your town back together while it's in pieces. It's alright, I'm sure it's been a really exhausting last couple of days for you." *Aw, why does he have to be so sweet and understanding?* I thought to myself.

"It really has, and I'm right back at it tomorrow, too."

"Tell you what, where's your phone?" he asked. I pulled it out of my back pocket.

"Take this number, five-oh-four, five-five-five-, two-one-six-zero." I dutifully punched it in and hit send, his phone rang a moment later. "I'll call you in a day or two, and if you're not busy, maybe we can meet up. My business here is almost over, but I like it here. I might stick around a few days extra, especially if I knew I might score dinner and drinks with a certain pretty girl."

I laughed, "Okay, you win. I'll try to call you."

"Sound's good, maybe in the meantime, I'll see you around, Charity."

"Yeah, maybe..." I agreed. He got up and with a nod, wandered off in another direction into the crowd.

Faith appeared and sat down next to me, "He looked cute," she said with a faint smile, "Seemed nice, too."

"Yeah, he *is* nice, easy to talk to..."

"But he doesn't set your panties on fire like Nothing, or intrigue you, or flip any of your 'I want to fix it' switches," she said nodding her head.

"Oh my god!" I gasped incredulous.

Faith shrugged, "I was sold into human trafficking; I didn't die, and I'm probably more observant than I ever was, I'm just a lot quieter about it than I would have been before." My sister shifted a bit uncomfortably.

"Therapist tell you to confront it and be open about it?"

"Yeah, it's easier said than done, I don't want to upset you," she made a distressed face and I knocked my shoulder into hers.

"You say whatever you gotta say, Faith. I'm not judging you and if it makes me uncomfortable," I shrugged a shoulder, "So what? I can live with that as long as it helps *you*. I'm just happy to have my favorite sister back."

"I heard that!" Hope quipped and came up to sit on my other side.

"Neeah!" I made a childish sound and leaned away from Hope and into Faith; Faith laughed.

"Woah! Hold up! Need a picture of this," Marlin cried and whipped out his phone. He framed the three of us up; all smiles, leaning into each other, plates of food in our laps and drinks in hand, and snapped a picture.

The rest of the evening passed in a blur of warmth, happiness, and such a feeling of *family* I don't honestly think I'd ever experienced before. Not even when my family had been whole, with Mom, Dad, Hope, and Faith all living under the same roof, gathered around the same table. It was educational to say the least.

"You look tired," Nothing's voice startled me. I hadn't realized he was there.

"It's been another full day. I guess I'm out of shape, too much time on my ass studying."

He chuckled and stood beside me, where I stood, watching bonfires light on the beach.

"I happen to like your ass," he said so softly, really for only me to hear. I felt myself blush, then shiver.

"Thanks," I murmured.

"Want me to take you back to the house?" he asked.

"What about your bike?"

He smiled, "Have a drink, relax a little longer, and hold that thought," he said walking backwards towards the part of the parking lot loaded with bikes.

I laughed, and nodded, "Okay," I agreed and he jogged a pace or two backwards before spinning and trotting into the throng of people. A moment later his bike fired up and I watched him pull out and down the street towards Cutter's.

I did what he asked, I had another drink, and mingled with some of the MC and a woman named Miranda who ran one of the bed and breakfasts, an upscale one called the Nautilus. True to his word, Nothing returned, sidling up behind me to rest a warm hand at the small of my back.

"Ready to go?" he asked and I looked up.

"More than, I'm tired."

"Give me your keys," he murmured and I handed them over. He walked me to my Jeep and held my passenger door for me. I got in, and when he was sure he wouldn't catch me with it, he closed the door, jogging around the front to get in on the driver's side.

"What did you do, park your bike and run here?" I asked, noting his hair was damp at the back of his neck. He smiled over at me.

"Maybe."

It struck me, *how incredibly sweet!* He'd literally run back here, just so he could drive me home. *Who does that?* Certainly no man I'd ever met. I liked this Nothing. I wished he were around more than the sad, lonely, tortured, Nothing.

"What?" he asked, freezing in mid motion as he was about to put the key in the ignition.

"Nothing, no pun intended."

"What was that look for?" he persisted.

I laughed a little, "Just surprised, is all."

He frowned, "At what?"

"You."

He started the Jeep and leaned back, clearly expecting me to elaborate.

"You rode to Cutters, parked, and ran all the way back here just so you could give me a ride home?"

"So?"

"So, that's quite possibly the most sweet and genuine thing that anyone has ever done for me."

"Did I earn points?" he asked.

"Oh yeah, you earned beaucoup points."

He smiled and laid his cut, which he was in the habit of taking off anytime he got into my Jeep, across my lap.

"Good, I'm glad," he said and shifted gears, pulling us carefully around and out the drive, onto the boulevard.

We rode the short distance in silence, and when he got out, he told me to wait, and came around opening my door for me. I handed him his cut, and he swung it on, before taking my hand and helping me out. I smiled, and he kept my hand in his.

"I really am sorry," he murmured and I nodded.

"I forgive you."

"Yes, but it still doesn't make what I did okay. I'm a screwed up head case, Charity. I think meeting you, has made me realize I need to start working on that."

I simply nodded; I mean what could I say? It was true that Nothing clearly had some unresolved issues regarding the loss of his family, but Cutter had been right to a certain extent. I couldn't help Nothing until Nothing *let* me help him, and we just weren't far enough along in any way shape or form for that to even be a possibility.

He led me inside and up to my bedroom door, where I had every intention of letting him leave me, but like that morning, he surprised me, bending to place a chaste kiss against my lips. When he lingered just a touch too long, I took the risk, flicking my tongue against his lower lip.

My body yearned for another round of his hands on my skin, and what can I say? I was a total sucker for those deep, gray eyes of his. I wanted to soothe his hurt, and smooth the pain in them away even if it was only for a little while. The smart part of my brain was screaming at me to knock it off. To stop things before they went too far lest he have another attack of conscience, but the rest of me was totally like, *take the risk girl*.

His hands slid around my waist, pulling me into his body, as his mouth worked mine and I think we were *both* lost for a minute, in each other, and neither one of us were a responsible adult enough to pull back or stop. After saving that boy on the beach, after fucking in Nothing's kitchen, I think I realized that both of us were adrenaline junkies with a heart, to a certain extent. Otherwise why would each of us have chosen emergency medicine?

Nothing broke the kiss and I felt a twinge of disappointment which flared into a white hot desire when his lush mouth moved from mine to the side of my neck, lips gliding against the skin, teeth nipping sharply, his tongue hot and wet and soothing the sting until he found that spot *right there* that turned my insides liquid and my knees to jelly.

I gasped, my arms reflexively going around his shoulders, and he lifted me with ease. I either wrapped my legs around him, or this was going to get awkward really quick, so I complied. When I did, he took a step inside my room, kicking the door shut behind us.

It was dark outside, the golden glow from the small, bedside lamp, making the space seem smaller and more intimate. He set my ass on the edge of the bed and I disengaged my legs, sitting while he straightened and took off his vest.

Desire, a naked want, filled his eyes and I felt an answering want flood my own. I reached up to touch him, letting my hands glide down his body in a caress until I found the waistband on his jeans. He tossed his head back and gave a shuddering sigh, as my fingers hooked into the front of his waistband, working the button free of its confining loop.

"Charity," he gasped and I shushed him.

"Shh, I want to do this for you," I murmured. I unzipped his pants and worked them down his thighs until his cock sprang free, thick and long, standing at attention. I wrapped gentle fingers around him, stroking him softly, looking up at him so that he could see that yes, I really wanted this, as I took him into my waiting mouth.

Slightly salty, with a hint of musk, was how he tasted and I was in heaven as I let him travel over my tongue to the back of my throat, careful not to choke. There was an art to giving head, one I had perfected as a teenager, and it was really something I loved to do. What I couldn't fit of him in my mouth, I kept wrapped in my fingers, letting my saliva lubricate him on my withdrawal; I worked him gently, making love to him slowly with my mouth.

"Oh, god!" he cried, perfectly sculpted chest rising and falling with quick breaths, in and out, pausing and crying out when I worked a particularly sensitive spot on the underside of him, near his head, with my tongue. He kept his hands on the back of his neck, fingers laced, a tension to his body, head bowed and those beautiful gray eyes watching me and I slowly descended, taking him in, working him inch by inch into my mouth, holding him until I had a need to breathe only to back off of him swiftly when it became paramount that I do.

He fought himself not to thrust, but I didn't mind if he did. He dropped his hands to his sides, balling them into fists, careful not to grab my head, trembling with the exertion not to do so, and while I appreciated it, it wasn't required. I let my hands find his, twining my fingers with his, letting them find the spaces between his when he let his hands relax out of the tight fists he'd been making. I locked our hands together as I took away the aid of my hand on his cock. Relaxing my throat, I swallowed him whole, all the way down. When his head rested in my throat, I swallowed around him, his hips jerked again in reflex, all on their own, and I backed off quickly so that I could breathe. Nothing kept his head bowed, his eyes squeezing shut as he gasped, and struggled to maintain control. He wanted to thrust, he wanted to thrust so badly, but he didn't.

I couldn't imagine how long it'd been for him since a woman last did this for him, especially given what he'd told me, so I have to admit I was impressed at not only his level of control, but his staying power as well. I licked and sucked him patiently, his hands gripping mine so tight, they trembled, the skin of his fingers mottled red and white, the split in his knuckle nearly opening up again. His whole body held a fine tremble to it now and his cock jerked reflexively in my mouth telling me before he could that he was nearly at the end of his rope.

He tried to warn me anyways, "Oh god, I'm gonna come!" and I swallowed him down. He spilled down my throat in a hot wash and I took it, backing off and taking in air only when I was sure he was done. He slipped from my mouth, a glistening strand of saliva between my bottom lip and the head of his cock which I found both alluring and erotic, but then his hand was under my chin, tipping my head back and his mouth was on mine, plundering, exploring; taking with a frenzy borne of need.

He pulled me up and I kicked off my shoes, his hands at my waist, were already lifting my tee and I raised my arms above my head, letting him have it. He stripped it off, mouths crashing back together, lips and tongues clashing, each fighting to dominate the kiss. Nothing was winning by a landslide and I really liked that about him.

Before I could even lower my arms, his fingers were scrambling at the back of my bra, going for the clasp. He unhooked it and I let it fall. He kicked out of his boots, stepping on the hems of his pants to pull first one and the other leg free, while his hands smoothed over my skin, roaming my torso, kneading my breasts. I was letting my hands do every bit the same amount of wandering, stuttering when I found a seam of scar just below his waistline at his back; wrapping around his thigh running down the side of his leg, I think, nearly to the knee. I tried to draw back, to look, but Nothing stopped me. His hands going to either side of my face, cupping it, keeping our mouths locked until the resistance left my body and I moaned leaning into him.

He found my waistband when he knew he had me back under his thrall and worked the button and zipper on the front of my shorts, pushing them down until they fell at my feet. He broke the kiss we'd been feeding one another's fires with and pushed me backwards, going to his knees at the side of the bed. I fell back and before I could push myself up, he wrapped powerful arms around my thighs just above my knees and pulled me until my ass rested on the very edge of the bed.

"Just relax, baby, and keep your ankles high," he murmured and pulled my panties aside, licking a wet line from my opening to my clit. I cried out and arched my hands finding the silk of his hair and pressing his mouth right where I needed him. He hummed in appreciation and my hips jerked of their own volition, much like his had.

He lapped at my clit, finding what sent shivers through my body, what sent me to shuddering beneath him, and then followed through by exploiting the ever loving hell out of those spots until I lay sopping, begging him for a deeper touch. I craved him like I craved no other. He wound me up and watched me go, his gray eyes full of all the right kinds of evil. He knelt up and pulled me down again, only this time he paused to ask, "Condom?"

"Fuck it," I responded and he grinned and tilted his head to the side, ripping my panties *off* and tossing them aside, before driving himself into me to the hilt. I arched, back bowing to damn near the breaking point which served to drive me even further onto his penis and oh, holy *god*. I now knew what it meant 'to see stars,' flashbulbs of pleasure going off behind my eyelids.

"You, didn't come, the last time, we did this, did you?" every pause in his speech, punctuated with a hard thrust.

"No!" I gasped out.

"Gonna, have, to make, that up, to you!" he said and drove me fucking wild. He set a strong, near punishing, rhythm. His thumb finding my clit and rubbing it as he towered over me. Just looking at the long, lean, fine as hell line of his body as he worked himself in and out of me was enough to get me halfway to orgasm. The way he fucked me, he was running himself over that sacred spot inside of me, turning me on, tuning my body up, until my toes curled and that sweet pressure built, it only took a few teasing strokes of his thumb to send me hurtling into that abyss no one ever wanted to come back from.

I was vaguely aware, that in the really real world, my back was arching again, my body bent nearly double backwards as he encouraged me to keep coming, to milk his cock for everything it was worth, and I was pretty sure my body had this, because my mind was nowhere near being able to handle his commands.

Holy, god almighty.

It was intense, *he* was intense, and you never would have known just how intense by looking at him or by his day to day interactions with people.

He let up on my clit, thank god, I didn't think I could take anymore I was so hypersensitive. His gray eyes swept me from the crown of my head all the way down, lingering on my heavy lidded eyes, which I could appreciate. He'd slowed his rhythm to slow, lazy strokes, letting me recover, letting me catch my breath and I could appreciate that too.

"Come on, come up here," he took me by the hands and pulled me up into his arms, winding my legs around his hips. I twined my arms around his shoulders, and he picked me up, getting his feet under him and lifting me, arms shuddering for just a moment until he got the weight and feel of me. I was enamored by the fact that he hadn't pulled out of me.

He walked us up onto the bed on his knees and laid me down more comfortably, joining me on the mattress, leaning over me, smoothing stray strands of hair from my ponytail away where they clung to my face. He was gentle, far gentler than the moment before; than he had been in his kitchen.

He picked up his pace and I almost mirrored him in a way, combing my fingers through his hair and holding it out of his eyes as this incredible connection, this shared moment, this shared energy, built between us. He closed his eyes, turning his face to nip lightly at the inside of my wrist and I felt myself contract around his cock in an unexpected aftershock. He bowed his head and moaned, picking up pace and I pulled him down from where he was bracing himself off of me with his arms.

He folded against me, and we held each other, him moving inside of me, the frantic energy of before winding into a softer, sweeter thing. We went from fucking, to a languid sort of sex and edged right into, dare I say, making love in the span of only a few minutes time. It was a strange sort of feeling, making love to a near perfect stranger, which is what we were, really. Intense attraction aside, we hardly knew anything about each other and really had only spent a handful of days near one another... *God this was moving fast!* In all fairness, Hope had warned me...

"You're thinking," he uttered.

"I'm sorry?"

"I'm not doing this right if you're thinking," he murmured and kissed the side of my neck, worrying at that spot that sent a wash of tingles all down my body. I shuddered and felt his lips curve into a secret smile against my skin as he quickened his pace, thrusting into me that much harder, hard enough that I thought he was trying to come through me.

He boosted himself back up onto his knees, his hands curving under my ass, supporting my lower body so that he could go searching for the right angle to penetrate me at, the one that would send his dick riding over that, *oh my god*, he found it.

The head of his cock slicked over and over my g-spot and I swear to god, that warm golden glow of ecstasy built twice as fast as the first time. He licked his thumb, the devil in his eyes and sent me crashing into that warm bath feeling. I was drowning and I never wanted to come up for air. I could stay good and drowned in this man's arms. I didn't care. Here felt like heaven.

CHAPTER 18
Nothing

She slept, tucked close against me in my arms, her head on my shoulder and it'd been so fucking long since I'd had this feeling of contentment. Only problem was the soul crushing guilt that came along with it. I held up my hand and stared at the gleam of my silver wedding band, now living on my right hand after the guys had ridden me so hard about still wearing it. The switch from left to right had only come last year and still felt weird.

I sighed into the night, and looked down, pressing a light kiss to the top of Charity's head. I couldn't explain to myself, let alone her, what had compelled me to do her again. She didn't deserve this. She didn't deserve a guy who couldn't make up his mind. Who couldn't let go. She deserved someone who could give her all of them, or at least most.

It was what was keeping me awake. The guilt made up of equal parts betraying my wife's memory, and betraying Charity's good will and kind heart. I knew a little something about that. I used to have a good heart, too. Saved as many as I could, always doing the right thing, even after joining the MC.

I'd joined about two or three years after Corrine and I had gotten here, before she'd gotten pregnant with Katy. Cutter had been the one to talk me into it, saying he had great plans for The Kraken. Mac, the previous president, had still been president when Cutter had approached me and asked me to think about it. The Kraken had a real different reputation back then. One known for their human trafficking. Not sex trafficking mind you, no, these guys were more smugglers, smuggling human cargo along with expensive and illegal Cuban cigars out of their country of origin. For a nominal fee, of course.

Cutter hadn't wanted me involved with the heavy illegal shit as much as he could avoid me being in it. He knew what it would do to Corrine, and to my livelihood as a paramedic. No, Cutter wanted to keep me on the down low, wanted to start giving the club a better image, one of civility, one of respectability. He'd convinced Mac that The Kraken had needed it, and he wasn't wrong.

The other reason he wanted me? To give some much needed medical attention to some of the refugees from the communist country. Some of those poor people got out by the skin of their fuckin' teeth, and they didn't always come out of there healthy. On that front, I'd been happy to help. A real fuckin' humanitarian effort.

I started to drowse, listening to the cadence of Charity's deep and even breathing. What I hadn't counted on, which I should have expected given how stressed the fuck out I was over this new woman in my life, unexpectedly dropping in from the goddamned ceiling, was a recurrence of the dream.

It was late, the rain coming down in sheets so thick the headlights almost hurt my visibility rather than helped it. Katy was asleep in her booster seat in the back and Corrine and I? We were having the same fight we'd been having, about me working the night watch.

"I need you home. Katy needs her daddy home, why can't you see that?"

"Is this about the club?"

"No! It's never been about the club. I love Hossler, I love the guys, the club is like a real family with the way Cutter and Pyro and the rest are around to help. That's just it though; it's always your damn brothers fixing things around the house. You're either working, or asleep! No, Dominic, this is about the hours you keep. You're always putting work first, and you need to be paying attention to what's going on at home. I'm sick and tired of you being tired all the time, I want my husband back and Katy wants to spend some with her dad that isn't the five minutes before you go out the door for your shift, or the two before you drag yourself into bed to die for the day."

"Corrine, I don't understand why this is even a thing, I've always worked the night watch, since before I even met you, that's how I met you,"

"Right, that was nine years ago, Dominic! You have a wife, and a beautiful daughter and there's more to life than just work, and me now, you have to stop this! I need you to grow up before you find we've moved on without you, I'm sick of being the only one trying here! I want my husband and Katy wants her father. We don't want anyone else."

My frustration was mounting, Corrine had no idea I was giving help to illegal aliens and I'd worried my time away from her had more to do with the club than my job, but she'd been so quick to deny it. I felt something stir in the center of my chest, something about what she'd said, how she'd said it. I turned to her, a flash of light from oncoming traffic went across her, angry, pleading, lavender eyes that I loved so much and she whipped her head forward.

"Dominic, look out!" she screamed and I reflexively swerved. I was tired, I was too slow. Sparkling glass and the unholy scream of tearing metal. I think I blacked out, I can't be sure. A terrible rending agony in my right thigh, the world tumbling end over end and the awful, frightened screaming of my baby girl.

Sparkling glass, and the feeling of being weightless, end over end, a total loss of time and space and the agony burning through my leg... lights out.

Warm. Wet. Blackness absolute. The revving of an engine, steady and loud, I opened my eyes, a crushing weight on my chest from where the seatbelt had locked up. I ended up just turning my head, feebly, to stare into the wide, fixed stare of my beautiful wife, her lavender eyes glassy, face a bloody mask.

My daughter's voice...

"Daddy?" she began to cry and I screamed, struggling, hands holding me down, lights blazing in my eyes.

"No!" I screamed, struggling against the hands of the rescue workers, flinging my weight, sitting up, "Corrine, no!" I screamed.

"Nothing, wake up!"

I reflexively drew back a hand to fight off the rescue worker trying to press me back down. I backhanded the paramedic, except there *was no* paramedic…

Charity!

She went flying, landing on the carpet of her bedroom, skidding to a stop. Her bright, blonde hair fell around her shoulders, framing her face that was all wide, icy blue eyes; and thanks to me, a now red and soon to be swelling lower lip. A bead of crimson dotting her pale skin where I'd split it.

"Fuck!" I scrambled out of the bed towards her and she flinched. I stopped myself from going to her, stopped myself cold, and shuddered. I bowed my head, pulling on the back of my neck and snatched my jeans up off the floor, ripping them up my legs.

"Nothing, I'm sorry, it's okay. It was just a dream," she was climbing to her feet and I shook my head buttoning my jeans, pulling up the zipper, grabbing my boots off the floor.

"Don't fucking touch me," I said, furious with myself, my chest heaving. She froze, her lovely breasts rising and falling with adrenaline and fear. "You need to stop; you need to stay away from me. This can't happen again. I can't. You understand me? I won't." I was shaking my head and she was making soothing noises, her hands out like I was some kind of feral dog.

"Nothing, it's fine! Really, I'm okay it was just a dream, aie!" I'd cut her off, grabbed her by the upper arms a startled sound coming from her lips. I leveled my gaze with hers, and she was all wide, startled blue eyes. A knife twist of guilt almost stopped me, almost made me let go, but this was important; she needed to understand.

"It's not just a dream, it will never *be* just a dream," I snarled and she opened her mouth to speak, "No! Forget it, Charity, this can't be. This can't happen ever again, now leave it!" I thrust her away from me so hard she hit the bed with the backs of her knees and sat down abruptly. "Now do yourself a favor; find someone who's not going to hurt you, because I sure as fuck will." I gave one last look to my white fingerprints against her lovely skin filling in pink. Son of a bitch! I snatched up my cut and put my arms savagely through the holes. Grabbing up my boots that I'd dropped, first one then the other. I threw open her bedroom door and headed down the stairs.

Radar was on the first landing coming up as I was heading down, worry and confusion on his face, "Nothing, man, what's up?" he asked.

"Check on her, make sure I didn't hurt her," I grated and blew out the front door, leaving it swing wide.

I jumped up and down on one foot, ramming the other into its boot and repeated the process on the other side, heading to my bike. I fired her up and laid rubber, going for the street and the fastest way out of there and away from Char.

Fuck, I'd fucking hit her. I hadn't meant to, it was a fucking accident… I hadn't meant to swerve into the guy coming our way either so I did the only thing I could think of. I tore the fuck out of there before I did anything else to hurt that beautiful girl.

All my fault. All my fucking fault, if only I hadn't been so fucking tired.

CHAPTER 19
Charity

I sat on the bed, my face stinging from the slap, my chest heaving with equal parts adrenaline and panic when Radar knocked on the edge of the open door frame. The door had swung mostly shut when Nothing had blown past it to bound down the stairs and I had just enough time to snatch the comforter to cover my nudity before Radar looked around the corner.

"Charity, you – shit," he sighed out and nodded, turning his head to the side and up to stare at the ceiling. "Right, do me a favor and put something on while I go grab some ice."

"Sure," I said and sniffed, the first tears gathering and starting to fall.

He turned to go out the door, and back to me asked, "You want me to call Hope, or Faith? They stayed at the marina on the boats."

"No, I'll be okay," I said.

"K, be right back."

As soon as he was out of sight I dove for the closet and swept an oversized tee over my head and shrugged a pair of leggings up my legs. I was as covered as I was going to get. He knocked twice and waited for an answer before returning to the room.

"Yeah," I said and dashed at the moisture in my eyes.

"What happened?" he asked.

"Nothing –"

"Don't tell me nothing happened, something clearly did."

I laughed, "No, I wasn't, I was telling you that Nothing, the person, was having a bad dream; I tried to wake him up, but he was flailing," I took the proffered icepack from Radar who let out in a string of Spanish that was clearly an impressive long line of swear words, but his angry posture diminished. "Yeah, that, anyways, he was really upset, cried out a couple of times for Corrine and Katy before I woke him up, I think he was having a flashback."

"Yeah, it's been a long time since he's had one. We thought he was over it."

"No one said he was in the accident with them, I always just assumed…"

Radar sat down on the edge of the bed with me and searched my face, wiping off a tear with his thumb and absently off on his long denim shorts.

"Well if you're going to get beat up over it, you have a right to know," he said but didn't sound happy about it.

"It wasn't his fault, the same way it isn't a soldier's fault when they have a flashback, my sister has them sometimes."

"Yeah, we tend to forget she was deployed, anyways, Nothing was in the car that night, was the one driving, but it wasn't his fault. This drunk guy hit them head on, on Corrine and Katy's side. Nothing was trapped and couldn't do anything. Corrine was killed on impact, Katy died later at the hospital before Nothing even got out of surgery. His thighbone got busted in two places and they had to put some metal in there to hold shit together. He was laid up for weeks in the hospital."

"His heart never healed," I observed.

"It was a stupid fucking accident he had no control over, but he likes to blame himself. If he hadn't looked away, if he hadn't worked that extra shift, if he hadn't been so tired… Man, excuse after excuse but it doesn't change anything. Dude's lucky to be alive."

I pursed my lips and nodded, pulling the ice away from my face; Radar had a look and moved my hand with the icepack in it back in place.

"Then I come to town…"

"Yeah, and for a minute, like thirty seconds today, it was like having the old Galahad back."

"Galahad?" I asked.

"That was his road name before he started insisting everyone call him 'Nothing.'"

"I see, let me guess,"

112

"White knight, out to save everybody," we said in unison. I hung my head and sighed.

"You really like him, huh?" Radar asked.

"Too much information, but he's hot as fucking hell and I'm a white knight too. Just something about the tortured bad boy image really got me."

"We all make mistakes," he joked and I shook my head.

"This isn't a mistake. We have a crap ton in common, and I can see he's a really good guy, just really fucking confused."

"That's putting it mildly. This mean you aren't giving up?"

"Seems to me, there's been a lot of giving up on Nothing, don't you think?"

"Ouch," he put his hands over his chest as if I wounded him. I met his eyes and didn't flinch, and he shifted uncomfortably.

"Compassion fatigue is a thing," I murmured and Radar gave a nod, taking the out I'd given him.

"Yeah, and we've been in it to win it since it happened, there just comes a point where you gotta let go of the bike and watch 'em pedal on their own."

"Spoken like a father," I said dryly.

"Daughter, just turned eighteen."

I raised my eyebrows, "Yeah, I started young."

"Nothing isn't a child," I said.

"No, he's a grown ass man that needs to start behaving like one."

"Seems like I've done a bang up job of shaking up his whole world." It was my turn to let out an explosive breath, and stare at the ceiling.

"Yeah, but Honey, truthfully, Nothing needs it. He's been stuck like he's been for far too long. Now, that's not to say I'd blame you one bit if you walked away now – okay." Radar held up his hands in defense of my withering look.

"I don't give up at the first sign of trouble, and I'm fairly convinced that Nothing needs my help. I'm going to do what I can for him, I just need to think on how to approach it so he won't spook or bolt on me."

"Sex was that good, huh?" he asked looking at me dubiously.

"Mind blowing," I said without missing a beat then frowned, "What are you still doing here anyways? Don't you have a house of your own?"

He shrugged, "All my equipment is still here, plus my place doesn't have a generator. The cable and internet lines are underground, so they weren't as affected by the storm, and I can't go longer than five minutes without my web fix."

I took the icepack off my lip and Radar tipped my chin, turning my face into the light to have a look.

"Eh," he shrugged and moved my hand with the icepack in it back toward the minor injury; I sighed and kept icing the lip.

"I'm not used to being the patient," I grumbled and his eyes darkened. I sighed, "It was an accident," I reiterated.

"Yeah, but I can't help but feel responsible somehow, too." A look of real disappointment and frustration crossed his face and I nodded.

"Cutter said something to me. He said that none of us could help Nothing, not until Nothing was ready to help himself. He's right, you know."

"Yeah, I know. I just can't help but wonder if there was something more we could and should be doing as his brothers. Letting him fucking stew for three years hasn't exactly helped him any." He eyed me carefully. "Then you show up and he's all shook up." He paused for a long minute searching my face. "Piece of unsolicited advice?"

"Sure," I agreed softly.

"It's pretty clear you like our boy, and it's pretty clear he likes you, too. Give him a few days to get a grip. Don't go looking for him. You're bound to run into each other, it's a small town, but if I know Nothing, you go looking for him it's just going to make him retreat even further."

I nodded, "Makes sense, and you're right. I do like him. We really have a lot in common, this insane attraction aside. Plus, I can't help it. The wounded bad boy routine really is hot as hell."

Radar laughed, and nodded. "Fair enough, Trouble, fair enough."

We sat there, comfortably, quietly, before I thought to ask, "You aren't going over there to hand him his ass again, are you?"

He chuckled, and it sent a bit of a shiver down my spine, "No, he didn't do anything wrong, this time if it is, as you say; an accident." I nodded emphatically, and he nodded too, bobbing his head up and down in a parody of me. "I'll go check on him for you in the morning if it would make you feel better."

I nodded, "It would, thanks."

"You know, I like what you do to our boy, Charity. It really was almost like having Galahad back today."

"I think I'd like to meet Galahad," I murmured.

"You have, by the sounds of things going on up here."

I blushed a deep pink which he thought was hysterical, "I know I opened the door a minute ago, but can we not commentate on my sex life anymore, please?" I asked.

Radar wiped tears from his eyes, "Spoken like a true woman, but if it makes you do that, then the boys'll smell blood in the water. They'll tease the hell out of you. You'd best get used to it with a lot like us. Gotta give as much as you take."

"Fun," I said and sighed.

"Seriously though, you gonna be okay?"

I nodded, "Yeah. It was an accident, the adrenaline will wear off and I'll be good as new."

"Atta girl," he said, all smiles. I handed him the icepack and he stood up. "You need anything, I'm right downstairs."

"Thanks, but I'm a big kid now," I said with a half-smile and he shot me a little salute.

"A fast learner, too."

"Good night, Radar... and thanks."

"Night, Trouble, and think nothing of it," he waggled his eyebrows and I rolled my eyes.

I couldn't sleep. I kept thinking about the raw naked pain in Nothing's eyes. His violent reaction after having hit me spoke more of a fear on his part that he'd actually hurt me. I touched lightly, the corner of my lip and sighed. He'd been in the throes of a full on flashback, I didn't for a minute think it was me that he'd been fending off, I just think that I'd gotten too close when I should have backed the hell off.

I closed my eyes and sighed, but it was all for naught, my bedroom's overhead light came on and I looked over to see Hope and Faith, their men right behind them, all piling into the room.

"Good lord, Radar," I sighed out rolling my eyes.

"What happened?" Hope demanded.

I shook my head and just came clean, ripping it off like a Band-Aid, "Nothing brought me back to the house, one thing led to another, got our freak on, went to bed and he had a nightmare. There's really nothing to tell."

She touched the corner of my lip with a thumb, gently cradling my chin with her fingers and I frowned, jerking my head back.

"Looks like one hell of a bad dream," Marlin commented dryly and he didn't look at all happy.

"More like a flashback, I think." Hope and Cutter exchanged a look. "I figured the two soldiers in the room could appreciate what those are like," I said just as dryly as Marlin had been the moment before. "Look, legit, it was an accident and I think he's taking it really freaking hard."

Faith sat down next to me and poked at my arm; I scowled at her and jerked it out of her reach. "And those?" she asked softly. I looked and sure enough, there were bruises on my upper arms from where he'd gripped me.

"I tried to comfort him, it didn't work out. He just wanted away from me."

"Don't worry, Trouble; I get it," Cutter said soothingly.

"Glad someone does," I muttered.

Cutter's phone rang and he pulled it out of his leather vest, checking the screen. "Yeah?" he answered it. "Uh huh, good to know. No, keep him there, let him drown his sorrows, take the keys to his bike though, me an' Marlin 'll come and get him. Yep, Thanks, man."

"Is he okay?" I asked.

"Seems you were right, Trouble. Nothing's drowning his sorrows at one of the places on the boulevard that has a generator going.

Charlie says he's kind of a wreck. Let him drink some, Marlin and me, we'll get him home. Don't you worry none."

I nodded, "Cool."

Marlin and Cutter left after some more checking with me, finally taking their asses out when I started to get irritated. Hope searched my face and Faith giggled.

"Well, Nothing's fucked," Hope said and I scowled at her.

"In more ways than one," Faith said and put her fingers over her mouth. I rolled my eyes so hard I saw brain matter and flopped back into my bed.

"Move it over, Blossom," Hope ordered.

I obliged with a "Whatever you say, Corporal Badass."

"Neeah!" she said and stuck her butt out at me which of course made me move faster.

"Seriously, you okay?"

"Scared the shit out of me, but I'm pretty sure it scared the shit out of him, too. It was an accident and I'm fine. I'm worried about him though."

Hope sighed and we three sisters snuggled into a cuddle pile, "He'll be fine, but Jesus you two came together in one hell of a passion-plosion, didn't you?"

"He's so freaking hot," I moaned like it was the hardest of hardships.

"Hey! Don't say I didn't warn you."

"Mmm! You did. I just don't know where to go from here."

"My advice?"

"Hmm?"

"Don't let him get away with shit. Spend time with him, don't shy away."

"Radar said I should give him a day or two, otherwise he might retreat further."

"Pfft! Fuck that," Hope said but it was Faith that stopped us both.

"You know Einstein's definition of insanity?" she asked quietly.

"What, doing the same thing over and over expecting a different result?" I asked.

"That's the one," she said.

Hope huffed a sigh, "Seems to me these guys have been giving Nothing, nothing *but* time to sort himself out. It doesn't appear to be working, though, now does it?"

"Not really, no."

"So what are you going to do that's different?" Faith asked.

I thought about it, and made a decision.

"Something different," I uttered.

"That's my girl," Hope said and got up to switch out the light. It'd been a long time since we'd all tried to squeeze into one bed. It was kind of nice.

CHAPTER 20

Nothing

The bed bounced twice as someone flounced down on it and I winced, pushing myself up. A cup of coffee was thrust under my nose and I looked up into a pair of very guarded and very serious icy blue eyes.

"The fuck?" I asked.

"Time to get up," Charity said.

"Charity, I meant it, I'm not –"

"Save it. The boys are outside to put your house back together."

I glared at her but she just kept looking at me with her cool, level gaze. My eyes fixated on the small split at the corner of her mouth, and the little bruise there.

"You should see me when I'm naked," she stated dryly, "Oh! That's right; you already have. Now come on and get dressed. I'm right here and I'm not going anywhere. So take this coffee monstrosity with no sugar, drink it, get in the shower and move it."

"I'll ride, I'll meet you there." I said trying to think through the haze of my pounding head. Hangovers were a bitch.

"No dice, your bike is back at Cutters. Marlin rode it there; you were too drunk last night. Do you even remember how you got home?" she asked.

"Not really," I grated out.

"Are you even listening to me? I said that the guys are all *here*. It's your house we're doing today. They're outside waiting." She set the coffee cup on the nightstand and flung a leg over my hips, straddling me. I turned my face and stared at the photos around the bedroom mirror. "You really think they'd want this for you?" she asked, voice husky with a sort of sadness that brought me back around to look at her.

"What would you know?" I demanded and she raised her eyebrows at me.

"Let's see, I know that you're sick and tired of hurting, for one."

"Yeah, how do you figure that?" I challenged, and she kissed me. Fuck, I couldn't not kiss her back and I winced knowing that after a night of hard drinking, I probably tasted like ass.

She drew back and I was throbbing where I was pressed against her heat through our clothes. She rested her forehead on mine and I closed my eyes and just basked in her soothing presence.

Someone once told me that it takes a special woman to soothe away all the rage and pain. If that was the case, Charity was definitely something special.

"Come on, they're waiting for us," she whispered and I nodded, our foreheads still together, that healing aura of hers working it's magic. I let myself savor it for just a moment longer before I gently gripped her upper arms to move her back off me. She sucked in a sharp breath and I froze.

Her eyes were a little wide and I cocked my head, "What was that for?"

"Nothing," she clearly, lied. She wore a light hoodie, long sleeves, in the muggy heat of Florida? I didn't think so. I pushed it off her shoulders and sighed at the ring of bruises on her upper arms.

"Fuck, Charity. I told you, you need to get –" she put her fingertips to my lips, and shook her head.

"You don't get to tell me what to do. Remember that," she said, steel in her voice.

"Get off me," I said and she arched a delicate brow, we stared in a proverbial stand of until I exhaled sharply. "Get off me, please."

She moved off my lap and I had to adjust myself. She smirked and handed me the coffee again. "Shower, and let's get a move on. Yours isn't the only house that needs attention."

"Mm," I uttered around the first slug of lukewarm coffee. A sugar free vanilla late. She'd remembered. I squeezed my eyes shut and shook my head, pulling on the back of my head to ease the tension in my neck and between my shoulders. I was finding it difficult to concentrate and had to believe it was because I still might be drunk.

"Did I just earn points?" she asked, her voice breaking through the fog like the sun. I looked up at her, an easy smile painting her lips that I couldn't help the smile that tugged at mine. She made it hard to wallow, made it hard to stay a miserable bastard.

"Maybe you did, but just a couple of 'em," I conceded.

"I'll take what I can get," she said, rolling her eyes, and just like that, the atmosphere eased, became something more bearable for the moment; almost friendly. She had a way about her. I wanted to pull my anger and my hurt around me like a cloak, but around Charity, it was next to impossible. She just had that *way* about her. It was easy to lay down the hurt, and it seemed that no matter how much I tried to drive her away, to protect her, she just came gravitating back with a stubborn set to her chin that reminded me a whole lot of her sister Hope.

I went and took a shower, when I came back to the bedroom, clothes had been laid out for me and Charity stood leaning against one wall, her shoulder pressed neatly to its painted surface, her arms cradling her breasts, one foot planted firm, the other crossed in front, toe of her Keds canvas sneaker resting on the hardwood.

She was model perfect, and my dick stirred just looking at her. I had the feeling she felt the same, given the way her eyes roamed my body, lingering where the towel was slung low on my hips.

"A little privacy?" I asked.

"You sure? Because last night we got pretty intimate," she said with a wink.

"I know, and it was a mistake," I said. A glint of hurt flashed in the depths of her eyes but she covered it with an easy smile.

"Well, I don't regret a thing," she said softly, pushing off the wall and making easy strides. I caught her sleeve between thumb and forefinger and she looked up at me.

"This is a dangerous game," I murmured.

"Doesn't have to be, Nothing. You're the one making it that way, so why don't you just stop?"

Her words hit me like a ton of bricks, I mean, I hadn't quite thought of it that way but at the same time, "It's not that simple, Charity."

"Why not? The only one I see complicating things, is you."

"Just what do you want from me, anyways?" I demanded, scowling. This was getting uncomfortable for me.

She stopped and looked thoughtful for a moment, "I want you to stop acting like a dick and start using your dick," she said and I scoffed, incredulously. "Let me ask you something," she said, before I could recover.

"What?"

"Does it feel good?"

"What?"

She gave me a look, like 'don't be stupid,' "Do you seriously want me to get into the gory details?" she demanded.

"No, I mean yes, it feels good; it feels really good when I'm with you." She had me off kilter and she knew it, but I couldn't figure out what she was trying to get at through my fog of a hangover.

"Okay, then. Fuck me, use me, do whatever you want as long as you keep the orgasms coming," she fucking winked at me while I stared at her slack jawed. "We'll figure out the rest as we go along, because let's face it, if it's one thing we've figured out, we're good together when we're in the sack. It's probably the one uncomplicated thing about us."

I laughed incredulously, "Are you fucking kidding me?"

"Serious as a fucking heart attack over here," she said. "Now get dressed," she slapped me on the ass as she went by and I jumped, grabbing for the towel that was coming unhooked at my hip.

I thought to myself, *did she just tear a page out of fucking Hope's playbook or what?*

CHAPTER 21
Charity

My body very nearly hummed with how anxious I was. I had Nothing off base, for sure, which was my goal. I mean, really, the only thing I'd accomplished was talking faster than Nothing could think, given his hung over state. I stepped out his garage door which was just finishing trundling up its track and walked out into the bright sunshine.

"Did it work?" Hope asked and I gave a one shouldered shrug.

"We'll see."

Cutter and Pyro exchanged a look and Pyro said, "I'm not sure if I feel bad for Nothing or if I'm cheering for him."

"I'm thinkin' a little of both," Cutter winked at me and I rolled my eyes.

The rest of the guys were already at work cleaning up the yard, and I looked around. Flowerbeds were weed choked and overgrown, bordering the walkways and beneath the boarded up windows. Some of the guys were already in the garage opening up what appeared to be packages of replacement shingles against one wall.

I looked over at Faith, "Fancy planting some flowers with me?" I asked and she lit up, smiling. There were a lot of smiles and the sound of industry filled Nothing's small side street as we all picked up something to do and got to work.

It was a long day, but a satisfying one. By the end of it, Nothing's roof had been repaired, as had his small front stoop. The shutters he had piled off to the other side of the garage, that he'd never gotten around to installing, had been put up, and the paint in places on the outside of his house had been refreshed. The weeds had all been pulled, but most importantly, Hope had led the charge indoors and every floor had been swept, every picture frame and piece of furniture had been dusted and, thanks to the power coming back on, all of the bedding and curtains had been laundered.

She'd taken charge of the indoor operations with Pyro's girl and Hossler, while Faith and I had brought the flowerbeds in line. There was one, lonely little circular bed in the front that had nothing growing in it. I'd gone to Nothing and had touched his shoulder. He'd jumped and turned to look at me, expression grave. He was sweating, in the heat and from his efforts to clear a fallen tree in his back yard.

"What was in the round flowerbed in the front yard?" I asked.

"Nothing, it died. Just leave it alone."

"Do you mind if I plant something in it?"

"Yes, just leave it alone, please."

I sighed and put my arms around his waist and looked up at him until he capitulated, his eyes closing, "It was a lemon tree. Corrine and I planted it when we found out she was pregnant, it was supposed to be so she and Katy could make lemonade, for a lemonade stand on the corner when Katy got old enough. A drunk took it out last year with his truck while I was out on a run with the guys. I just haven't replaced it."

I went up on tiptoe and gave Nothing a quick, soft kiss. "Thank you," I said and he frowned.

"For what?"

"Sharing that with me, I know it was hard."

Some of the tension drained out of him and he sighed, nodding. I left him and went back around front. Faith was waiting for me and she asked, "What'd he say?" I got close to her before I told her, repeating what Nothing had told me. She stared at my face intently for a long minute and chewed her bottom lip. She pulled out her cellphone from the back pocket of her shorts and said, "Give me a minute," before wandering to the curb and making a call. I shrugged and went back to work.

She came back and I asked, "What was that for?"

"I called a friend and asked him a really big favor," she said and I raised my eyebrows, pushing my new sunglasses that Hope had bought for me, up my nose.

"What kind of favor, and who's this friend?"

"Bobby, he's a friend of Marlin's. He has an orange grove about an hour away."

"Okay, but what does that have to do with anything."

She rolled her eyes so hard I thought she might have glimpsed gray matter, "He doesn't just grow oranges, silly. Orange grove is a misnomer, it really should be called a 'citrus grove,' he grows limes and lemons too. I asked him for a tree."

"You did what?" I asked, blinking.

"He grows them for plant nurseries, so why not?" she asked.

"Big sister, I could kiss you," I said and she blushed.

"It's not that big of a deal, I like Nothing... he helped get me better. I'd like to help him get better, too."

I hugged the crap out of Faith and whispered, "You're the best sister anyone could ever ask for."

"Thanks," she said softly and hugged me back just as tight.

We ended up *just* working on Nothing's house. There was so much that'd fallen into disrepair that it needed the attention. Even his brothers seemed surprised at how much the house needed done. It was worth it, though. By the time we were through, it looked like one of the nicest houses on the block. It was amazing what you could accomplish when you had an entire team of people working together.

Nothing and I hadn't seen much of each other throughout the day, and when I found him again, it was him standing in his kitchen, a bottle of water in his hand and a faraway look in his eyes.

"Hey," I murmured.

He shook himself, like a dog coming out of water and his gaze focused on me, a mask falling into place, shuttered, guarded.

"Hey," he said simply and I sighed inwardly, steeling myself for the rejection I just knew was coming.

"Place looks great," I said.

"Yeah, got a lot of stuff done that Corrine wanted," he said and looked at the bottle of half empty water in his hands. "Kind of wish I'd done it while she could appreciate it," he said, punctuating the statement with a heavy sigh.

"Yeah, I get that." Silence ensued and it held that oppressive weight, the feel of an impending storm, only instead of thunder and rain, I pictured yelling and tears.

Here we go, I thought. *Radar was right; I should have given him space...*

"Listen, Charity..." I perked up and waited for the hammer to drop, thinking to myself, *just get it over with.* "I really like you, but I really can't do this. It's..."

"It's not you, it's me? I'm sorry I was weak? Let's just be friends?" I asked, my tone was sharper, more sarcastic than I'd meant it to come out, but I was surprised at just how much I found that this inevitable speech was hurting. Bewildered at just how much I'd emotionally invested in Nothing in such a short time.

"Pretty much all of those things," he said quietly.

"I really want to help you," I said.

"I know that, but I'm not one of your patients, and I'm sorry."

"No, you're not," I murmured and stared up at the ceiling, tears pricking the backs of my eyes.

"*Yes,* I *am*. You're a beautiful girl, and any man would be lucky to have you –"

"Really? Well what about you?"

"I'm just not that guy," he said with a shitty half assed shrug.

"Do you think you're being noble right now, Galahad?" his head snapped up and his gray eyes flashed with anger.

"What did you call me?"

"You heard me."

"That's not my name anymore."

"No, I suppose it's not," I uttered, then heaved a big sigh. "Strike three, you're out. Have fun being miserable, Nothing. I'm just not on board anymore. I can't be the only one trying here. Things just don't work that way."

I turned and walked out of the kitchen, through the open space of the living room, and out into the bright sunlight. I didn't know what sucked more, the total sense of failure, or the fact that despite all of his asshattery, I still *really* liked Nothing. I felt like we vibed on the same frequency, or whatever, in those rare moments when he wasn't letting his grief be all consuming.

I couldn't help but wonder if I was giving up too easily, but at the same time, I couldn't help but wonder if I was saving myself a lot of heartache in the long run. I got in my Jeep and drove off, the few remaining guys loitering around Nothing's place eying me with sympathy. Radar's face flat and unreadable except for the slight nod he gave in my direction. I wondered vaguely if they'd heard the exchange, but couldn't bring myself to care. Might as well make my humiliation complete on that front, eh?

CHAPTER 22

Nothing

I stood in my kitchen, everyone gone, and stood at the counter that I'd bent Charity over what seemed like forever ago, but shit, must've only been a few days gone now. A fresh bottle of Jim Beam rested within reach, an empty whiskey glass next to it but I just wasn't feeling it. I felt shitty, I really did and decided I needed to shelve the fucking bottle this time.

Still, that didn't mean I wanted to stay sober tonight, so I busted out my stash of weed instead, rolling a joint. I'd never been good at it, Corrine though, she'd gotten pretty decent at it. I went out back and dropped into one of the wooden patio lounge chairs, propping my feet up. It was peaceful, the crickets and frogs starting their serenade, the smell of fresh cut grass filling the air. I stuck the joint in my mouth and lit up, sucking in a lungful of green, sticky smoke and holding it until my lungs screamed and the mellow effects rolled out from my center.

I turned my head up and back when the screen slid back, Cutter coming out to join me. I frowned, "Back again, Cap?"

"Figured it was time you and I had a talk, man."

I nodded, figuring that I was about to have my ass set straight, but honestly, I had no clue what the Captain was gonna say. You never did when it was Cutter. He dropped into Corrine's lounge chair and set a six pack of cheap beer between us. I passed him the joint.

"Don't mind if I do," he said, taking a hit and propping his booted feet up.

"Come to tell me I'm bein' an idiot?" I asked.

"Of the highest order," he said, voice strained as he held his breath. He exhaled sharply and passed me back the weed. I took another hit and pinched off the cherry, figuring the tongue lashing I was about to get was gonna be epic.

Cutter pulled a beer from the pack and twisted the cap off the amber bottle, he leaned back again, crossing his booted ankles, frayed denim against worn leather. He'd ridden over here.

"Let's have it," I said.

"I think it's time," he said, "to set the record straight."

I frowned and leaned my head back against the back of my chair, rolling it over to look at him, "What d' you mean?"

"We've been waiting a real long damn time for you to show any fuckin' signs of waking the fuck up out of this," he gestured with his beer, "whatever the fuck it is."

"Grief?" I supplied, and he gave me a flat, stone cold look like I was *the* biggest fuckin' tool.

"Whatever you've been doin' to yourself these last few years? The word 'grief' ain't even come close to covering it, neither does wallowing, whatever you been doing, they ain't got a name for, Dom."

Oh shit, he used my real name… I sobered almost instantly, "You stripping my patch?" I asked and he frowned.

"Hell fuckin' no! Once a brother, always a brother, lame ass. Point I'm trying to make is you lost your wife and baby girl, and ain't none of that your fucking fault." He raised his hand when I opened my mouth to protest and barked, "Shut it! I'm talking now, and you've had your fuckin' turn. You've had your fuckin' turn for three goin' on four fuckin' years now. Now it's *my* turn. You feel me?"

I shut my fuckin' mouth and swept out a hand in the classic 'after you' gesture and he nodded once, curtly.

"This back and forth you got going with Charity –"

"That's done now," I interjected, shifting uncomfortably.

"The fuck it is, I see it written all over your face. You forget I'm fuckin' her sister? I know how addictive these women are. Hell, don't believe me, just ask Marlin.

"I don't have to," I grumbled.

"That's my point, Dom. You've got Corrine put on this pedestal so fuckin' high ain't no mortal woman down here on the ground ever gonna compare, and its fuckin' bullshit."

Charity's words echoed back to me, "*I can't be the only one trying here...*" which harkened back to what Corrine had said to me that night, before the crash.

"I blame myself for some of your marriage falling the fuck apart," he sighed.

"We weren't falling apart, Cap. It was just a rough patch, I would have pulled my head out of my ass and things would have been fine."

"We'll never know," he said with a heavy sigh, "but Corrine came to me a few days before your accident. She told me she loved the club, but she loved you more and that we needed to let you go. We were building an empire back then, trying to help people, for profit, sure, but tryin' to help 'em none the less. She asked me to let you go, and I told her we needed you. Selfish as fuck, I know but it was true. You were pretty irreplaceable to the operation. She threatened to leave you and I told her she didn't want to do that." I was staring at him open mouthed as he dug around in his cut.

"Man, this whole time we wanted to tell you, but you've been on that fuckin' razor's edge and we were afraid if we did, you'd just end it." He extracted a manila file folder, folded in half long ways and said, "Then Charity showed up, and we thought with how you two were magnets for each other, that you'd finally let Cor and Katy go, but then you had to go and fuck it up today, and I just don't know what to think."

A cold knot of dread took up residence in the center of my chest, my eyes locked on that fuckin' file folder, and I asked, voice hollow, "What's in the folder, Captain?"

"You ever wonder why we run Hossler's ol' man outta here?" he asked.

"You said he'd stolen from the club."

"Yeah, about that, I'm sorry to have to do it this way, but it's *what* he stole."

He handed over the folder and I took it with numb and shaking fingers, opening it up to eight by ten glossy photos of my former brother, balls fucking deep in my wife. I dropped the folder, the photos sloshing out onto the fresh cut grass and shaking I put my head in my hands.

"Oh my god, man. This can't be happening!" I said and tried to suck in deep and even breaths, except I couldn't get any air. Cutter put his hand on the back of my shoulder giving it a squeeze.

"Take it easy, brother. I need you to breathe."

"The fuck? What the fuck? Why would you keep this from me!" I shouted and Cutter sighed.

"I told you, man. We were afraid of what you would do. You weren't in any kind of place to fuckin' *hear* it."

I launched to my feet and staggered to the edge of the grass, falling to my knees and puking up whatever was in my stomach. I'd only wretched once before on a super emotional call that involved a child that'd been exactly Katy's age.

"This isn't fucking *happening!*" I repeated and looked up at my Captain, the President of my club. The resignation was written all over him, and I could tell what a burden he'd been carrying all this time in keeping it secret from me. I asked him, "Why are you doing this to me? Why now?"

"Because you've got a real chance at something here, and I don't want to see you fuckin' piss it away on some illusion of what you *thought* you had. It wasn't fuckin' real, Dom. Maybe it was once, but by the time the shit got really real, it was pretty fuckin' broken."

I bowed my head and couldn't hold the flood of grief and loss back any longer. Cutter came over and lent support, and I fuckin' lost my shit, as much as any man would on discovering his entire fucking life had been a goddamned lie. My reality lay shattered around me, winking in the dying afternoon light.

CHAPTER 23

Charity

"Hello?" I gripped the towel at my chest and tried to hold the phone so it didn't come in contact with my wet hair.

"Hi! It's Greg." I paused, several heartbeats going by before he said, "Is it lame that I'm calling you like the very next day? Because I'm suddenly feeling like I'm pretty lame," he laughed nervously.

"No! Hi, um, you just caught me at a bad time; I just got out of the shower."

"Oh, hey, if you don't mind me saying, I guess that's just a matter of perspective," his tone was teasing and I laughed a little.

"Can I dry off and give you a call right back?" I asked.

"Sure," he said, sounding skeptical.

"Call you *right* back. I promise," I said.

"Okay."

I ended the call and blew out an explosive breath. *What is wrong with you?* I thought to myself. I dried off and got dressed. A lace top that was long sleeved, but off the shoulder. Perfect to hide the bruises but cool enough for the sultry afternoon outside. I paired the black lace top with a pair of short light colored denim shorts and a pair of black, strappy wedge sandals. Not too dressy, but not totally casual either. I dried my hair, straightening it with my flat iron, and spent an extra few minutes covering the light bruise at the corner of my mouth with makeup. That done, I decided *fuck it* and did my whole face. I'd perfected the natural look, and with some light pink, bordering on nude lip gloss I was done.

I went back to my bedroom and picked up my phone off the bed. I needed a little 'me' time and had planned on heading down to the boulevard to have a drink by myself, but I fancied a bit of company, so long as it was company who wasn't Nothing or the MC. I needed a break from the drama and Nothing's club brothers kept casting me sympathetic looks that'd like to drive me crazy.

Greg picked up on the second ring, "I didn't expect to hear from you," he said.

"Yeah, sorry. I'm a girly girl. Hair and makeup take a minute."

"I see, does that mean you're going out?"

"Actually, if you're free for that drink, I'd love to meet up."

"Absolutely!"

So it was that I found myself down on the boulevard parking my Jeep down the block from one of the more tourist trap bars. An open air affair right off the beach with a spectacular view of the water and the sun hanging low in the sky, deepening on towards sunset. Greg was at the bar, and I slipped up onto the stool next to him.

"Hey stranger," I greeted and he turned, all smiles, his mouth dropping open. *Success!*

"Wow! Look at you," he said, "I know it's forward of me, but can I have a hug?" he asked.

"Aww, that's sweet you would ask," I said with a laugh and held out my arms. We hugged, a friendly greeting that was neither too quick nor did it linger.

"So what did you do today?" he asked me, by way of conversation starter.

"Oh, you know, more storm clean up."

We chatted amicably, and he bought me a drink, I went with a tried and true, Pina Colada, and sipped it slowly. As far as drinks went it was cool, sweet, and fruity but sort of on the weak side, which I was okay with seeing as I had every intention of driving home after a bit.

The bartender came by and asked if I wanted another drink. The first one had absolutely zero effect, so I nodded, smiling.

Greg was good conversation, he said he worked for a development company and that he'd been sent out to Ft. Royal to see if it was a prime location for a resort. I'd laughed at that, and he'd smiled ruefully.

"Yeah, I'm kind of feeling like I was set up to fail out here. The townspeople aren't exactly welcoming with open arms when I mention that."

"Can you blame them? It feels like this place is the last bastion in Florida when it comes to corporate development."

"You are not wrong," he said with a sigh.

The bartender set down my drink and I took a sip, smiling.

"So, what do you plan to do now that you have your degree?"

I scoffed, "Find a job before the student loans try to eat me alive."

Greg cringed, "Oo, that bad?"

"Ahhh, not really. I pretty much had a full ride when it came to tuition, it was the text books that kill you. Some of them were more than four hundred dollars!"

"Yikes, why didn't you get them used?"

I looked at him like 'are you serious?' and told him, "That *was* used."

"Holy shit, are you serious?"

"As a heart attack," I slipped off the stool, "Can you excuse me for a second? Ladies room is calling."

"Absolutely, I'll be right here." He smiled brightly and I found the restroom to break the proverbial seal. I knew the science behind why you had to pee when you were drinking, I mean, that's all alcohol was; a diuretic, and subsequently, that's what a hangover was, a combination of dehydration and your body reacting to, essentially, the poison you put into it.

I freshened up my lip gloss in the bathroom mirror and went back out to the bar, retaking my seat.

"Where were we?" he asked and I smiled.

"Lamenting how stupid it is to get an education just so you can turn around and spend the rest of your life paying for it."

"Ah right, I believe that's the new American dream, isn't it?"

"Something like that."

I took another drink and Greg sipped his beer, both of us lapsing into the natural lull in conversation.

We made more small talk and I nodded at something he was saying, only the room started to spin, causing me to frown.

"You alright?" Greg asked.

"Yeah, that's strange." I looked over to the bartender who was in the back corner behind the bar, on the phone looking over his shoulder at me and Greg.

"What's strange?" Greg asked and I swallowed hard.

"Guess this second drink was just a little bit stronger than the first, just got a bit dizzy there for a second."

Greg frowned, "You want some water?" he asked.

"No," I closed my eyes squeezing them shut and opening them again. I was seeing double. Something was really wrong. I slipped off my bar stool and nearly went down, my wedge heel turning under me, or maybe I was just that unsteady on my feet.

"What the hell?" Greg asked, and sounded genuinely concerned.

"Can we just get out of here?" I asked.

"Sure, absolutely."

He put an arm around my waist, only it wasn't right, it was too tight, and he began to usher me towards the door.

"Ow, Greg, ease up, you're hurting me," I said.

"It's okay, I've got you."

I looked back at the bartender, head swimming with confusion. He nodded and spoke rapidly into the line and before I could call out, Greg had swept me out the door and onto the street, leaning me up against a parked car.

"Just a second," he said and opened the passenger door on the nondescript gray sedan. The Gray of Nothing's eyes.

"No, I don't want to go anywhere with you," I said but my voice came out slurred nonsense.

Oh... oh shit.

Greg shoved me into the passenger seat of the car, and I think I must have passed out, because I can't remember anything after that.

CHAPTER 24

Nothing

"I'm tired of getting fucked in ways that don't end with me getting off," I said miserably.

"I know, brother, and I'm sorry. I never wanted you to find out let alone like this, but you have to understand, we didn't want you to remember her that way. Corrine made a monumental mistake, but there was no denying she loved you."

I closed my eyes and sighed out, "I don't want to think about this anymore."

Twilight was invading my back yard and I'd mostly pulled my shit together from this latest soul shattering mind fuck. I was on my second beer and the light buzz wasn't enough. That Jim Beam was looking awfully tempting but getting obliterated hadn't been doing me any fucking favors lately and I needed to lay off the sauce.

Cutter's phone started ringing and he pulled it out of his cut answering, "Yeah Charlie, what's up?" His expression crushed down into a frown. "You fucking kidding me? Uh huh. Uh huh. Did you get the plate number? Yeah. No, give it to me. Uh huh, yeah text it through," he pulled the phone away from his face and then put it back saying, "Yeah, I got it man, good lookin' out." He hung up the phone with a gusty sigh and immediately tapped out a message.

"Come on man, life ain't done fucking you yet, me either for that matter. You good to ride?"

"Why, what's going on?"

"Charlie down at Tiki Steve's just watched someone roofie and take Charity."

"You fucking kidding me?"

A mixture of adrenaline and fear chased the low grade buzz from the beer and the weed right out of my system.

"As your girl would say, as a heart attack."

I got up bent double and screamed "Fuck!" as loud and long as I could to just *get it out*. "Let's go, where we headed?" I asked.

"The Plank, let's move, I gotta call Hope. Son of a fucking bitch," he said and I didn't fucking envy him *that* call.

We rode, and we met Hope, her Ducati screaming down the boulevard, winding down as she pulled up and fell in with us the rest of the way to The Plank. Her deep, dark eyes were snapping fire and mayhem and I had no doubt that some motherfucker was going to die. I was surprised to realize that it was going to be a race as to which one of us got there first.

We piled into The Plank, Trike opening the door for us and locking it behind us. The place had been cleared of anything not in Club colors except for Faith; she strode right up to me and slapped me soundly, the clap of her palm against my flesh echoing off The Plank's open rafters.

"Woah! Marlin, buddy, control your property!" Beast called out, but Faith was inconsolable, her face streaming with tears as she screamed at me.

"This is all *your fault!*" she shrieked and resignation settled like a lead weight on my chest. She made to come at me again but Marlin got behind her, catching her wrists in his mitts and pulling her back, cradling her against his chest, holding her by the wrists.

Hope pushed past me and they took her back to the throne room. Cutter gave me a meaningful look, but the accusation stood, stinging in a fiery line from forehead to chin on the left side of my face.

"She's not wrong, and I'm gonna fix it. Radar, what have you got?" I asked.

No one said a word about my overstepping the Captain by asking. Radar gave a curt nod, "Glad to have you back, Galahad," he said and turned to his bank of laptops on the corner of the bar.

"Radar," Cutter intoned.

"Right, Charlie got the plates on his surveillance camera. The car belongs to a rental company out of Miami-Dade International Airport. Looks like it was rented by a Grigori Rossoff, natural born American citizen to first gen Russian immigrants."

"Fuck, how did we miss him?" Lightning asked.

"Don't know, doesn't matter, what else?" I asked.

"Grigori used a corporate credit card for an Iron Horse Holdings LLC. It's a shell corporation owned by a Sergei Rimini, who *also* owns four *other* shell corps one of which's corporate card was used to rent a hotel room at the Sunglade Motel off of the 595."

"Good work, man!" Lightning clapped Radar on the back.

"Hunting people; it's what I do." Radar gave us the plate number, just in case we got lucky and Cutter gave us our marching orders.

"Marlin, you stay with Faith, she needs you. Hope, Nothing, Radar, and Lightning; let's roll. Trike, get the first aid kit and medical bay set up in here, just in case."

"Aye, Captain!" Trike got is ass out from behind the bar and to work.

We piled back out the front door and mounted our bikes, starting them up and falling in behind the Captain. We rode hard, but obeyed the speed limit when we needed to. I was so tempted to split lanes and cane it the whole way, but resisted.

I irrationally kept looking for the fucking plate number. It was stupid, they had a head start. Not much of one, but a head start is a head start. The motel we were after was something like three exits ahead of us when I spotted the fucking car. I was dumbfounded that we'd caught up, but sure as shit, after checking the plates twice from the number Radar had rattled off, that was the car.

"Captain!" I bellowed into the wind, and resorted to the risky move of breaking formation to ride up alongside. I pointed out the car and he nodded. Hand signals were traded, and the consensus was to fall back and to get onto the surface streets with him before attempting a takedown.

There's an art to getting a car to stop that doesn't want to when you're on a motorcycle and the opposition is in the car. I hadn't ever had a need to perfect such an art, but Radar in his line of work had, and Cutter had done it too, so I dropped back with Hope and Lightning to leave it to the pros. My expertise was in putting men back together when the shit went sideways, and for the first time that

I could remember, that frustrated the hell out of me.

Never had I ever been so fucking righteously pissed off. It was like three plus years of rage and pain had just found a convenient target and he was behind the wheel of that car. My last chance at salvation was in that car too, and I wanted to fix things, give her the chance she deserved, be a better man, and I never would get that chance if we didn't stop these motherfuckers.

The car took the exit for the motel, so it looked like Radar's information was spot on. I didn't know what to do with the feelings of doubt that were clouding me, it was a new thing brought on by the fucking bombshell the Captain had dropped on me. My brothers, my whole club had been lying to my face for *years*. Good intentions being what they were, the doubt I harbored now? It was that road to hell those intentions had been paving for close to four years. *No good deed goes unpunished.* I thought back to the smuggling work we'd done, to all of the medical care I'd provided to those refugees, and at what cost? *The cost of your marriage, you jackass. Corrine couldn't get it from you, she went elsewhere.*

We dropped back further, and tried to avoid being an obvious tail. Easier said than done when you were a pack of bikers and the dude behind the wheel stealing your woman was probably aware that bikers were the big bad in his world.

Cutter gave signal that he and Radar were going in, once we were more towards the glades versus heavily populated areas. Hope fell back next to me, her face unreadable behind her black, full face mask helmet. It was a good idea, concealing identity for those of us with legit jobs to worry about, but I painted houses for a fucking living. Radar had the bottom half of his face covered with an orange bandana. We all wore our colors, but that was the beauty of brotherhood. If we got pinched, one of the boys with a record would step up to take the fall.

My belief in these guys was rattled, but on some things? It remained true. That was one of them. We rode, me and Hope up front, Lightning acting as our tail gunner. It was getting dark, but we could still see Cutter and Radar split and go to either side of the car. Cutter'd disengaged his getback whip from his clutch lever and with a mighty overhead swing, brought the lead ball the tip contained down hard on the driver's side of the windshield.

The sound of the crack it made against the safety glass traveled all the way back here. The Captain kicked out, his boot making contact with the driver's side door. The guy in the car swerved towards Cutter, who evaded, but just barely. Hope revved her Ducati and leaning down over her tank, punched it. The engine whined and she shot forward. There wasn't any stopping her, but I think she and the Captain had some kind of accord because he dropped back and let Hope pull up.

She waved at the driver of the car to pullover, but he swerved at her instead. She punched it again and he missed her, but it was close. Cutter pulled up, and took another swing, only this time Radar pulled forward out of the driver's blind spot where he'd been hiding and took out the passenger side of the windshield. The driver braked hard, tires squealing, brakes screaming and both the Captain and Radar kept going.

Lightning, who had pulled up next to me, shot me a hand signal for 'get ready' and I gritted my teeth, sure I wasn't going to like this even as smoke rose from the screaming rear tires of the car and it shot forward. Fuck, he was making a run at the Captain.

Pop! Pop! Pop!

I looked up, past the car at Hope in the road, feet shoulder width apart, smoking gun in hand, she ditched off to the side, rolling, even as the car tipped up onto its side, it's momentum carrying it along on its passenger side into the ditch on the side of the road.

"NO!" I screamed and torqued down hard on my accelerator. I braked hard, rolling to a stop by the car, barely having the wherewithal to put down my kickstand. Cutter and Radar were there and Cutter hoisted himself up onto the driver's side of the car. He reached into the busted out driver's window and seized the driver by the collar, slashing through the seat belt holding him.

"Charity!" I screamed. Cutter threw the injured driver down and Hope, Lightning, Radar, and I put our shoulders to the roof of the car.

"One, two, three, push!" Hope's muffled cry from beneath the black carapace of her helmet. We put our backs into it and shoved the car the rest of the way over onto its wheels.

"Charity!" I screamed and thumping and bumping alerted us to the rear of the car.

"The trunk, man! Pop the trunk!" Radar cried and Lightning dove into the busted out driver's side window. I was already there, the trunk flew open and Charity's ice blue eyes, wide with a combination of fear and rage met mine.

"It's okay, I got you, Baby. Do you think anything's broken?" I asked her, running my hands over every part of her the awkward position she was in allowed me to reach.

I pulled the gag out of her mouth and she said, "No, get me out, get me out of here, now!"

"Hold still," I put my arm beneath her knees and one behind her back, lifting with my knees. I turned and set her down carefully in the grass. "It's okay, you're okay; I've got you."

"I know I'm okay," she snapped and she demanded, "Untie me." I flipped open my folding blade and sawed through the zip tie cutting into her wrists, and through the strips of material around her ankles. She pushed to her feet.

"Woah, woah, woah! I need to check you out, Baby, steady." She wobbled on her feet for a second and pushed me off of her, making strides to where Cutter had the guy that'd kidnapped her. The first thing she did was march over to him and stomp one of her sturdy wedge heeled shoes down on his balls.

"Oh!"

"Ooo!" Lightning and Radar said in unison and we drifted over to where the guy was cradling his family jewels.

"We've got to move before we're seen, Captain. Someone could come down this way any minute."

"K, we're going to the hotel," he said and Charity stood, nodding, chest heaving in her outfit that she'd put on special to go have drinks with this asshole. *Because you hurt her. You rejected her.* The thought made me feel sick, but it was true just the same. She and I stared the distance between one another.

"Charity," Hope called and flipped up her visor on her helmet,

"Charity!" she barked. Charity tore her eyes from me and looked at her sister.

"Go with Nothing, back to Ft. Royal. We'll handle this. Okay?"

Charity nodded and I held out my hand to her. She walked unsteadily to me and took it. I led her to my bike and asked her in a low, soothing tone, "You okay, Baby?"

"I'm not your fucking 'Baby' hotshot. Just take me home. Faith has to be freaking out."

"She is, and I want to check you out. Adrenaline has you going, you're gonna crash."

"I know that, asshole!" she snapped and I took it. I deserved it.

"Can you ride?" I asked. She was shaking so bad, I had my doubts.

"I'm gonna have to; let's go." I got on my bike and she got on behind me, holding onto me tight, her body trembling against mine. I didn't like it.

"Hang on tight," I told her, she turned her head and the mercenary side of Charity came right out in the open. The part that was all her sister, Hope.

"Kill that son of a bitch!" she screamed, and I fired up my bike and took her home, to Ft. Royal.

CHAPTER 25
Charity

Nothing was right, I was running on pure adrenaline and it was a problem, if I crashed before we made it back to Ft. Royal... well I didn't want to know what that would look like. Nothing hurt yet; that scared me a little bit too. I'd woken to the sensation of being slammed around like a fucking rag doll in the dark, and then there was Nothing, lifting me out of the trunk of that asshole's car. I shuddered and held on to Nothing tight, the lean, corded muscle of his body both familiar and a lifeline in a blur of scenery and scary.

He put one hand over both of mine and I buried my face against the colorful patch on his back, shutting my eyes tight against the wind, using his body as a shield. He drove us to The Plank and I looked up.

"I want to go home," I said.

"Faith is here, and I want to check you out."

"I'm fine," I said but I wasn't. The tears were threatening and my throat was closing up. He tapped my hands twice and I startled; shaking myself, before climbing off the back of his bike. He shut it off and got off the front, putting arms around me and tucking my head beneath his chin.

"Shh, it's okay. I've got you now," and I couldn't hold myself together anymore. I fell apart into this shattered mess and Nothing was right there to catch all the pieces.

I sobbed into his tee shirt and cut and he held me tight. I must have been making more noise than I realized, because the door to The Plank opened and my sister Faith was holding me from the back, Marlin hovering protectively over the three of us.

"Charity, Baby, I gotta get you looked at, Honey. Make sure you're good, come on, Honey, let's go inside?" Nothing's voice was at once soothing and pleading. I sniffed miserably and nodded against his chest and Faith backed off of me. Nothing walked us through the door and into the back with the electric chair. He sat me down in the thing, a tray set up next to it with all of the essential diagnostic trappings.

He started by taking my pulse and then blood pressure in both arms and both legs. He took my pulse in both my feet, too.

"Nothing... Nothing!" he looked up at me, "Nothing's broken."

"Okay, Babe, okay. Just let me check anyways." I nodded and he turned on a pen light shining the light in my eyes, running through all the routine questions, running his fingers through my hair, feeling for lumps along my scalp.

"I expect some delayed onset muscle soreness tomorrow," I said and he nodded.

"I've got some drugs for that," he said and I winced.

"I have no idea what he dosed me with, should we worry about interaction?" I asked.

He shook his head, "Shit they use for roofies, GHB, Special K, that shit has a short half-life, it should be out of your system by morning."

"You seem to know a lot about it," Faith murmured. She was hovering nearby, Marlin kneading her shoulders.

"Paramedic for over ten years in a county known for its college spring break appeal? I'd better know more than a thing or two, or I'm not doing my job right."

Faith sighed, "You paint houses for a living."

Nothing bowed his head and nodded, "Yeah, I do that, too."

He was holding my hands in his, thumbs stroking gently across the backs of my fingers and all I could do was stare at him. Something was different, but I couldn't put my finger on it.

"Take me home?" I asked and he nodded.

"Prospect!" Marlin bellowed and we all jumped at the unexpectedness of it. When there was no immediate answer, we all looked at each other confused. Marlin reached into the back of his waistband under his cut and thrust Faith towards me. I took her hand and he went out front.

"Prospect!" he called again, and the front door opened. Trike put up his hands, my spare Jeep keyring dangling from his fingers.

"Woah, she can't ride, I went to get her Jeep so you could drive her."

"Good lookin' out, Trike. That's what I was gonna have you do." Marlin put up his gun like he hadn't just been brandishing it a second before. He held out an arm and Faith went to him automatically, tucking herself into his side.

"Right, I'm going to take Charity home."

"We'll wait here for the Captain and the rest," Marlin said, "Faith you want to stay with your sister?" he asked. She looked at me and I shook my head.

"Stay with Marlin, Faith. You'll be safer with him and I just plan on sleeping."

She nodded, and looked as torn as I'd felt staying up at my university all that time. I reached out and we pulled each other into each other's arms hugging one another fiercely.

"I love you, Blossom."

"I love you, too, Bubbles."

Nothing touched my back lightly and I jumped slightly. I turned and he said, "Let's get you to where you can get a hot shower and some sleep, Baby."

"Okay," I nodded, and just felt *drained*.

My Jeep was waiting outside, and he helped me up into the passenger seat. I closed my eyes for the short drive to Cutter's but opened them the moment I felt us make a wrong turn.

"Where are you going?" I asked, anxiety spiking.

"Taking you home."

"Not your home, my home."

"Exactly," he said and I turned to look at him.

"You're one of the club now, all our homes are your home," he said and pulled into his driveway, reaching into the inside pocket of his cut. The door to his garage opened.

"Cutter's. Now." I ordered and he rolled us to a stop.

"Make you a deal," he said.

"What?"

"I'll take you to Cutters, as long as you let me stay with you."

I shook my head, "No dice, you already made your position clear, you told me to fuck off so I fucked off. I don't want to do this back and forth." He swung us around and made for Cutter's.

"I was wrong," he said.

"Yeah? What changed your mind?"

"A lot of things, but the biggest one? The thought of never being able to touch you, or see you smile again. I'm freaked the hell out, Charity. Scared shitless. Can you let me have that, please?"

I stopped arguing for a second. He'd pulled up to the stop sign right before the turn on the boulevard and was staring at me. His beautiful gray eyes as solemn and *frightened* as I'd ever seen them.

"That car flipped on its side, on *the passenger side* and I thought I was gonna get to you and you were going to be gone. Dead. I thought I was never going to see those gorgeous eyes of yours sparkle again."

Oh. Well crap.

"Take me home, please?" I said much softer this time.

"Okay."

We made the drive to Cutter's in silence and he let us in the front door, Stoker and Beast were in the living room, and they were armed. Nothing nodded to them.

Beast looked me up and down, "You look like hell, Sweetheart. Why don't you come sit down before you fall down?"

"Thanks, but I really just want a shower and my bed."

"We're going to stay down here until we get word to do something else," Stoker said.

"Thank you, I feel safer already."

"Sure, thing." Stoker tossed back his dyed black hair and Beast nodded.

Nothing guided me to the staircase and I moved slowly up the stairs. I was already beginning to feel stiff in a few places.

"Let me draw you a hot bath," Nothing suggested outside my bedroom door and I shook my head, wincing.

"Shower. I don't like baths."

"Good to know, find what you want to wear. I'll get you some towels and the water started.

He went down the hall to the linen closet and pulled down a couple of towels, disappearing into the bathroom. A second later I heard the water tap turn on and a second or two later, the shower begin to run. I pulled down an oversized tee and a pair of boy-short panties out of the drawer and trailed down to the bathroom.

Nothing pulled the curtain and turned around, sighing as I slipped into the bathroom.

"Lean up against there," he said indicating the sink's counter. I leaned my butt against it and he went to one knee in front of me, his hand gently cupping my heel as he slid first one shoe, then the other, off my feet.

I watched him, transfixed. Partially because I was still loopy from whatever that asshole Greg had dosed me with, and the rest because something was *different*. The look on his face, the energy around him, something had changed in our short time apart; something significant.

"What happened?" I asked, the words out of my mouth before I could stop them.

Nothing looked up sharply, "You were drugged and kidnapped..."

"No, with you. What happened with you?"

He searched my face, him looking up at me, me looking down at him and his hands gliding up my leg in a *very* distracting manor. I closed my eyes and held onto my line of questioning, stopping his fingers with mine when they went for the front of my shorts.

"Can we talk about it later?" he asked and I opened my eyes.

"Do you promise?" I asked softly, and he gripped my hips, one hand on each and gave me a little shake.

"I promise. Now, will you let me take care of you?"

I nodded and he smiled, and it held something akin to shyness rather than sadness. Something had indeed happened, and I'd just about reached my limit when it came to trusting men, especially given what'd just happened, but for Nothing...

"I guess I have room for one last do-over," I murmured and his face lost that easy smile, his eyes growing so very serious.

"I don't deserve it, Baby, but I'll take it for the gift it is and I promise not to disappoint you this time."

We stared at one another for a long time before either of us dared move. When I did, it was to nod slowly, "I believe you," I whispered and he nodded, breaking eye contact and working the button out of its loop on my shorts.

He stripped me the rest of the way gently, his hands whispering over my skin, sending shivers and goosebumps in a wash over my flesh. He lifted the hem of my lace shirt and peeled it over my head, letting it fall to the floor before slipping his hands into the back of my panties, nudging them so they would fall in a pool at my feet.

I felt exposed, being so nude while he remained fully clothed, but at the same time, safe. He pulled back the curtain to the shower and steadied me as I stepped over the edge of the tub into the warm spray.

"I'll be back to check on you in a minute," he said and I nodded. The curtain whisked across the rail and Nothing disappeared.

I leaned against the shower wall, palms flat to the cool tiles and soaked my head. Eventually I leaned my forehead against the wall too, and just let the warm water cascade down my back, the pulsating showerhead gently beating the tension out of my knotted shoulders.

I don't know how long I stood like that, I didn't really care, but when the curtain rustled and hands gently started prying at the residual tightness and knots I didn't care. I just let the whole world spiral down to the gentle kneading touch and Nothing's healing presence.

He pulled me back against his chest and simply held me for long moments, his lips tracing up and down the side of my neck in the steaming rush of shower water from the nozzle. The sound steady and even, a white noise that made me give up the ghost on trying to hold onto any of the thoughts in my head. I turned around and put my arms around his neck and let him hold me for a little bit.

He was a gentleman, even though he really didn't have to be with me, and when I tried to kiss him, he put a finger to my lips to stop me.

"Why?" I asked.

"Because the drugs that S.O.B. used are designed to lower inhibitions, the next time we go there, I want to be sure you're going there with a clear head and that *you* want it. Not because of some drug in your system."

The fact that he said this to me with a raging boner pressed against my stomach only made me think more of him, not less.

"Okay," I whispered, nodding despite how fucking horny I was all of a sudden.

"I'm here to take care of you," he said, punctuating the remark with a chaste kiss against my lips.

He did. Take care of me, I mean. He started by washing my hair, then my body; his hands slicked with soap. He was careful of me, and by the time he was through, and I was rinsed and clean, I was nearly asleep on my feet, so lulled by the relaxing sensations he wrought with those hands of his. *Magic hands, magic fingers.* I thought to myself.

He dried me, and towel around his lean hips, helped me to dress in what I'd brought from my bedroom. He walked behind me, pressed to my back, keeping me safe in the circle of his arms from tripping over my own feet, or from curling up right there on the bathroom mat, which sounded like a *really* good idea.

The adrenaline had worn off a long time ago, and rather than the shakes, anxiety, and fear I should have been left with, Nothing had provided just the right combination of presence, support, and care needed to lull me into an almost perfectly relaxed state, so I let him take the reins and lead; which he did, right into my room. He lost the towel and ushered me into bed, climbing in after me and reaching up to switch out the light.

I lay against him, head on his shoulder, and he kneaded my neck, at the base of my skull between forefinger and thumb. I recall sighing out, then nothing as I fell into, what I presumed was, a deep and even sleep.

CHAPTER 26

Nothing

The door to Charity's room cracked open, light from the hall spilling across the carpet. I didn't know how long I lay here with her, but it'd been hours; that was for sure.

Hope poked her head into the room and looked us over, a scowl carving deep, shadowed lines in her forehead. She slipped in and shut the door behind her, dipping us back into a deep twilight.

"I swear to fucking Christ, Nothing, if you hurt my baby sister again, I'm cutting your balls off." I tried not to smile, amused by her overbearing sisterly protection, mostly because I knew if I smiled now, she'd skip waiting on me to hurt Charity and lop off my balls right here and right now. I sort of liked where they were.

"It was never my intent to hurt her in the first place, Hope."

"Then what were your intentions? Because you damn sure did a bang up fucking job of *not* hurting her." Hope crossed her arms over her chest and leaned her back against the door.

"Just wanted to spare her," I muttered and Hope leaned her head forward on her long, graceful neck.

"Excuse me?"

"You heard me."

"Yeah, I was kind of hoping I hadn't heard that right, you jackass," she threw up her hands and let them drop to her jeans clad thighs with a slap. "Seriously, *what is your fucking deal?*"

"I have a lot to sort through, new information, a lot has happened in a short amount of time for me," I swallowed hard, "I promise when I figure it all out, you'll be the first to know."

I stroked Charity's hair and she shifted in her sleep. Hope and I both froze solid, and exchanged a look.

"Right, I don't want to wake her up. You," she stabbed a finger in my direction, "Figure your shit out pronto, because I'm not doing that again."

I nodded vaguely, eyes on Charity as much as I could for the angle, and Hope slipped back out.

I sighed, wasn't that what I'd been laying here doing all this time? Trying to figure my shit out?

I didn't know what to think anymore. Not after the bombshell the Captain had dropped on me. For three years going on four I'd been heartsick, dying a slow death on the inside, plagued with guilt for not having saved my wife and daughter. My own club hiding from me that she wasn't even faithful to me. Did I get why they hid it? Yeah. Did it still kill me that they did? You bet your life on it.

And Charity... I'd pushed her away, and *fuck* was I completely mental? It sure felt like I'd lost my fucking mind, man. I closed my eyes, these thoughts chasing themselves around the inside of my head until I felt sick.

Corrine... why?

Her words from that night drifted back to me, as they often did in the dark and quiet moments before sleep. Only this time, they didn't carry with them the torturous guilt, this time they were there for me to analyze and to rip apart, before they got a chance to tear at me...

"*...it's always your damn brothers fixing things around the house.*"

"*...you need to be paying attention to what's going on at home...*"

"*I need you to grow up before you find we've moved on without you... We don't want anyone else.*"

With the new information to put them in context, I realized now why her words had unsettled me so. Our last words to each other had been said in anger and the guilt was still there, welling up out of the cracks and eating at me, but not like before. With new context I understood, clearly now, what Corrine had been trying to say.

If you don't get your act together, I'm leaving you... and not only was she going to leave me, she was going to leave me for one of my brothers.

Fuck. Why had the Captain and the rest of the guys kept this from me? Which circled me right back around to the bitter as hell truth – *because you couldn't handle it.* Cutter had been right. I would have lost my shit completely, I was already riding a dangerous line. Chilling on the edge of a precipice, with only one way to go; down. Straight down, right to hell and gone.

Charity shifted slightly in her sleep, a soft moan escaping her lips that sounded auspiciously like distress. I smoothed a hand over her golden hair and she settled and I thought to myself, *but then she looked at me.* Charity had looked at me and one look was all it'd taken and I didn't understand the why of it.

I'd never understood the why of it when it'd been Corrine's look that'd knocked me left of center either, but as my grandfather had always told me, 'There are some things in life that you just go with, that you don't ask questions and just accept them for the gift they are.' I'd seized it when it'd come to Corrine, so why had I resisted it so hard when it came to Charity?

The answer to that had come to me when that fucking car had flipped up on its side with her in it: because I was scared. Because if I'd let it happen, I was setting myself up for the same kind of pain that'd taken me over when I lost Katy and Corrine and I was damn sure I couldn't live through that a second time... but I'd nearly had to, tonight.

I held Charity a little tighter and kissed the top of her head. Corrine had been right about one thing, when it came to her final words... she, and now Charity, couldn't be the only one to try. I needed to try too, or this gift I'd been given, this second chance, would be gone forever. 'Nobody ever said that life was easy,' was another thing my gramps used to say. It was the truth, and it was time I stopped waiting for my life to run out so I could see my wife and girl again, and time I started living it so that when I did, they could greet a man they could be proud of.

Eventually, I managed to sleep. Decisions and some peace made with myself over some things. I closed my eyes and let Charity's deep and even breathing carry me down into the dark.

CHAPTER 27
Charity

I woke up first, and when I lifted my head, it was to light streaming through the slats of the blinds, falling across Nothing, who was sleeping beside me. I sat up carefully, and studied his face. Slack with sleep, it was like he'd tripped and fell headlong into being beautiful. I swallowed hard and pressed my thighs together beneath the sheet. I'd been dreaming, just before I'd woken up, dreaming of his hands on my breasts and his lips on my skin. I know, I know! I should be mad at him. I should hold out on him and make him prove himself before giving him any, and all that psycho female bullshit, but I wanted him. I wanted him *bad*, and he was right *here*... he was *still* here.

I carefully sat up, pulling my tee up and off over my head, letting it fall to the floor by the side of the bed. I contemplated him a moment more, and decided to try and wake him with a smile, what guy didn't like that? I skimmed my panties down my legs, arching to do it and Nothing didn't stir one bit. He didn't stir when I lifted the sheet off his nude body, either. I was a little worried when I straddled his lean hips and lifted his cock gently, putting him inside of me, gliding down gently until our bodies met.

I closed my eyes, hands caressing over his chiseled chest, as I rocked my hips, a slow sensual grind. I concentrated on the full sensation for a moment, before the draw to open my eyes to watch him grew too great. He was still asleep, though he stirred, his lips pursing, his head twitching to the side before finally, his eyes flew open, his hands matching them for speed, going to my hips and gripping them tightly to stop me. His chest heaved with deep and ragged breaths and I stilled.

"Do you want me to stop?" I asked gently, suddenly feeling guilty for taking advantage. He focused his gaze on me and his head started to shake before he could give voice to his thoughts.

"No, I was dreaming. Just dreaming... caught me off guard. I... I like this." His grip on my hips eased and he smoothed his hands over my skin, his touch firm and warm as he swept them up my flanks and back down, along the tops of my thighs. I rocked my hips and his beautiful gray eyes drifted shut, his dark lashes even darker against his tanned skin. His breath left his mouth in a sensual gentle rush and I bent carefully to place my lips against his.

He seized me with a passion, one arm a bar across my lower back, the other curving protectively around my body, hand gripping the back of my neck tenderly, buried in my hair to hold me to him while we kissed. Something was different. It was as if whatever burden of sorrow Nothing had been carrying had been eased, or, for the time being, had been laid aside.

He thrust up into me, slowly, deliberately, while he kissed me and I felt myself melt into his embrace. I think this was Galahad, because the man holding me to his body so carefully, while he filled me and pleasured me... there was no way that this man was nothing. He was most definitely something, and I wish I could say I was surprised, but I really couldn't be... this man made me *feel* something. Something I couldn't claim that I'd ever felt before, but something, I none the less, wanted to feel every day. I wanted this. I wanted him. I wanted him like this, with no sadness, no worry, no fear... I wanted him to be happy. I wanted him to feel this contentment like I was feeling right now.

We parted, a natural lull in our impassioned kiss, and simply stared into one another's eyes. He kept moving, his hips thrusting up carefully and gently, body slipping in and out of me, the warm golden glow of pleasure building, like the hint of sunrise in the east.

It was incredibly intimate, both of us laid bare before the other, the secrets; so many things unsaid, slipping between us and rolling away. As if our two separate worlds suddenly snapped into focus and we were seeing each other clearly now, feeling one another, for the very first time. We'd had incredible, mind-blowing sex before but this was different. This held weight. This was something both incredibly complex, and simple at once.

I could see when it hit him, too. That this time was different from all the rest, and I could feel when he committed to this strange feeling, whole heartedly. He sat up, with me still straddling him, and claimed my mouth in a fierce kiss. He was fully seated inside of me, and I tightened around him, my arms wending around his shoulders, tears of something very like joy burning the backs of my eyes.

We both dissolved into action, me by grinding against him, needing more of him that was very nearly impossible to get lest there was a way to pull him *through* me. He used his surprising strength to turn me so I was on my back, and cradling me in his arms, thrust more surely. I wrapped my legs around his lean hips, locking my ankles together behind his back and pulling him in.

"Oh god, *Charity*..." he uttered and I think my heart very nearly soared out of my chest.

I gazed up at him and marveled, whispering "Nothing, *please*," in an impassioned plea for him to find that place, to make me come, and he did. He slipped his hand between us, slicking his thumb in my considerable wetness before teasing my clit.

That golden glow of promise erupted into full dawn, just like the sun bursting over the horizon, so too did this orgasm, rocking through me, burning away any doubt, fear, anger, or pain. Nothing was my anchor as I shuddered beneath him, clinging to him while my nervous system sparkled and flitted with little shots and jolts of pleasure.

The spots cleared from my vision to reveal his kind face, eyes alight with something warm and all-consuming as he smoothed my hair from my face. I panted and he shifted and I very nearly climbed his body with a yelp at the intensity of my over sensitivity.

I waited and nodded, and murmured, "Go ahead."

"Hmm, 'go ahead' and what?" he asked, kissing my throat.

"Finish," I murmured and he chuckled.

"I came with you, Baby."

"What?"

"I came the same time you did."

I blinked... *Oh...*

He snuggled me in his arms and kissed me, and I kissed him back, my heart thundering with quicksilver energy against the inside of my ribs. He drew back and leaned down to place his lips between my breasts, centered over my heart. He kissed me there, and the look of such tenderness, of such care and just *reverence* on his face when he did it, sent me over a different kind of edge.

It was the look every woman ever dreamed of seeing on a man's face as he handled her, and it brought a hot flood of tears to my eyes that welled and immediately spilled down my temples to see it. It was such an amazing *gift*. One that was unparalleled and it took my breath away. The hitch in my breathing snapped Nothing's eyes to mine and he *knew*.

He didn't ask me what was wrong. He simply smiled the most contented smile I'd ever seen and turned his head to lay an ear where his lips had been. I found my fingers then, tangled in the sheets, and let the poor material go so that I could run them through Nothing's dark hair instead. Combing it back from his face so I could marvel at the peace painted across his features as he listened, eyes closed, to my heart's slightly unequal rhythm.

"You have a murmur," he uttered and I felt myself nod.

"Non-life threatening, it's just kind of there."

"I like it; it makes your heartbeat something different, something uniquely you."

I fell in love with him. Right then. Right there. I fell in love with this difficult, sad, angry man and I wouldn't trade it for the world. I lost myself to him right then and there and you can't lose yourself to nothing... because he was most definitely *something*.

"What should I call you?" I asked softly, and he glanced up at me. Whatever was on my face made him still and consider me seriously.

"Dominic, or Shep would work."

"How about Galahad?" I asked and he considered me gravely.

"Who told you that name?"

"Does it matter?"

He considered me and raised his head slowly, shaking it gently back and forth, his eyes never leaving mine, "I don't suppose it does, but names like that one are earned. I earned it once and then I threw it away. I kind of feel like I need to earn it back, now."

I nodded carefully, "Maybe for them," I agreed, "But not for me."

He laid his head back down and closed his eyes listening to the blood flow through my body before he opened his eyes again, tongue flicking out to wet those sensual lips. He sighed and it took him a try or two, but finally he spoke.

"It was raining, the night... the night," his voice cracked and he stopped, swallowing hard and clearing his throat, "The night my family died. The night I killed them by accident."

I held very still, my fingers automatically and still gently, running through his silken soft hair. I nodded, afraid to speak and shatter his resolve.

"I'd worked, essentially, a double and I'd promised Katy and Corrine we would go see the alligators at the gator farm, and so we drove out there and spent the whole day. I was tired, I was *so* tired, but I pounded an energy drink and I said I was good to drive. It was dark and raining, a long drive and we weren't too far outside Ft. Royal when this car, it crossed the center line. I swerved, but I was beat and my reaction time, it was too slow and I swerved *into* the guy instead of away and he hit Corrine and Katy's side... I killed them. I..." he closed his eyes and he shuddered, his breath breaking on a brittle sob that he tried to force down. I soothed, I put my arms around him and I held him, and was his rock as he had been mine the night before as he spilled his bitter anger and pain in a hot wash of tears down my skin.

He'd promised, and he was making good on his promise, but what he told me next, made my heart break for this good and noble man. This man who had been giving so freely of himself as a paramedic before his world had shattered into a million shards of cutting agony.

"She was cheating on me, with a brother. I didn't know until the Captain told me last night, and then you were gone and I thought I had screwed up everything and all of a sudden you were in front of my face as everything I should have seen you as in the first place.

This beautiful, smart, intelligent, funny woman who was interested in *me*. This nothing and nobody. This beautiful, kind, and soft hearted woman who didn't want to give up on me and you were gone and when that car flipped, I thought it was my fault, that God was punishing me for wasting the opportunity he was gifting me and I thought sure you were gone, and that it was my fault for driving you away. I'm so sorry. I'm so sorry..." he was babbling, his emotions running over the dam he'd spent so long building to stem the tide and so I did the only thing I could do.

I held him, and I opened my heart, and I took it all in and locked some of his burden away where I could carry it for him, so he didn't have to carry it alone any more. He looked at me and I smiled, cradling his face in my hands, smoothing my thumbs through the tears and he stared at me with soft wonder until I stripped his fear that I would laugh or turn away from him by kissing him, his mouth warm and salty beneath mine.

"I don't want to be alone anymore," he said dully and I smiled and rested my forehead against his.

"You aren't," I said and it was as if that statement alone lifted a thousand pound boulder off of his shoulders. If one of his brothers hadn't already held the name Atlas, I might have suggested it in that moment. Of course, Atlas could never set his burden down while Nothing? Nothing sighed with relief and held me close, while I held him.

I finally thought we might have a good start here. Time would tell.

CHAPTER 28
Nothing

We held each other and dozed and I didn't think I could deny it. It'd been a long time since anything like love stirred in the center of my chest, but it was there now. It was like Charity had drawn the two fractured halves of me into alignment, like she had the touch and the skills, where no one had before and the real break that'd happened the night my family'd died, had finally been set. I felt like, with a little more time, and with hers and my brothers' support, that I could start to mend. That was, if my brothers had it in them to be around me anymore.

The door to the room opened, and I looked over from Charity's angelic face where it rested on the pillow across from mine. She'd fallen asleep again, and I had simply stared at the golden morning light through the blinds as it shimmered in her golden hair and wondered how on earth a man like me could be so lucky twice in one lifetime.

Cutter stood in the doorway and looked us over, he swallowed, and said "Club meeting, The Plank, twenty minutes." I nodded and tried not to let my heart drop at how grave he sounded. I turned back to Charity's ice blue eyes looking me over.

"Hey," I intoned softly.

"Hi."

"You heard?"

"Mm-hm."

"You gonna be okay, here?"

She smiled and kissed the tip of my nose. It was cute, and made me smile, which I think was her goal.

"Should get dressed and get going, twenty minutes isn't a lot of time to do both that and get down there."

"True enough."

"I'll be here when you're done, maybe on the beach," she said.

"Promise?"

She smiled again, "Promise."

It was enough to make the knot of anxiety in my chest ease some. I got up, got dressed and with a final, lingering kiss, got myself gone and down to The Plank.

***

The Captain had called us all together to debrief us on the whole Russian situation. Hope was invited to this little soiree being as she was as involved as the rest of us. They'd taken out the dipshit who'd kidnapped Charity and disposed of him accordingly, however, when it came to the hotel, they'd gotten there too late to be any good. His comrades had gotten out before they could catch up with them. It left us all a little bitter and more than on edge.

"Hypervigilance is our only option at this point. We're as on the defensive as we can get," Marlin grated. He didn't sound at all happy about this turn of events and I could reliably say, I knew *exactly* how he felt. Our girls may have had a couple three years separating their birth dates, but they might as well be twins for how alike they looked. Hope shifted where she leaned against the archway leading back to the Captain's chair. The rest of us all sat at our hodgepodge war table.

"Galahad," Cutter drawled and I looked up sharply, shaking my head.

"I have to earn that name back, Captain, but what would you have of me?"

Some of the guys around the table groaned and rolled their eyes. I gritted my teeth. Cutter hung his head and smiled, shaking it some.

"We'll have to agree to disagree on that," he said. "What I need is to know if you're on board with the program. Think you can stay sober and out of self-destructionville long enough to see this through?"

"I do."

"Look man," Radar drawled, "We all know you've got way more food for thought than you should be able to handle right now... No man could handle the dose of reality you just got without going a little off the rails-"

"It's fine, if I need to talk or deal, I'll reach out, I promise. Just, what are we gonna do about this? We can't have these assholes hanging over our heads forever. That's no way for Faith and Charity to live, no matter how used to living on the edge or the fringe *we* are."

"You ain't lyin'," Marlin stated, and I heard the 'but' coming. "But it comes with the territory when you get involved with an outlaw by citizen standards. If it ain't this, something else'll come along."

"Yeah, but 'something else' usually involves just us, and not the women and children," Atlas supplied.

"You aren't wrong Atlas, and I'd like to see us get back to our regularly scheduled programming," Cutter drawled.

"Never thought I'd miss the rum running and coyote days," Pyro muttered.

"I'll take illegal salvage and tomb raiding any day over this shit," Atlas agreed.

"So what do we do about it?" Cutter asked and I could see the strategy behind it.

He was met by fierce stares from around the table, "We go on the offensive," Radar said judiciously.

Cutter nodded, "Nothing, Marlin, you two are as invested in this as anybody, but seriously you need to stick with your women on this. Marlin, Faith is still too jittery and with good reason. Nothing, I think you and Charity have some things to work out and a little ways to go. Plus, if shit goes sideways I'd rather it *not* be our medically proficient brother who ends up shot, stabbed, blowed up, or worse; you feel me?"

"Like a virgin on her wedding night," I said and didn't bother to deny it. I kept up on my certs for a couple of reasons. One, because I wasn't entirely sure I wanted to paint houses for a living forever, and two, because a lot of the guys and their families couldn't always afford health insurance. I filled the gap for them, and for some of the town. It just was what it was. It'd been a while since we'd done any covert immigration operations, but it was worth it to keep the certifications up for that, too.

At my core and in my bones, I helped people. No matter how bad I fucked up or how guilty I felt, no matter how bad my damage from that accident... I helped people. It was what I did.

"Operations like what the Russians are up to... they don't die easy. They're just going to keep comin'," Lightning said grimly.

"Only way to kill it and kill it for good is to cut off the head of the snake," Radar agreed.

"Well, the boys in New Orleans might just handle that for us. Ruth and the rest of the Voodoo Bastards are involved in the mightiest of turf wars over there, and by the looks of it, all things considered, they're winning thanks to us." Cutter said. "Now they're doin' it for themselves, so it ain't like they're going out of their way to do us no favors —"

"That doesn't mean they won't want somethin' from us down the line," Marlin said with all practicality. Cutter tapped his nose twice and pointed towards his second.

"What will we do if they want to collect on something they haven't exactly earned?" Gator voiced, he'd been quiet up to this point, along with Beast and Stoker. I was curious myself about the Captain's answer.

"Well fellas, I think it best we don't borrow trouble afore it gets to our door, but it's like anything else we take on. We vote on it. Of course, it's hard to project what any of 'em might want from a little outfit like ours and so far away. So it's best we let sleeping dogs lie for now lest we get bit."

"Captain's right, deal with it when and if it comes to pass, and not before, but the Voodoo Bastards, like us, are an honorable lot as far as outlaws go." Hope said from the wall.

"My Lady's right. They may not be as honorable as the Sacred Hearts boys, but they did us some good turns—"

"Yeah, that aligned with their own self-interests," Stoker muttered.

"Be that as it may, they helped us out plenty with that lawyer and getting Hope outta jail, scot free and all. I think we legit have a friend in Ruth and his crew. I project the most they'll want is to come to our neck of the woods for some R and R once the dust has settled in their neighborhood."

"A good party, now *that* we can provide," Pyro said with a grin.

A raucous cheer went up around the table and several of us had our faces split by smiles. Cutter rapped his gavel on the arm of his throne.

"Alright, alright! I guess on *that* note, our business here is concluded unless anyone else has any questions?" He waited but no one piped up. "Right, get your marching orders from your Sergeant at Arms and let's get back to life as we know it for now. Go on, git."

Cutter called the meeting with a few more raps of his gavel, and the guys got up, chairs scraping back and bodies dispersing to go do whatever it was that needed doing. I sat, lost inside my own head for a long time, before realizing not everyone had gone. Radar still sat at the table with me. I looked to my brother and sighed.

"A lot of things make sense now," I said.

"Like?"

"Like you wanting me to get over Corrine. I thought it was just frustration on your part for the time dragging out... but it was more than that wasn't it? You knew, didn't you? Before anyone else."

"Where do you think the pictures came from?" he asked with a sideways, self-deprecating smile.

"I figured, what I can't figure is why you started looking into Corrine in the first place. What happened?"

"You sure you're ready for the full story?" he asked.

"Truthfully? No, but there's no real good time for things like this is there?

"I don't know, Charity came along and made it the right time for a lot of things for you," he said slyly and I felt embarrassment heat my face.

"It shouldn't have had to come to that," I uttered and Radar reached out a hand and squeezed my shoulder, giving me a shake.

"Bro, we all know how in love with that girl you were, and are.

What she did doesn't change that, and it certainly don't change a damn thing about how you feel about your baby girl. We get how much the accident, them..." he groped for a word and I sighed.

"Dying, they died, man."

"See, that's my point. Two, three weeks ago, if any of us put it that way? You'd have flown off the handle. Charity's changed things for you."

"I don't understand it," I said grimly.

"What?"

"How a guy like me could be so lucky twice in one lifetime."

Radar snorted, "Maybe because it's *a guy like you.* When you going to stop torturing yourself long enough to realize that *you're a good guy,* Nothing? Better 'n over half of us motherfuckers. We're the lucky assholes to have *you* watching our backs."

We stared at each other and a chair creaked, we both looked over to the bar and Atlas leaning back in his high backed barstool in front of his and Radar's laptop getup.

"Light show!" he declared grinning and Radar and I smiled and bowed our heads laughing.

"That son of a bitch is gonna get hit again one of these days," he said.

"You and I both know it, and you and I both know I'd better be there if he does, except now, the lucky bastard has two of us to bring him back from death's door."

"She good?" Atlas asked from the bar.

"We saved this drowned kid last week on the beach. She's really good. I have to say though, I think she'd make a better paramedic than a nurse," I gave it a second thought, "Maybe an *ER* nurse, would do it, but she's an adrenaline junky, like me. Paramedic would be better."

"Trouble," Radar said, nodding judiciously.

"Sounds like the Captain had her pegged from day one with that nickname."

More like salvation for me... I thought to myself.

"How long until the light show?"

"Meh, a couple of hours by what the Doppler's spewing."

Radar nodded, he and Atlas were partners in the bounty hunting field and Atlas, in addition to having a thing for maps and tracking had a side thing for weather which worked out well for the Captain's salvage outfit, and Marlin's fishing gig. He picked up the handset to the ham radio on the bar and radioed out to the marina and its harbor master, imparting the information. Just one more reason the town loved us, too. Share and share alike. They got the latest and greatest on impending weather before the news stations could even get it out, and in return, when we put out a B.O.L.O. or a 'Be On The Lookout' on someone or for something, they came through for us.

Everyone liked to think the worst when it came to this town's willingness to give us the information we desired, or the willingness to withhold information from outsiders. They liked to think we held this town in thrall, under our thumbs using fear and intimidation tactics. No one ever counted on how this town's love ran deep for us, and no one damn sure counted on how deep our love ran for *it*. So it was, when it came to citizens and the outlaw life, and I and my brothers had a motto for that: Fuck 'em.

"C'mon, boys. Let's go see what the girls are up to, and watch Lightning get his ass fried."

"Hey, he makes a killing on those things if he gets one." Atlas pointed out.

"Yeah, *if* he gets one and when they finally sell, he *does* rake it in. Not like it's consistent."

I listened to my two brothers' banter back and forth about a third as we headed out the door, and got on our bikes. We rode back to the Captain's house, and I felt a growing excitement in the center of my chest. An effervescence I hadn't felt in a really long time as my spirits lifted and I thought about seeing Charity again.

Second chances didn't come along every day, and I learned my lesson last night. I wasn't going to cast a blind eye or turn away from this one again. No way.

CHAPTER 29
Charity

I put on a bikini and slid a wrap around my hips and a light matching swimsuit cover-up onto my shoulders. My hair I threw into a haphazard messy bun, before I slipped down the back stairs down into the dining room. The club's prospect, Trike, was in the kitchen, drinking greedily from a glass at the sink, a rifle leaning against the counter at his hip. It gave me pause at the bottom of the stairs.

I caught the corner of his eye because he turned to look, "Hey," he said out of breath. I smiled and inclined my head, trying to act naturally in the face of the obvious, and larger than life gun. I hated guns.

"Hey, yourself. Everyone at the meeting?"

"Yup."

"Left behind with the women and children, huh?"

He grinned, "Women, anyhow."

"Seen my sister?" I asked.

He inclined his head to the closed water closet door and I smiled, "Ah."

"Water?" he asked.

I shook my head, "No thanks, I was wondering if it was alright if I went outside."

"How far?" he asked, and I felt a trickle of unease go down my spine.

"The hammock?" I asked.

"Sure," he started, eyes sliding over me, "You're not a prisoner, you know. I'm just set to make sure both of you are okay, and I'm only one guy. I was just gonna ask that if it was a walk you wanted to go on, that you wait for Faith."

I felt my smile slip and surge back to life although a little more watered down than it had been the moment before, "I'm not used to all of this," I murmured. He picked up his rifle and slung the strap over his shoulder.

"That makes two of us; it's never been quite like this before, even when the Sacred Hearts girls were here."

I shook my head, not understanding the reference, and a small grin flickered to life, "I don't know what that means," I admitted.

"Sacred Hearts are an outfit up north; they got into it with another club, extreme disrespect. The other club hurt one of their women. For their girls' safety, they stayed down here for a while, while their men took care of business."

I raised an eyebrow, "Should you be telling me any of this?" I asked.

He flushed a deep red, and went to the sliding glass door, opening it up for me. I heard the toilet flush and the water run in the bathroom. I took the last two steps and drifted towards the portal to bright sunshine and fresh sea air. The door at my back opened and Faith stepped out.

"Probably not, but don't tell on him, okay? I don't want to see him get in trouble for things we aren't going to ever repeat anyways."

I held out a hand and Faith drifted up to me, I hugged my sister and she smiled, I smiled back and smiled at Trike.

"Who would I tell?" I asked.

"Exactly," Faith said with a nod.

"Nothing, maybe. He is our secretary." Trike shifted uncomfortably.

"What would I tell Nothing?" I asked mock-innocently.

"That I told you –" Faith and I giggled and Trike stopped mid-sentence, understanding dawning on his face. "Oh! Right." He said and stepped aside. We slipped past him into the bright warmth of the sun and I paused, letting the daystar warm me.

"You okay?" Faith asked and I nodded.

"A little stiff, a little sore. I was going to lounge out here in the hammock."

"Sounds good. I could use some cuddle time with my favorite sister."

"I'm telling Hope."

"You better not!"

Trike grinned at our banter as we slipped across the patio and down the steps. He lit up a cigarette and perched on the low wall to one side of the stairs while Faith and I hung up our wraps and cover-ups on the hooks at either end of the chains holding the hammock up. It took some laughing and a couple of attempts for us to get into it right, and it spun and dumped us on our asses at least twice, but in the end it was worth it for us to lie side by side in the sun, Faith's head tipped and resting on my shoulder, talking like we used to when we were kids and it was late but neither of us could sleep.

We raised our hands and traced each other's matching tattoos on the insides of our wrists and giggled over memories. Finally we settled into staring into the blue sky and talking about the here and now.

"You love him?" I asked her, and glanced at her face. Her eyes were closed but the smile that spread across her lips told me everything it needed to before she used her voice.

"Very much, I don't know how I would do this without him."

"You would, you know. You're stronger than you know."

"You think?"

"You're still here, aren't you?"

Her face lost its easy smile of a moment before, and she sighed.

"A lot of girls didn't make it," she murmured.

"Yeah?"

I was pretty sure I didn't want to know this, but if Faith could live it for going on two years, I could hear about it and not flinch. It wasn't a fair trade, but it was all I could give her, and so I would.

"Some were killed, some they accidentally overdosed, some tried to run one too many times, others just never came back from their..." she groped for a word and I wanted to help, so I picked one of the most sanitized ones I could.

"Assignments?" I suggested.

"Johns. Customers," Faith gave a one shouldered shrug. "My therapist says I shouldn't try to marginalize anything that happened to me. That plenty of people would, to suit their own comfort level and that I shouldn't do that. That by acknowledging the really horrible things that happened, that by confronting things head on, it will allow me to deal with them better than hiding from them, you know?"

I nodded, "Makes sense, I'm sorry."

She shook her head, "Don't be. You didn't know."

"Now I do," I said and knocked my shoulder into hers.

"What about you?" she asked, changing the subject.

"What about me?" I asked, grinning.

"You think you love Nothing?"

The question made me think and finally, I answered her as truthfully as I could, "I think something is there, besides just the absolutely bat shit insane attraction. He's kind of a hard man to get to know."

"I didn't ask about *getting to know* him. I asked if you were falling in love with him." She rolled her eyes and I laughed.

"Yeah, I think I am, but he's so damn mercurial," I admitted.

"I know, I wanted to ask you to be careful, but I didn't want to upset you."

"I'm not offended, and I get why you would ask. He *has* hurt my feelings and he *has* been a dick, but…"

"But?"

It was my turn to roll my eyes, "He sets my panties on fire with a look and his dick is magic?" I tried and Faith burst into laughter.

"Marlin's the same way; I think Cutter is the same way for Hope, so I get what you're saying."

"Something changed between yesterday and today," I said.

"I should hope so!"

I made a face, "Leave her out of it, I'm surprised she hasn't gone all Corporal Badass on him and beat him up for being a douche the last time."

"I think she's letting you fight this particular battle on your own, but word; she's not happy. You deserve better than how he's been treating you with this hot and cold routine."

"I know," I said softly. "Somehow I think the cold tap has been shut off, though."

"Why?"

"He promised to talk to me," I said and it came out sounding childish and skeptical even to me. I winced.

"Yeah, well, we'll see if he does," Faith said and sounded skeptical too.

"That's just it, he did."

"Yeah? When?"

"This morning," I said.

"What did he tell you?"

"A lot of things, but I don't feel like I should share, you know? Nothing is a private person."

Faith nodded, but I could tell she was a little disappointed. I tilted my head and rested it on top of hers.

"Sorry, Bubbles."

"It's okay."

"Hey girls!" Lightning marched past us dragging what looked like long lengths of rebar topped with neon plastic flags through the sand. Faith and I burst out laughing.

"What are you doing!?" she called out to him; he turned to face us, carrying on with his antics, dragging the long lengths.

"Storm is coming in! Gonna be a light show!" he called back and for some reason, my sister and I looked at each other and found that to be hysterically funny. Dissolving into a fit of giggles that damn near tipped us right back out of the hammock again.

Shadows descended on us and we blinked up at Marlin and Nothing.

"Hi!" I said and both of them smiled down at us.

"Hey, didn't Lightning tell you? Storm's coming," Marlin said.

"What is he *doing?*" I asked curiously.

"Up and at 'em, and we'll show you," Marlin said grinning and with a yelp, he scooped up my sister. I cried out as the hammock tipped and threatened to spill me out, and Nothing was suddenly there. I hadn't seen him come around to my side, but his hands were wrapped around mine, and his body blocked mine enough to allow me to get my feet under me.

"Whew! Thanks," I said smiling, and gingerly got to my feet. "Ouch!"

"What's wrong?" he asked frowning and it warmed me, the concern in his voice.

"Sore from yesterday, I think. Delayed onset muscle soreness, it's to be expected after getting tossed around in a trunk."

He pulled me against his chest, his arms going around my waist, and I held him too, taking comfort. I frowned over his shoulder at Lightning who'd put on a pair of work gloves and was thrusting the long, long pieces of rebar deep into the sand of the beach, at random intervals. The neon pink, construction marking tape, fluttering in the stiff breeze coming in off the water. Dark clouds were on the horizon and moving in fairly quickly.

"What is he *doing*?" I asked again.

"One of his favorite, odd jobs. Dangerous as hell, too. Come on, let's go inside and I'll fill you in." Nothing shook his head at his brother as he came trotting towards us across the sand.

"You done?" Nothing called.

"Hell no! Just grabbing more." Lightning panted and disappeared around to the side of the house.

"That fool is going to kill himself, *again*." Atlas uttered from the back patio. I gathered up my wrap and cover up, slipping into them and walking with Nothing to the back steps. Atlas handed an unopened beer to Nothing but Nothing shook his head.

"No thanks, man," he said and gave me a squeeze around my waist where I was tucked into his side.

"Oh, my god! You're killin' me! What is he *doing*?" I cried.

"Fulgurites," Radar said opening up the back slider. "Come on, let's watch this fool fry himself."

"Folgers what?" I asked, "What's coffee have to do with anything?"

Nothing laughed, "Not Folgers, *fulgurites*."

"What's that?"

Radar answered me, "When lightning, the phenomenon, not the brother, hits the sand; it superheats it and turns it into a hollow glass tube. They're really cool looking, and really rare. When the storm conditions are right, Lightning helps God along by driving in the rebar. If he's lucky, one or two will get struck, the lightning travels down the rebar, superheats the sand and he'll get a fulgurite out of the deal. He makes a killing on 'em in one of the local, high end gift shops on the boulevard. If he manages to sell one, he's good for a month or more."

"Wow!"

"Like he said, they're really rare."

"Fragile too. If he gets one, he'll be lucky to keep it whole getting it out of the ground. That's why they go for so much," Atlas took a drink out of his can.

"I guess if he's unlucky, lightning doesn't hit one of his bars?" I asked.

"Nah," Atlas said.

"If he's unlucky, the damn fool gets hit, and Nothing has to run his ass out there and save him." Radar said with a grin.

"Wait, he stays out there during the storm?" I asked.

"Stupid motherfucker," Stoker said from behind us and laughed.

"How many times has he been struck?" I asked incredulous.

"Just the once," Nothing said. "And once was enough."

"Oh my god, I don't know who's more insane, him for doing it, or you guys for *letting* him!"

"Probably a good mix of both, Trouble." Cutter said, and I turned to look up at him. He winked at me, and grabbed a couple cold beers from the fridge. "You're welcome to join me, your sisters, and Marlin in my private box for the show," he said and I frowned.

Nothing chuckled, "He means the master bedroom upstairs. Floor to ceiling windows, you get a better view of the shenanigans."

"I think I'd better stay down here, in case something goes wrong," I said. The first rumbling of thunder rolling in distant came in from the water. The breeze carried with it the scent of ocean, rain, and ozone and Lightning was *still* out there running around the beach like zippy the squirrel, driving rebar into the sand. I felt myself grow tense.

"Suit yourself, Trouble. Enjoy the show," Cutter said with a grin, and took the back stairs two at a time, disappearing. Most of the brothers had crowded in behind me, standing at the sliding glass doors and watching Lightning, drinking beer and taking bets and I was mollified.

"Isn't he in very real danger?" I asked.

"Yep, and that's just the way he likes it," Atlas said.

"You're all crazy." I stated matter of factly.

"You ain't lyin'." Beast observed and all of the men burst out into laughter.

I tipped my head back against Nothing's shoulder and rolled my head back to look up at him, startled to find him looking down at me, a faint smile gracing his lips.

"This is like, totally normal for you, isn't it?"

He gave a one shouldered shrug, "Lightning's been doing this for years; its how he got his name, way before he was ever hit. This is part of the divide between our lives and that of your average citizen. We do what makes us happy, with the full support of our brothers. *This* makes Lightning happy, so here we are. If something goes wrong, we help him. It's just the way it is."

It was food for thought, and those thoughts were interrupted by Trike saying, "Here he comes."

Lightning was hotfooting it across the sand even as the first drops of rain started to patter against the glass. Thunder boomed and he leapt up onto the patio and turned around to watch progress.

"Isn't he coming inside?" I asked.

"Nah, it took a lot of work just to get him to get on base," Beast said.

"Base?"

"The patio."

"Oh."

Light flashed, brilliant and blinding enough for me to throw up a hand and it hadn't even dissipated when the thunder boomed hard enough to shake the very walls. I jumped and Nothing held me tighter against his body. The guys were all laughing and looking at me and I blushed. Lightning was pacing back and forth in front of the glass, muttering to himself.

"This is insane," I said just as a bolt leapt from the ground and crashed from the sky onto one of the pieces of rebar in the sand.

The thunder was deafening, and you could *feel* the crackle of electricity on the air. I clapped my hands over my ears and flinched back into Nothing, who I could feel shaking with laughter. When my hearing returned it was to the guys cheering and clapping. Lightning leaping up and down on the other side of the glass shouting like a teenage boy who'd just beaten the hardest boss on the hardest mode of the game.

I shook my head in disbelief as Nothing's warm hands drifted up my body to rest on my shoulders, his thumbs digging slightly into the base of my neck, easing the tension in my shoulders.

"Oh my *god*, this is crazy!" I said but I couldn't deny the smile on my face, or that the jubilant glee of the men around me wasn't seriously infectious. My heart lifted in excitement for Lightning even as more electricity lit the sky, sheeting through the clouds.

I suddenly found Nothing's hand at my throat, cupping my chin and drawing my face up to look at him, even as his lips descended on mine and a whole, different, electrifying feeling took over. Sweeping through my body, stilling my breath in my lungs for a fraction of a second even as his tongue swept into my mouth and swept all inhibitions away. I twisted, turning in his arms; my arms going around his neck even as I leaned my body into his, wanting more. More of this, more contact, more of his warmth, just *more*.

The guys were shouting and cheering, whistling and rowdy around us, but I was sure it had nothing to do with the sparks happening outside and everything to do with the sparks igniting in Cutter's kitchen between me and Nothing.

"Come home with me tonight," he murmured and I nodded, readily. I likely would have agreed to anything he asked in that moment. Such was the spell he had on me. *God, I was such an epic sucker for this man and his bad boy image.*

I rested my head on his chest, tucking it beneath his chin and folded myself into his welcoming embrace. He held me, turning so that we could still watch the dwindling show outside the glass.

Atlas set down his beer on the table and jogged back to the living room. Lightning was watching where he'd gone from outside the glass, his hair and clothing soaked, plastered to his wiry frame.

"He clear!?" Radar called.

"No! I'll tell you when."

Lightning was bouncing on the balls of his feet, and Radar rapped on the glass, Lightning's gaze switched from their intent focus on the living room to where Atlas was standing and making a cutting motion across his neck. Lightning very nearly deflated and bobbed around impatiently.

Several minutes went by, and the sky began to clear. Lightning looked very nearly ready to come out of his skin when Atlas called, "Okay! He should be good!"

Radar knocked on the glass again and gave two thumbs up; Lightning whooped, grabbed up a five gallon bucket from under the patio table and tore out onto the beach, looking up at the tops of the rebar.

"What's he looking for?"

"See the flags? The ones that got hit, they're going to be melted. It's not perfect because a lot of the ones close to the one that took the hit will be melted, but it tells him which ones to dig up carefully, so he doesn't break it," Radar explained.

"Can we go out there?" I asked Nothing.

"Yeah, you want to see?"

"Yeah! This is fascinating."

He smiled and huffed a laugh, "Yeah, it was my first time, too; come on." He slid open the sliding glass door and we stepped out onto the patio, washed clean by the rain. I drew in a deep breath that was tinged with ozone, the smell of wet earth, with just a tinge of the acrid smell of burning metal.

"Come on out! Don't touch any of 'em yet though, still might be hot!" Lightning shouted from down the beach.

We spent the rest of the day digging up fulgurites with the care and consideration one would use to unearth ancient treasures. Lightning even had an assortment of different paintbrushes to use to brush sand away from their twisting, corroded looking surface. They were beautiful. Sparkling when you turned them this way and that, under the sun. They looked like a living thing of fire and sand, like coral. Wild and warm to the touch, I could understand with both how fragile and unique each one was, how they fetched such a price.

The piece of rebar that had taken the direct hit, had the biggest one, but there were more, smaller and much more fragile ones from where the bolt had split among a few nearby poles and done its magic.

"Here," Lightning said and laid a small, spidery fulgurite, delicate as spun glass, though not nearly as clear, into the palm of my hand. "Keep this one, it'd never make it in the gift shop with people picking it up and handling it all the time."

"You sure?" I asked.

"Absolutely! Gotta have something from popping your fulgurite cherry."

"You just *had* to ruin the moment, didn't you?" Hope asked from over Lightning's shoulder and he nodded happily. Hope rolled her eyes and winked at me.

Out of the three of us, I'd taken to this the most, Faith being happy just to tuck herself against Marlin, a look of contentment on her face.

I yipped with girlish excitement at my new treasure and carried it up to my room in my cupped hands. Finding a safe place for it was a bit of a trick, but that accomplished, I stood back and admired it, sitting atop my night stand in a protective curve of the base of the iron lamp there.

"Beautiful, like you," Nothing uttered from the door. I hadn't realized at first that he'd followed me up.

"Thanks," I replied, blushing.

"Come home with me tonight," he said again. "Pack an overnight bag; let's leave now. I want you to myself." I swallowed hard and met his gaze and saw sincerity and heat there.

"Okay," I murmured.

"I'll go tell the guys and your sisters we're headed out," I smiled a little half smile.

"Good luck with Hope, better you than me."

"I think I'd brave a lot more than Hope for you, now."
"Yeah?" I asked softly.
"Yeah."
"How come?"
"Let's just say I've been given one hell of a wakeup call," he said and turned, heading down the hall toward the back stair. I think I sort of liked the sound of that.

I took my time, putting together a proper overnight bag with options according to what the bipolar weather of Florida might be the next day. Nothing reappeared in the doorway.

"You ready?"

"Yeah, just let me grab a pair of flip flops, I figured I'd follow you in the Jeep?"

"Sure, whatever makes you feel more comfortable," he agreed.

"Thanks, that obvious, huh?"

He nodded, "I've been a dick, I realize that, but I promise, that's over. Still, I get it, once burned twice shy. Were I you? I'd want a bug out option of my own too."

I felt like a jerk, even though I knew I had no reason to, so I said the only thing I really could say in a situation like this one: "Thanks."

"Think nothing of it," he murmured and held out his hand to me.

I grabbed a pair of flip flops off the closet floor and dropped them to the carpet, shrugging my feet into them. I picked up my gym bag and took his hand. He took my bag from me and shouldered it, which I thought was sweet. I scooped my phone up off the night stand and popped the charger out of the bottom and let Nothing lead me down the front stair. My phone buzzed twice in my hand.

Hope: You text me if I need to come kick his fucking ass!

I rolled my eyes and ignored the text, following Nothing out the front door.

CHAPTER 30
Nothing

I opened her Jeep's door for her and tossed her bag over to the passenger seat before stepping aside to let her in. She paused before getting up into the driver's seat and leaned out to kiss me. I took it for the gift it was, and swore to myself to treat her with the utmost care tonight. She was trusting me, when she had no fucking reason to, and I was blessed for it.

I shut her door, ensuring she was safe in her Jeep, making sure I didn't catch any of her with it. She rolled down the window and leaned down as I leaned up. A quick, chaste kiss and she started up the engine. I jogged over to my bike and got on, starting it up and leading the way.

Once we were at my place, I hit the button for the garage and watched it trundle up. I'd pulled off to the side and waved Charity in. She put the Jeep in gear, pulled smoothly inside and I pulled the bike over and into the driveway, letting down the kickstand and thumbing off the motor. I took my keys and ducked under the garage door before it could finish closing, just as she got out of her Jeep.

"You got anything sturdier in there to wear?" I asked.

"Um, like what?"

"Jeans, better shoes like sneakers maybe?"

"Yeah, why?"

"I don't have food, and I don't know about you, but lunch was a while ago."

"Oh... wait, are you asking me out to dinner?"

"And for a ride on the bike," I said and had to smile.

She turned and looked at the door leading into the house and back to me, "I'll be right out," she said and smiled. I nodded and followed her into the house so I could freshen up myself. She disappeared into the guest bathroom, closing the door behind her and I headed into my bedroom. I changed into fresh jeans and a clean shirt, shrugging my cut back on over the tee.

I was sitting on the edge of the bed pulling on my boots when she peeked inside my bedroom door. She wore form fitting jeans and a pair of women's canvas tennis shoes. Her top was one of those form fitting ladies cut tees that clung to her curves, the light peach color giving her skin a healthy glow, her eyes standing out to perfection. She was beautiful, without the benefit of any makeup, in just jeans and a tee shirt. I liked that about her.

"Ready?" I asked her, and she smiled nodding.

"Do I need anything other than phone, bank card and I.D.?" she asked.

"You don't even need the bank card; phone and I.D. should be just fine."

She blushed lightly and said, "I don't like to presume."

I pulled the cuff of my jeans down over the top of my last boot and stood up, going to her. I pulled her lightly by her denim clad hips into my arms and smoothed my hands over the delicate curve of her ass.

"I said I was taking you to dinner, no presumptions there. You got your stuff?"

"Yes," she said, and held up her phone in one of those cases that had places to hold her cards on the back. Three of them were stacked neatly in their cases. I gave her a swat on the ass and she yipped, laughing.

"Cool, let's go."

We left out the front door and I locked up behind us, she let me back the bike out of the drive and got on behind me, snuggling up close. I liked that too, that she wasn't afraid to ride or afraid to get close. We rode to the boulevard where I found some easy parking along the strip. I figured we'd go back to the place we'd been last night. I owed the bartender, Charlie, a big fucking thank you. Charity stopped and tugged on my hand when she saw where I was headed.

"I don't know about this, can we go somewhere else?" she asked, skeptical.

"Hey, it's okay." I pulled her into my arms and couldn't get enough of the feel of her there. "Haven't you wondered how we found you?" I asked, and she blinked several times, bewildered. I saw the gears turning and her shoulders lost their tension.

"I totally didn't even think about it, no. How *did* you guys find me?" she asked.

"That's why we're here," I said and ushered her the last few steps up the sidewalk and through the door.

She put her sunglasses up on her head and I did likewise, letting our eyes adjust to the dim interior. Charlie was behind the bar and looked up to greet us.

"Oh, hey, good! You got her. How you doing, Sweetheart?" he asked Charity and she didn't even miss a beat, she went around the bar and hugged Charlie tight.

"Thank you, I saw you on the phone, I just didn't realize *you* realized."

He hugged her back, shooting me a stricken look over Charity's head. I waved him down and he relaxed. She drew back and slunk back around the bar quickly, like she was afraid to get Charlie in trouble.

"It's no worries, just doing my part," he said. "You guys staying for dinner?"

"Yeah, man, we are."

"Cool, find a seat anywhere, know what you'll have to drink?"

We went through the motions, ordered some drinks and some food, talked quietly for a while, and just tried to relax which was easier said than done when all I wanted to do was get her naked and writhing underneath me. Charity had been right about one thing, our sexual chemistry was off the charts.

Dinner ended up being equal parts delightful and torturous with how bad my cock raged against the inside of my zipper. I couldn't even care that I was sporting full wood in a public place. All any of these motherfuckers would have to do was take one look at Charity to understand, so I didn't sweat it.

The conversation was light, as we studiously avoided any topic of conversation that involved any of the down and dirty fuckery to have gone on as of late. Mostly we kept it to where we had come from and where in life Charity wanted to go. It was nice. Her dreams aligned perfectly with what I used to want and what I'd given up. She wanted a career in the medical field, and no surprise, emergency medicine was her main focus. Kids were neither here nor there for her. If she had one or two, great, if not, that was okay too. She was focused and driven, like I had been once, and I felt an almost excited pull to try and go back there again.

I thought I'd given up the ghost when Corrine had died, when I'd lost my wife and child. I slammed the door, as I always did, on thoughts of Katy. That was too painful, and I tried like hell not to think about that particular gaping hole that would never heal.

"Nothing, are you okay?" Charity's soft warm hand covered my own where it rested on the table. I snapped back to the here and now.

"Yeah, sorry." I cleared my throat, "Thinking about my little girl."

"Oh, I'm sorry. What made you go there?" she asked.

"You did, sort of. You're eager, a real go getter, out to save the world and I remember when I was that way. You make me want to go back to it, but I thought those days were over, you know? They kind of ended when I couldn't save her." I dropped my eyes to where her hand rested on mine, and moved my hand, letting my fingers find the spaces between hers, playing with our entwined hands; idly twisting my wrist back and forth.

"You miss her the most."

It wasn't a question, so I didn't answer but I had to ask, "How do you figure?"

"Because you don't talk about her, like at all. It's too hard. It was the same way for me when Faith was missing. I could talk about my dead mother, but bring up Faith and I couldn't speak. I thought it was awful and strange, but then I went to counseling. The counselor told me it was because we knew mom was going to go, and that I'd had closure there. There was no closure when it came to Faith. She was just gone… so I couldn't deal with it as easily."

"Except we found Faith," I said shifting uncomfortably.

"Not when I was having the feelings. She'd been gone over a year. There wasn't anything to go on, and I just... I lost hope that we'd ever know."

She leveled me with a gaze so solemn it made my chest feel tight. I gave her hand a reassuring squeeze and we finished our meal in a comfortable, if weighted, silence.

I paid for our meal, and we slow walked back to the bike, taking in the fire of the sunset over the water. Charity sighed and I smiled.

"Ready?" I asked after a few minutes and she nodded. I got on the bike, and turned her over. Charity climbed on and signaling, I pulled us smoothly into traffic. We took a bit of a ride, all the way to the edge of town, around and back down. I could have turned us around at any of the intersections, but a little wind therapy seemed to be just what the doctor ordered. Sometimes you just needed to put your knees in the breeze and just ride.

When we got back to the house, I pulled into the garage alongside her Jeep. There was enough room. It was a two car, and I didn't store a whole lot of crap in it. We went into the house and Charity asked me, "Have anything to drink? The food was good, but a bit salty."

"Uh, yeah." I opened the fridge and hung my head, "Beer or water?" I asked. Smooth, real smooth...

"I'll have a beer," she said with this adorable as hell little pixie grin.

"You old enough?" I joked.

"I'm twenty-four, jackass."

I stood up and held one out to her, "Now I feel like a dirty old man," I said and she raised an eyebrow.

"What are you? Thirty-four?"

"Thirty-six," I answered.

"So we have a little bit of an age difference," she gave a one shouldered shrug, "I always knew I would end up with someone older."

"Yeah?" I asked.

She set her beer down and placed her palms flat on the counter she stood against and hefted herself up and back onto it. She twisted the cap off her beer using the hem of her tee and took a drink.

"Mm-hmm," she uttered around the neck of the bottle.

I wasn't thirsty, at least not for anything to drink, so I shut the fridge door. I went to her and stood between her knees, letting my hands rest on her hips.

"Why did you figure you'd end up with someone like me?"

"Hmm, I didn't think I would end up with someone like you, I said I knew I would end up with an older guy. Ending up here, with you, is just a bonus," she murmured and she stole what I was gonna do and kissed me first.

I pulled her to the edge of the counter, closer to me, her body right up against mine; pressing hot through the mutual denim of our jeans. She tasted crisp and clean, like the hops from the beer she'd just drunk. Her mouth was cold and eager and the combination of sensations drove me wild. I hauled her even tighter against my body and she wrapped her legs around my hips, an awkward motion on her part, and her tennis shoes hit the linoleum of my kitchen with a loud slap; one after the other as she toed them off.

She pushed at my cut and I stripped it off, laying it on the counter beside her and had to vaguely wonder *what was it about my kitchen?* All thoughts left my brain and I turned it over strictly to feeling when she lifted my shirt over my head. I let *that* fall to the floor. I didn't care about the shirt. Her hands were cool against the heated skin of my shoulders and I broke apart so I could search her face.

Those beautiful eyes of hers were heavily lidded with lust and I felt an answering spark in my own. I lifted her tee and stripped it off her, her bra hitting the edge of the counter and dropping to the floor right behind it. I took a nipple into my mouth and spent several seconds worshipping it with my tongue. Charity arched, forcing more of her breast into my mouth as I let my hands work at her jeans.

I backed off her breast and said, "Lift your hips for me, Baby," and she did, placing her palms flat behind her on the countertop to give herself the leverage she needed. God this woman could arch like a cat, her body all sleek, toned, lines. I hauled her jeans and panties away as one and she yipped when her ass touched the cold Formica.

"That's cold!" she complained and I took her other nipple into my mouth, because you know, symmetry.

That distracted her, although it didn't diminish her squirming, if anything, it intensified it. I finished my descent onto my knees by kissing down her body, my hands finding the curve of her ass and lifting her, settling her on the edge of the counter from where she'd squirmed off of it to give me easy access. I licked a wet line from her opening to her clit before settling on just that little bundle of nerves, giving it a proper tongue lashing. I have to say, I loved the reaction. Wantonly, Charity grabbed me with one hand by the head and ground her pussy into my mouth. It was hot. Incredibly hot, and I stiffened to the point of pain in my jeans.

I held out though, licking her pussy like it was the last meal I was ever going to have. After a few minutes of her moaning, fingers buried in my hair, I decided I had better up my game or suffocate. Not that I was complaining, I loved her enthusiasm. It was hot as hell. Still, I wanted to get her off at least twice and if I didn't get my dick inside her, and *soon*, I was afraid of somehow causing myself some permanent damage.

I slid my middle finger inside of her, bracing her thighs open with my shoulders so I could better use my hands.

"Oh, god!"

Yep, I found the spot. I curled my finger just so, in that come hither motion and Charity jumped and whimpered. She clenched down around my finger and I knew she was close, so I came up for air with some long, lingering laps of my tongue, took a deep breath, and mercilessly teased her clit, stroking her g-spot, until she came apart completely, her knuckles white with the force she used to grip the edge of the counter. I stood up, wiping a hand across my mouth and her cunt honey off on my jeans, even as I bent to rip off my boots and to drop the offending pants off my hips.

Charity looked dazed, her eyes glazed with pleasure, but I wasn't done with her yet. I dragged her back to the edge of the counter and she yelped, her arms going right where I wanted them, around my neck and shoulders.

"Hang onto me," I said and lifted her legs around my waist. She locked them behind me, just like I wanted and with a few false tries, I slid inside her. Charity moaned and my eyes closed with the intensity of how good it felt. I rested my forehead against hers for a heartbeat, stroked in and out of her a few times, and repeated, "Hold onto me, hold on tight."

She did as I asked, and held onto me tight, I supported her weight with my hands on her ass, hitching her up my body, and trembling with the fine exertion of carrying the weight of another person, I made long strides down the hall to my bedroom.

I kicked open the door, and went right for the bed, laying her down on it, and taking the opportunity to press myself deep. She cried out, voice sultry and breathy, that right combination that told me I was doing everything right, and I wanted her to keep making that sound for as long as possible. I adjusted her position on the bed so I could join her, laying over the top of her, smoothing that golden hair of hers away from those luminous eyes. I kissed her, made love to her, took my time with her, and tried like hell not to go too early on her. It was a fine balancing act, and worth the effort.

She was beautiful, laid out in my bed on the black sheets, hair fanned out around her head, a golden halo; my personal angel. She held onto my shoulders, her eyes for mine, her voice a plea that was soothing to the ear as she begged me to make her come again. I obliged her, I couldn't deny her, and with every panting breath, I think I was falling even more in love with her.

I slid my hand between us, teased her clit, and lit the match that sparked the inferno inside of her. Her pussy clenched around me, hot and wet, milking my cock until I just couldn't hold back anymore. I came with her, sparkles and little white flits of light taking over the edges of my vision as synapses overloaded. *Jesus* she was fucking amazing. Beautiful, warm, caring, and everything I needed right now. An anchor in the light, a chain to follow out of the dark and self-loathing.

I collapsed on top of her and gathered her close, her slender arms going around my shoulders, pulling me down on top of her, holding me even closer as we panted together, our heartbeats pounding from the rush that we found in each other's bodies. Her lips found mine and kissed them softly and I withdrew from her body, shuddering at how sensitive I'd become. I lay beside her, and pulled her tight against my chest and swore, that I'd never let her go again. That I'd work on me, and work on making us a thing, because I wasn't sure, after having this taste, I would ever be able to go back to doing the alone thing without imploding.

Charity had quickly become a need in my life that I just never expected.

CHAPTER 31
Charity

We slept, close and warm in each other's arms, which was a feat considering how high Nothing had the AC up in his house. Sometime in the morning, a mechanical sound woke me. Or maybe it was Nothing, who'd gone stiff beside me.

Men's voices filtered through the front of the house and Nothing bolted upright, reaching into the bedside table's drawer and drawing a pistol. I froze.

"What's wrong?" I asked. The gun making me uneasy.

"Someone's in my yard," he said. He pulled on a pair of jeans, setting the gun down on the nightstand to do it. I stared at it for several heartbeats and jumped when he snatched the firearm up again.

"Stay here," he ordered. As soon as he was out the bedroom door I scrambled for my gym bag and pulled on a pair of shorts and a loose tank top, forgoing a bra or panties. I needed a shower, so as soon as things were sorted, I would be handling that.

I found Nothing standing in his front doorway, gun hanging limp and forgotten in his hand. Outside, men worked to offload a foreign piece of machinery off the back of a giant flatbed truck. Towards the front of the flatbed, near the cab of the big rig, a tree sat, the ball of roots wrapped in burlap.

"What's going on?" Nothing called out to one of the men, confused.

"That Charity behind you?" the man called.

Nothing looked back over his shoulder and frowned, but I was grinning, "Yes! I'm her, are you Bobby?" I asked.

"Sure am, sorry it took me so long to get out here, I had to do some digging through the assessor's office to find out where the utility lines are buried. They're on the other side of the driveway, so we should be good to go. Is this a bad time?" he asked, glancing between Nothing and the gun in his hand.

"Bad time for what? What are you doing, bro?" Nothing tucked the gun into the back of his waistband and I smiled.

"Faith called Bobby for a favor for me," I explained.

"Favor? What favor?"

"It's a lemon tree," I said and wrapped my arms around his waist. I kissed the back of his shoulder, "It's Katy's tree," I murmured against his skin.

One of the men called out and Bobby turned, "Got the tree spade all ready to go, should only take about an hour to do this, you good?" he asked Nothing, who was standing there a little shell shocked I think.

"Good?" he asked, staring in disbelief at the tree on the back of the truck, "Yeah, good, we're good…" he said and Bobby gave him a nod, turning and striding back down the driveway.

Nothing twisted and raised an arm and I ducked, tucking myself into his side.

"You did this?" he asked.

"Yeah, it was Bobby's idea to bring a tree as old as Katy would be, though. I can't take credit for that."

"I can't imagine what this cost you, Baby…"

"Nothing, I mean, it didn't cost me anything… Bobby wanted to do it."

He leaned on me heavily, as if the wind had just been knocked out of his sails and I smiled, kissing his cheek.

"A lot of people love you," I observed and he just shook his head, mystified. We stood in his doorway, letting the air conditioning cool our backs as the Florida heat swirled in front of us, and watched the installation of the new tree. It took minutes with the giant tree spade machine, but then Bobby and his crew took the time to take up the sod around where the old tree had been and lay it in front of the new one so Nothing wouldn't have this giant bald spot in his lawn. That's what took the real time. When it all was done, Bobby came up to the porch again, smiling proudly.

"What do you think?" he asked and turned to look at the lemon tree, standing proud in the spot in Nothing's yard that the old one had resided in before the driver had taken it out, long before I'd ever resided here. The only giveaway that anything had been there was the sad, lonely ring of bricks that'd been left behind. Let's face it; I was a sucker for a rescue in any form, and right now, this felt like one.

"It's beautiful," I said with a smile, while Nothing stood mute. I don't know if it was a loss for anything to say, or if he were emotional, or what. His face certainly gave nothing away.

"I don't know what to say, man." Nothing scoffed, "I'm just... I don't know, I'm speechless."

Bobby's face split into a wide grin and he held out a hand. Nothing grasped it and they pulled each other in for one of those manly hugs, slapping each other heartily on the back.

"I can't thank you, *any of you*, enough for this."

"Just try not to let this one die, eh?" Bobby pulled a folded piece of computer paper out of his back pocket and handed it to me with a wink. "Care instructions," he said and I smiled.

"I'll do my best," I promised and with a backwards wave, he went back up the driveway to oversee the removal of the heavy equipment. Nothing pulled me back into his side and I cuddled there, comfortably.

"You're incredible, you know that?" he asked.

"How so?"

"You seriously did all this, even after I treated you –"

"Shush," I said and he looked down at me, raising an eyebrow, "It seemed like the right thing to do," I shrugged, "So I did it."

"Well thank you. I think she would love it. I know that Corrine would have..." he fell silent, his mixed feelings playing out in a war of expression on his face. I hugged him around the waist and looked up at him.

"Let's grab a shower," I soothed, changing the subject.

"Then what do you want to do?" he asked.

"I don't know about you, but it's been 'go, go, go, go, go' since I got here. I would love a lazy day in bed having sex, oh, say, two or nine times."

"Hmm, not sure we need a shower for that if we're just going to go and get messy again," he observed.

"Right, but that's half the fun, isn't it?" I asked.

"Good point," he smiled, and it was a genuine smile, one that warmed me from the inside out.

"So how about it?" I asked.

He kissed me as an answer and swung the front door shut on the outside world. I wrapped my legs around his hips and his hands on my ass, he carried me back to the bedroom. He set me down on the bed and returned the gun from the back of his waistband, to the bedside table.

"Is that really necessary?" I asked and he looked me over.

"Yeah, I'm afraid it is. The guys, however many of them, that were waiting for you and the one that took you back at the hotel, they're in the wind. Somehow they got tipped off before the Captain and your sister got there. Better safe than sorry, Baby."

My libido cooled a degree or two.

"Oh. Thank you for telling me."

"What?" he asked, my face giving me away.

"Did they kill him do you think?" I asked softly, and he gave me a sad sort of little smile.

"That's club business, he won't ever come after you or hurt you again, that's all you or I need to know."

"You sound so sure of that."

"I trust the Captain, and my brothers."

"Even after they held back that information?" I was genuinely curious and he nodded.

"Yeah, that was different," he said.

"How?"

He looked thoughtful, "It's hard to explain, honestly. There are certain things that are unshakeable in this life. Them hiding what Corrine was up to behind my back, I get why they did it. Does it make me happy? Not at all. Does it cast some doubt? On some things, yeah, but not on the really important stuff."

"The men who took my sister being more important?"

"And you, Baby. They're an outside threat. Let me ask you

something, you and your sisters are at a club, right?"

"Okay," I agreed, listening to his scenario, relishing that his hand had found its way to the top of my thigh, a warm weight full of promise against my skin.

"Say Faith and Hope start arguing."

I laughed a little, "Not hard to imagine, okay, go on..."

"Out of the blue, some random drunk bitch comes up and tries to start shit with Faith, what happens next?"

"Hope would probably smart off to the bitch, and put her in her place," I said.

"Right, but she was just fighting with Faith a second before," he said.

"Right, but Faith is Hope and my's sister, we get to say shit to each other, some hooker in a club doesn't." I said and Nothing smiled.

"Exactly."

"Same principle, huh?"

"Exactly the same. When the threat's over, we'll go back to our inner dealings but until then, there's a job to be done. The stupid shit, and really, it's all stupid shit, is on hold until then. When something like this is in our face, it makes us appreciate each other all the more."

"Like family," I intoned.

"Some family is related by blood, but sometimes, chosen family is a bond that's stronger. Fuck knows, I cut ties with a lot of my blood relations when they had a fit about Corrine and I still, to this day, don't regret that decision. It's a little ironic now."

"How so?"

"Pretty sure my folks would have loved you, nice college girl, goals in mind, studying medicine," he smiled and tucked some of my hair behind my ear.

"Corrine wasn't like that?" I asked softly.

He shook his head, "It wasn't that she wasn't like that, Corrine just didn't have a calling, not like you or me. She didn't know what she wanted to be, other than a wife and mother. She was phenomenal as the latter. I couldn't have asked for a better mother to my child. Just turns out she wasn't so awesome at the first."

That weight of sadness was back, dragging Nothing's shoulders down, but I was grateful he was *talking* about it. Even if it was just to me. He was fulfilling his promise, sure, but he was also, every time he talked, letting some of that weight go. I could see that his grief would always be a part of him, but it didn't have to be the totality of his existence. I was relieved that he seemed to be seeing that for himself now.

"Hm, thank you," he said, shuddering as if coming awake after a long silence.

"For what?"

"Sticking it out, being here now, mostly for listening and not judging."

"You're hurting," I said softly, "It would be pretty shitty of me to judge you knowing that, wouldn't it?"

"Mm," he nodded, "When you put it like that, yeah, I guess so."

"Did you ever think that maybe, just maybe, the other guys just couldn't deal?"

"How do you mean?"

"I mean, for three *years* they've watched you languish, knowing what they knew, afraid to tell you, and all the while holding it in and watching you spiral further and further down into your grief… I've only known you a short time, and insane attraction aside," I shifted, straddling his lap so I could look into his eyes from a scant few inches away, "I hurt for you, I can't imagine how the lot of them were feeling about it. I can imagine, a lot of those feelings translated to frustration and I know when I'm frustrated, it translates fairly easily to anger…"

"Smart girl," he murmured, hands smoothing up my ass, under my shirt so he could touch skin. I closed my eyes, relishing the touch.

"Like that?" he asked, voice husky with desire.

"Very much," I whispered.

"Hmm, me too."

He pushed my shirt out of the way and fastened his mouth over one of my nipples, teasing it with his tongue. I shifted, grinding myself against him until we both reached that fever pitch where it was all we could do to get rid of our clothes and join together in a frenzy of need and mutual heat.

As he was last night, so he was this morning, tender, careful with me and, *dare I say*, loving. He moved inside of me with a singlemindedness towards bringing me pleasure, with no obvious thought or care towards his own. It wasn't something I'd ever really encountered before and it upped my desire for him all the more.

I held his hair back from his face, so I could see him clearly, as he moved above me and begged him, when he'd held me on that precipice for too long, "Nothing, *please?*" and it was like my plea was music to his ears, his eyes drifting shut, head turning so he could kiss my palm.

"Touch yourself for me, Baby. I wanna see," he murmured and I let my hand drift down between us, teasing my clit gently with my fingertips.

"*Oh, god,*" he groaned and surged into me that much harder, hitting all the right points. I gasped and arched, coming around his cock in a tight, pulsating, rhythm. Nothing cried out and jerked, and I felt his dick twitch in counterpoint as we fell back to Earth together. He leaned down carefully over the top of me, and kissed me, a slow, languorous kiss that melted me into the dark sheets.

He felt just so damn *good*.

I wrapped my arms and legs around him and held him close, and he chuckled, cuddling me right back, that is, until my cellphone started buzzing across the nightstand. I groaned when he moved off of me, and out of me, so I could get it.

I grabbed it up, "Hello?"

"Charity, are you okay?" Hope demanded, and the urgency with which she said it sent up red flags.

"We're fine, why?" I asked sitting up.

"We as in the club, 'we', have problems," she rushed out.

"What kind of problems?" I asked, the warmth of afterglow chased right out of my bloodstream by fear.

"Is Nothing there?"

"He's right here," I said.

"Put me on speaker."

I did, letting her know it was done with an "Okay, we can hear you."

"Okay, first off, Faith is fine. Marlin stopped him, Hossler is okay, too. She took her's out with a shotgun blast to the chest."

"Jesus!" Nothing exclaimed.

"The cops are at Hossler's, and are dumbfounded by the home invasion, Marlin beat the one that got on his boat to within an inch of his life, and we're handling that one internally. Nothing are you armed?"

"Yes, sure am."

"Okay, we're on our way. We took care of one on the *Mysteria Avenge*, I don't think he was expecting I knew how to take care of myself. Didn't take much. Cutter and I have to take care of one or two things before we get over there, you two sure you're good?"

"We're sure, we're okay; who are they?" I demanded.

"Give you two guesses, Blossom. Pretty sure you'll get it on the first try."

"Nothing! Switch to the burner for all further communications!" Cutter called from the background.

"Aye, aye, Captain!"

"Shit, we've got to go," Hope said and the line went dead.

"Right," I said.

"Shower," we both said in unison.

"You go first," Nothing picked up the gun off the nightstand and went for his jeans, "I'll make coffee, burner phone's in the kitchen anyways."

"Does it ever stop?" I asked.

"Pretty sure this is the last stand, Baby."

"You think so?"

"I hope so. Go get a shower, get dressed, okay?"

"Okay," I nodded and grabbed towels out of my bag, and a change of clothes, heading for the bathroom.

"Leave the door open if you want, so you can hear," he called from the kitchen.

"Okay," I called back and started the water.

I stepped into the warm shower spray and sighed, letting it beat some of the new tension from my shoulders. I sincerely hoped that nothing else would happen, but at the same time, at least *this time* if something did, I was in a better position to *do* something about it.

After Faith had disappeared, the first thing Hope had done, was enrolled me in an accredited Krav Maga class near my university. Whenever we'd gotten together in the intervening years, you'd better believe Corporal Badass had tested my ass on my learning, and had also given me a few pointers to impress my instructor with.

I was pretty good, though nowhere near as hardcore as Hope. When it came down to it, there just wasn't any comparing with my sister who had trained since she was a child. While she'd been whooping ass, Faith and I had taken dance classes. It just was what it was. Right now, I was simply grateful for my education in the martial arts, and that there was a total lack of drugs in my system, well, aside from Nothing, but that didn't really count now did it?

I shampooed my hair, and was in the midst of rinsing it, when I heard a footfall on the other side of the curtain.

"Nothing?" I asked, and the curtain whisked aside, the man on the other side, definitely *not* my lover.

I jabbed, and he caught my wrist, sidestepping just in time to avoid the throat punch I'd meant to deliver. I was in the shower, so slippery, and as I began to fall, I pitched myself towards him in a bid to both knock him off balance and save myself. It worked, to an extent, both of us crashing to the bathroom floor. The curtain and rod, crashing down on top of me. I scrambled over him and reached for the door frame trying to pull myself out into the hall, but the stranger grabbed hold of my legs and hauled me back, climbing my body.

I felt a surge of panic, and in my terror, bleated out, "*Nothing!*" but I had no idea where he was or even if he was okay...

Shit.

CHAPTER 32

Nothing

I stashed the gun in the junk drawer and pulled out the burner phone, turning it on and setting it on the kitchen counter. I made a point to keep it charged and it lit up, ready to go. I set about making coffee, and honestly, I didn't see it coming. I was getting into the fridge to grab the creamer one second, and the next I was on the floor seeing stars.

Charity, was my first thought, my second was that I didn't want to get hit again, or go unconscious, so I played possum, and made like I was down for the count. Whoever was in my house, predictably, went for the bathroom, and my woman, leaving me to my own devices. I got lucky he didn't tap me, really lucky. I guess 'unconscious' was enough for him.

"Nothing?" I heard her call, and then the curtain rattle; her short shriek of fear twisted the knife in my heart and had me pushing to my feet. My vision swam and I fought down nausea, as I went for the drawer with my gun. I got it in hand just as there was a crash, and it sounded like the whole damn curtain and rod came down.

"*Nothing!*" Charity screamed and I was around the corner and down the hall. She was on the floor, trying to pull herself out into the hall but whoever'd hit me had a hold of her.

I rounded the bend, and aimed down at him, "Let her go," I said with authority.

"Or you'll what? Shoot me, and risk hitting your bitch?" his accent was thick, and he looked up and sneered. His head was shaved, and his thick, black eyebrows were drawn down into a frown.

"Shoot him!" Charity screamed and kicked back, catching our friend in the mouth. *Good girl!* I thought savagely. He let her go and she scrambled out of the bathroom around my legs.

"Still want me to shoot him?" I asked, knowing if she rang that bell she wouldn't be able to unring it, and neither would I.

He snarled and lunged, taking the decision away from me. I pulled the trigger, and I honestly felt nothing about it. No regret, no guilt, he was trying to hurt the woman sheltering behind me, the woman I loved, and I wasn't about to let that happen.

The shot took him high, in the upper left anterior quadrant of his chest. Charity screamed and jumped, clapping her hands over her ears. She stared wide eyed as our attacker fell backwards against the tub, and left a red smear against the white bath.

"Okay, we have a gunshot to the upper left anterior chest, with a posterior exit wound to the," I tucked my gun into the back of my waistband and gritted my teeth against the burning sensation just above my butt, it couldn't be helped. I pulled the man forward and declared, "Left posterior, center mass, through and through, pretty fucking sure I clipped a lung. What do we do, Charity?" I asked, getting her brain engaged away from the fear, and as much as I loathed to do so, saving this fucker's life became the top priority.

"Heartbeat?" she demanded.

I checked, "Yeah."

"Here, apply pressure, I'll call 9-1-1," she ripped the towels off the floor where they'd fallen and I pressed them to the wound. The son of a bitch coughed, and started to come around.

"Phone's on the kitchen counter, try and find some clothes, Baby. I got this for right now."

"Okay!"

She ran down the hall to the kitchen and I heard her voice, frantic on the line, "Yes, please help, a man's been shot... I don't know, Nothing, what's the address!?"

I pressed down hard on the wound, the man crying out and glaring murder at me, "Trying to save your life, you sack of shit," I told him, before calling out my address to Char.

"Why?" he demanded, in his thick Slavic accent.

"Because, it's what we do... her and me... you picked the wrong house to come rob and the wrong girl to attack. You live through this, you can tell your boss and the rest of your boys."

"*Niet*," he said, and spit blood onto my floor.

"Could always let you die here," I said easing up on the pressure, his eyes widened and I saw defiance, no fear. He was a cold piece that's for sure. Charity's voice dimmed as she went, presumably, into the bedroom, she returned a moment later.

"He attacked me, in the shower, my boyfriend, he shot him. Please hurry, he doesn't look good. No, I don't know who he is, neither does my boyfriend. He's a medic, and he's applying pressure, but we need more than that. No, I'm a nurse, we don't have any equipment to handle this kind of thing here. Okay, Okay, sure. I'm as calm as I'm going to get."

I risked a glance over my shoulder and Charity was in a light summer dress, her hair dripping onto it and still half soapy. I swallowed hard and returned my sight to my patient. I could hear sirens, and it sounded like they were an eternity away. Of course, I wasn't used to being on this end of things. I was the one used to riding to the rescue.

"Yes! I hear sirens, I'm opening the front door, now." Charity's footfalls pounded across the floor, and I heard her unbolt the front door and fling it open.

"Please hurry! Through here!"

"Shep!" I heard a familiar voice call.

"Yeah, Brody! Back here!"

"What the fuck happened man?"

"Dumb son of a bitch picked the wrong fuckin' house, that's what."

The guy was fading, but he would make it if Brody and whoever he was partnered with made good time.

"Shit, we've got to get him out of there." I helped Brody lift him and carry him out to where we could get his ass on the stretcher. His partner must've been green, because I'd never seen him before for one, and two, he wasn't a paramedic – no patch, so he was just an EMT.

"Right, we got it, man. Shit, I'm sorry it was you of all people," he said and glanced at Charity, "Ma'am," he said and shook himself.

"That's my girlfriend, Charity," I said and Brody looked pole axed.

"Sorry to meet you this way, Ma'am, but if you could see fit to get Shep here to come back to the team, we'd not only appreciate it, but we'd be in your debt."

"I'll see what I can do," she said and smiled wanly. Brody and his partner finished strapping the guy down and hustled the hell out of there, just as a couple of cops pushed through my front door. I held my arms open and Charity rushed into them, holding me tight. I held her back and soothed as best I could while the cops waited a moment for us to collect ourselves.

"*Charity!*" Hope screamed from outside and she and Cutter were through the door next.

"We're good, Captain," I said, and leveled Hope with my gaze, "We're good, I got her."

Hope nodded at me, and Charity flung out an arm blindly to her sister, who joined us. We huddled around Charity who shook, but didn't cry. My brave, beautiful, fucking girl.

CHAPTER 33

Charity

"Well we touched a nerve with that Grigori guy, that's for sure..." Cutter said quietly, peeking out the curtains at the cops retreating down the drive. They took Nothing's gun into evidence, and took photos of the bathroom and red marks on my skin that may or may not turn into bruises.

I sat, shuddering on the arm of Nothing's couch. Post combat shakes, Hope called them. I was pretty sure it was just the after effects of the adrenaline wearing off, but then again, it should have worn off much sooner than this. The cops had been here for hours taking their fingerprints, dusting the house, taking their pictures, and evidence.

Hope rubbed my back in useless little circles, and I breathed out a sigh of relief. At least the investigating officers were from Ft. Royal's little police department, although I got the impression they were none too happy with The Kraken at the moment. Of course, I got the impression that The Kraken were none too happy with the current state of affairs, either.

"What's going to happen?" I asked dully.

"Nothing, Baby. We're good. The gun is mine, registered to me, and legal to have in my own home. He broke in here, and Florida has a King of the Castle law in place, just like most of the rest of America. They can't touch me. It was justifiable."

"Helps that y'all saved his life, not going to lie," Cutter said.

"That's if he makes it," I murmured.

"He will, I've treated a lot worse," Nothing said.

"What next?" Hope asked, dropping her head back and sighing, staring at the ceiling.

"Is Faith okay?" I asked.

"She's fine, Trouble," Cutter said.

"We're perilously close to club business," Nothing warned.

"Good call, brother," Cutter grunted and let the curtain fall back into place.

"Oh give it a rest, she's family," Hope said glowering at the both of them.

"Right, and given her profession, the less she knows, the better," Cutter said giving my sister a pointed look.

Hope stuck her tongue out at him, "I hate it when you stick me with a point that's right."

"Do it every night, might as well do it every day too."

"Gross," I uttered and the ensuing laughter eased the tension.

"So, what now?" I asked, wearily.

"Now, you go rinse the dried soap out of your hair, and we spend the next few days circling the wagons," Cutter said.

"What's that mean, exactly?"

"We all go back to the Captain's house on lockdown. It's not safe to be spread out throughout the town anymore."

"Do you think he'll deliver your message?" I asked.

"Probably, can't say for sure," Nothing said, and gripped the back of his neck, pulling.

"What message?" Cutter asked sharply.

Nothing sighed, "He asked why we were trying to save him, I told him to go back to his boss and tell him it was the kind of people Char and I were, and that he'd picked the wrong girl to attack."

"Heat of the moment kind of a thing," Cutter said, and there wasn't any question about it.

"Yeah."

"Shit, well, looks like I need to set Atlas and Radar to some digging, maybe get a hold of Ruth. See if we can't get these guys to back off of us. I'm pretty sure they're tired of losing men, and I want this to stop before we lose one of ours. The way we been going at each other, it's only a matter of time."

I think Cutter forgot I was still sitting there, but I knew when to keep my mouth shut. Even still, Hope nudged me and said, "Blossom, go get washed up, get dressed and let's get out of here for now."

I nodded, and went back towards the bathroom to clean it up, Nothing called out to me, "Leave it, Babe. Use the shower in my room. We'll get it."

I looked at the red ruin of my shorts and tank, spattered with the man's blood and the water pooled on the floor, tinged pink with yet more of his blood and didn't even put up a fight. I did what Nothing asked, and went to his room instead. I was chilled down to the bone, and I was pretty sure it didn't have anything to do with how high the air conditioning in the house was turned up.

I took yet another shower; the door locked tight this time, and wondered if there would ever be a time that I didn't lock the bathroom door in the future. I closed my eyes as I rewet my hair, and sighed out in relief. Thank god Nothing was there, that he hadn't been knocked unconscious, and that he'd managed to keep his wits.

Two knocks at the door and I nearly jumped out of my skin, "Char you alright?" Hope called.

"Yeah! Sorry," I called back, "Be out in a minute."

"No, take your time; I just wanted to check on you!"

"Thanks, sister-mom!" I called back, but I had to force the sarcasm into my voice.

"No problem," Hope called back and I shuddered and let it go, having a quiet cry to myself in the shower just to get the pent up emotion out.

CHAPTER 34
Nothing

"She alright?" I asked, and used my gloved hands to shove my shower curtain and liner into the trash bag Cutter was holding open for me. Hope leaned a shoulder against the bathroom door jamb.

"Shook up, probably harder than she's ever been, that includes her little adventure in the trunk of that whack job's car. She'll be okay though. She's like me, made of some tough stuff, just not quite as Teflon, if you know what I mean."

I did, being tough was one thing, letting it slide off was another. I finished shoving the curtain with its torn ring holders at the top away, and Cutter cinched the bag closed. The bloody, water soaked towels had gone in first.

"Garbage?" he asked.

"What the fuck I want to keep 'em for? A souvenir?" I grated then sighed, "Sorry, Captain. I don't mean to take it out on you."

"Hey, man, you did good. There's still more to do, but you followed through and maintained the main objective which was to keep your woman safe. She's a little scared, a little shook up, but it ain't nothing she can't and won't handle. Now let's just take a minute, get this mess cleaned up, and get her back to base. We'll go from there."

I nodded, surprised I needed the pep talk, but truthfully, I wasn't like a lot of the rest of the guys. I was used to violence in the way of coming in to mop it up after the shit had already gone down. I wasn't used to being in the thick of it, or used to being the one to dish it out. That was pretty much new territory for me.

Aftermath I could handle, but this shit? I don't know... I just didn't know.

Cutter slipped out past Hope, who handed me the mop, that I had sitting out in the hallway. I started running it across the bathroom floor, wringing it out into the bathtub until I had the worst of the flooding up. The cops had at least let us shut off the shower once shit had calmed down and our uninvited guest was well on his way to the nearest emergency department.

"Thank you," Hope said, and I nodded.

"Just glad he didn't knock me out and I had the sense to play dead. Really glad he didn't have the sense to tap me or finish me off while I was down."

"Newbie, you think?"

"I honestly don't know, it isn't exactly my area of expertise."

"Yeah, I know it's not, Galahad. Which is why I'm grateful you didn't hesitate."

"Guess it says something that I'm willing to kill for her, yeah?"

"You mean you were shooting to kill?" Hope asked, surprised.

"Out of all of us, Nothing always was a shit shot, so it doesn't surprise me he missed, just be glad he hit him at all." Cutter said from behind Hope, returning from his trash run.

"Yeah, fuck you, Cap. Like I said, putting holes in people has never been my thing." *I'm supposed to be the one patching holes up... not making them.* I thought to myself.

"Yeah, and we never wanted it to be," Cutter said, all joking gone from his tone, as if it never were. "We tapped you because we liked you, and because you're an honorable dude. The fact that you can patch certain holes up was just a bonus. We wouldn't have you any other way, and I'm sorry you got dragged into this shit storm."

"I'm not," I said and was surprised to realize I meant it.

"Yeah, and how's that?" Cutter asked.

"Because if I weren't ass deep in it, things could have and would have gone very different for Charity, and that's a thought I just cannot abide, Captain."

"There *is* that," Cutter agreed, but it was the admiration on Hope's face that caught my eye. She nodded, and it was something that didn't come out of the irreverent woman very often. She gave me a nod all the while her posture, and the look in her eyes, communicated respect.

I felt like I'd just passed some kind of invisible test, but I couldn't care too much about it just then. All of our heads lifted because the water had shut off in my bathroom. Cutter held out a hand past Hope and I passed the mop to him.

"Box of gloves under the sink," he told Hope, as I stripped mine off onto the edge of the vanity. Hope and I traded places, and Cutter said unnecessarily, "Go on, we got the rest of this."

I slipped down the hall towards my room and thought to call out, "Charity, it's me, you okay if I come in?"

"Yes, of course," she called back softly, and I rounded the doorframe to see her sitting on the edge of my bed body wrapped from armpit to mid-thigh in one of my towels, another turban style, wrapped up around her hair.

"How you doing?" I asked.

"I'm okay," she said quickly. A little too quickly, but I let it slide and didn't press.

"Cool, you need help packing up, or you got it?" I asked.

"I've got it," she murmured.

"Mind if I stay in here, change and pack a bag myself?"

"No, I think, honestly, I'd like the company," she said and when she smiled, it was a fragile, tremulous thing.

"Come here," I uttered and went to her. She met me half way, standing, her arms going around me. I folded her into my arms and sighed, just holding her. I don't think there was any doubt in my mind at this point that I was in love with her. It just really didn't seem to be the time to say it, so I just did my best to show it. I held her close to me, breathing in her clean, fresh scent, pressing my lips to the smooth, soft skin of her shoulder.

"I'm okay," she said, "really."

"I know, Baby, and I promise, I'm going to keep you that way." I drew back so she could see the seriousness on my face and in my eyes. She smiled, and pulled the towel from her hair, tossing it towards the dirty clothes hamper in the corner, before turning back to me.

"Then I promise the same thing," she murmured and held up a pinky finger. I couldn't help it, I laughed and obliged her, hooking her little finger with mine, bending and kissing them. She smiled and kissed our linked fingers too, and just like that, I think our first 'thing' as a couple was established and it was cute as fucking hell.

"I think those jeans are a lost cause," she murmured and I looked down, they were bloodstained for sure, but I had a few tricks up my sleeves for that.

"Nah, some hydrogen peroxide and they'll be fine if I can get 'em soaking in it quick enough." She arched one golden brow at me and I smiled, "Paramedic, remember? Blood is par for the course, that's why the uniforms are so dark, even still, blood gets on the patches sometimes. Hydrogen peroxide is color safe and breaks down the proteins in the blood if you can get it on the stain fast enough. Pretty sure you would've learned it as a nurse eventually, consider this your inside track."

She looked at me thoughtfully, and nodded slowly, "Thanks for the tip," she said softly, but I could see the wheels turning. I let it go for now in favor of changing, and getting this pair of jeans into a tub with a bottle of the aforementioned stuff. They were my favorite pair, so yeah, I wanted to take a crack at saving them.

Charity dressed in shorts and a tank top, the ones she had on earlier today, and shoved the rest of her stuff into her bag. I dressed quickly in a fresh pair of jeans and a clean tee, shrugging into my cut. I took the time and I threw a bag together, tossing my bloodied jeans into my bathroom's sink and pouring the industrial sized bottle of hydrogen peroxide I kept under it, over the soiled denim. It immediately began to froth, the stains beginning to lift.

"Huh, I'll be damned, it really does work," Charity said over my shoulder.

"Told yah," I said.

"Do you need to do anything else?" she asked.

"Antsy to leave?" I asked, deflating just a little on the inside. I didn't want her to not come back to my home. I didn't want this place to be a bad one for her, not when there was a potential to build new, less painful memories in it now.

"Just a little, I'm worried about Faith," she confessed.

Ah, of course, "Yeah. We're good to go, just let me throw these in the wash and get it going."

"Won't they go sour?"

"Not worried about that, I can always re-wash them later."

I shouldered my bag and Charity shouldered hers, we met Cutter and Hope in the hall, my soaked jeans dripping I shouldered my way through and into the garage, Cutter and Hope moving aside to oblige me. I dumped the jeans into the wash, added detergent and started up the machine.

"We good?" I asked the Captain about the bathroom and he nodded.

"We're good."

"You want to take your Jeep or you want to leave it here and ride with me?" I asked.

"I'll ride with you, if that's okay."

"It's more than okay."

"Gimme your bag, Nothing," Cutter held out his hands and I tossed it to him without a second thought. He slung it over his shoulders to ride along his back. Guess Hope had ridden over here on her own.

I hit the garage door opener and asked, "Front door and back slider locked?"

"Yep," Hope answered me.

"Cool. Let me back the bike out and you can get on," I told Charity. Cutter and Hope went to their bikes, sitting at the curb. I fired mine up and backed it out of the garage, Charity climbed on, her gym bag riding along her back in an imitation of what Cutter had done with mine.

"Hold on tight," I told her, and once the garage door was down, I pointed us towards the end of the drive, put her in gear and pulled smoothly into the street behind Cutter and Hope. We rode swiftly, back to Cutter's place and pulled into the tree and shrub lined circular drive, backing our bikes into the line of them parked around the outer edge of the drive.

Charity had hopped off to allow me to back in, and with a swift peck on my mouth, had made a beeline to the house's front door. It opened, Marlin, standing there with a frightened Faith tucked into his side. Faith cried out as soon as she saw her sister and in a flash, she and Charity were a tangled mess. Faith sobbed and Marlin stood grim behind his woman. We made eye contact, and something new and different passed between us. He nodded and I nodded back. No words needed. We'd done what'd been required of us to protect the ones we loved and it was a mixed bag. As shitty as it was to hurt or even kill another human being, we were two men on top of the world that the ones precious to us were *safe* and there wasn't anything more we could really ask for. It was simple, for as complex as it was.

"You good, bro?" Marlin asked me as I ascended the steps. I held out a hand and he grasped it. We pulled each other in and bumped shoulders.

"I'm okay," I said, unwilling to go as far as 'good' given the circumstances, "What about you?"

"As well as can be expected, was wondering if you could watch my girl and yours while me and a couple of guys handled some business."

I nodded, "Not a problem."

"Good deal," he said.

"Need me to look at any of those?" I asked, giving a chin lift to the impressive array of bruises blossoming across half of my VP's face.

"Maybe when we get back," he said and called out, "Pyro! Gator! Let's roll, guys."

I moved aside and let them file past me, Hope joining in on hugging Faith and uttering to her sisters that we should all move inside. Cutter and Hope corralled the girls, while I brought up the rear, shutting the front door on the roar of three bikes starting up.

"Guys heading out on clean up?" Radar asked, coming down the stairs and I put my finger to my lips, indicating the girls who were settling on the living room couch.

"Shit, sorry."

I lifted a shoulder in a shrug and Cutter dragged his eyes away from the trio saying, "'S okay, man."

I sighed and went around the couch to find a place to sit nearby, but far enough to give the women their space. Charity met my eyes above the heaving shoulders of her sister and I gave her a small smile. She gave me a single nod and mouthed 'thank you' and I gave a slight shake of my head, a 'think nothing of it' sort of thing. Her lips lifted a touch and fell, and she went back to focusing her full attention on Faith, the most fragile one of them all.

I hoped like fuck that a solution was reached and soon, because it wasn't fair for these girls to be living like this. In fact, it was a damn fucking shame.

CHAPTER 35

Charity

It was late and it was quiet, we were all still on the couch, the television playing some random movie quietly, but I don't think any of us were watching. At least, not really. I was sitting, bare feet propped on the coffee table, Faith's head in my lap, stroking her hair. She'd fallen asleep.

Hope was sitting on the floor, staring at Faith, and Nothing? Well, Nothing was sitting nearby watching me. Meanwhile, Cutter, Atlas, and Radar were in the dining room, piled around glowing laptop and computer screens. They were talking softly, but I couldn't be bothered to pay attention, though Hope was listening, looking over her shoulder every once in a while and frowning.

I jumped when the front door opened and I saw Nothing sit up sharply out of the corner of my eye. I cursed my jumpiness because it jolted Faith awake, although that might not be such a bad thing in this case.

She pushed herself up into a sitting position just as Marlin came through the door after Pyro, he smiled down at her tiredly, his face swelling something awful and mumbled out of swollen lips, "Hey, Baby Girl."

My sister instantly became weepy at the sight of him, and I couldn't blame her. He looked something awful. I sighed and pushed to my feet.

"Come into the dining room and let me have a look at you, please?"

"Thank you," Faith said to me and I smiled at her.

"Of course," I said and Marlin didn't argue, humoring me for my sister's sake. I think I loved him for that.

He dropped into a chair at the end of the table and I declared, "Light," in warning to the three piled around their laptops.

"Get anything?" Marlin asked.

"Getting there," Atlas declared, and Radar nodded.

"Gonna need the girls to go upstairs, and honestly, bro? You look like hamburger, so it's best you sit this one out."

"Fuck you too, Buddy."

Radar shrugged and Cutter cut in, "He speaks the truth, my friend. You look like shit, and we need a show of force on this end. Having a dude in front of the camera who looks like he was on the losing end of a fight ain't going to help our cause, even if *we* know you won."

"Yeah, yeah, I got better places to be anyways," he said looking at my sister.

All the while they were talking, I was trying to get a good look at him, Nothing already filling a Ziploc bag with ice. I shook my head and Marlin said, "Ow!" when I put my hand under his chin to get him to look into the light for me.

"Well! You going to let me help or not?" I demanded.

"Fine, you ain't gotta go all Nurse Rachet on me, shit."

I rolled my eyes, "Big damn baby," I jibed and turned to Nothing to ask, "Got any frozen peas in there? They'll mold to his face better and will be a little gentler than ice like that."

"No frozen peas, but I got a hammer and can crush it up."

"That'll work," I said.

"Use the counter, and don't fuckin' chip it. I got the storm shutters closed back here for a reason, so you can't go out back and use the patio," Cutter said and I looked out the sliding glass door. I hadn't realized the shutters were closed with the kitchen light reflecting off the inside of the glass like it was. I assumed it was so no one could see to shoot from the beach and I suppressed a shudder. Hope and I traded knowing looks over Faith's head who was glued to Marlin's side.

Nothing crushed up the ice finely and emptied it into another, sturdier, Ziploc. He passed it to me wordlessly and I eased it over the half of Marlin's face that would likely look worse in the morning. I pressed one of his large hands over it and he sighed.

"Got any anti-inflammatories around here?" I asked Cutter.

"Like what?" he asked, and Nothing answered for me.

"Like an NSAID, or Naproxen? Ibuprofen?"

"Check the medicine cabinet," Cutter said and jerked his head behind him to the darkened portal of the bathroom door. I went in and turned on the light, digging through the medicine cabinet which was well stocked. I came up with a name brand NSAID and shook two of the blue liquid capsules into my palm.

"Marlin, I'm going to need you to take the girls upstairs. Nothing, you mind staying down here for this?" Cutter asked.

"Not at all," he said and caught me around the waist as I went to go by. I looked up into his eyes, not at all happy about having to leave him down here. Frustrated but understanding why I was being sent to my room like a child while the adults had their talk.

"I'll be up as soon as I can," he murmured and I nodded. He kissed me, and I kissed him back. After all, it wasn't him or any of the rest of the guys I was upset at. It was the jerks that had us all in this situation to begin with, the fucking assholes.

"Come on, Honey. Let's help your man-child to bed," I said to Faith and she gave me a tiny secret smile.

"Ooo, sisters. Never done that before. See you guys," Marlin joked but Cutter was far too serious, waving us off absently. We took the back stairs from the dining room and kitchen as it was closer to the bedroom Marlin and Faith would stay in.

We helped him to lay down and I made sure his ice was working for him and told him how long to leave it on for. Faith hugged me tight and I smiled, "I love you, Sis."

"I love you, too," she said and we broke apart.

"Don't do anything I would do," I told them and left to go down the hall to my own room; as much as I wanted to sneak back down and listen in, I really didn't feel like pissing off Cutter or bringing Corporal Badass out of my sister. All of my ornery had just plain fled and I figured I would just go lay down and wait for Nothing.

It'd been a long and crazy, crazy, day. Hell, it'd been a series of long and crazy days ever since I'd gotten here. One right after the other, bleeding into the next until I couldn't really tell where one had left off and another began. Just so much had been happening in such a short amount of time I couldn't even keep track. It felt like I'd been here for months when in reality, it couldn't have been more than a couple of weeks.

Still, I was with my sisters, and I had met an incredible, if difficult man. One who, by all accounts, was just as crazy about me as I was for him; at least now that our shit had been straightened out and we were on the same page.

I slipped into one of my nicer sleep sets, a peach pair of satin shorts with a matching satin and lace cami, and got into bed. I left the light on and turned on my side, tucking my hands beneath my cheek and waited for my white knight, determined to stay awake for him.

You know what they say about best laid plans and all of that, though...

CHAPTER 36

Nothing

I knew better than to ask questions when the Captain was as engrossed as he was, and I caught Hope's eye to warn her off, but she was just as intent as the Captain was when it came to what was going on, on the screen.

"Pyro, Gator, get in here!" The Captain barked and we ranged out behind him. He had Skype up and ready to rock and roll. It looked like, for all intents and purposes, it was show time. We all dropped expressions into neutral badass territory and he triggered the call. We waited, and the screen flickered to life, the scowling face of someone who was clearly in charge filling the screen on the other end.

"Who is this?" he demanded in heavily accented English.

"Well, now! By and far, I'd say your worst nightmare. Now how many more men of yours you want to keep throwing in our direction, eh? Because we can keep right on disappearing 'em. By my tally, we're winning this game, and from what I hear, you really can't afford to lose any more personnel, now can you Mr. Tsaritsyn?"

The man on the other end looked suspicious, a glint of something akin to anger mixed with fear in his eyes.

"I do not understand what you mean..."

"Aw, cut the bullshit, will you? This is a secure line, I've got the best of the best on that. You stop sending your men to my town, you forget the girl, and you'll never have to think about us again." Cutter cut right to the chase, and I felt myself go on edge, hoping the Captain knew what he was doing here. This was a dangerous game and these were dangerous people that weren't prone to just letting it go...

"Let me ask you this, what is this girl to you?"

"Family," Cutter replied without missing a beat, "I'm sure you know what that's like, having family you would do absolutely anything for, am I right?" Cutter demanded.

"I do, yes. And what about my family?"

"You send some out here?" Cutter demanded.

"Niet, but my men, are they not family like your men are family?"

Cutter scoffed, "Not even fucking close, my friend."

The man scowled, "We are not friends, Mr..."

"Cutter."

"Mr. Cutter."

"No, no we are not, but there's no reason to not keep it friendly, despite our little difference of opinion. Now, your men took someone who didn't belong to them, and we tracked her down and took her back. That needs to be the end of this now, because I can't have y'all traipsing into my town. We can keep adding to the body count, or you can just let sleeping dogs lie. We got what we wanted and left y'all alone, it's time for you to do the same, now. Y'hear."

"I do not like to be told what to do," the man said.

"That makes two of us, but we ain't givin' her back, so you can just forget about that."

"We do not want the girl, she has become too much trouble," he said waving dismissively, and I could see Hope tense where she was standing off camera.

"Then I think that settles it then, now don't it?" Cutter asked and we all held our collective breath.

"I have lost many men, what is in it for me? As you Americans like to say."

"You don't lose any more, and you stop dividing your man power." Cutter said succinctly and the man frowned.

"I don't understand, how do you mean?"

"You're not a stupid man, Mr. Tsaritsyn," Cutter said leaning back nonchalantly.

"I am not," the man agreed.

Radar tapped his watch and held up three fingers off camera, "So, you leave us alone, and we'll leave you be and we part ways, here and now, before things get even bloodier," Cutter said.

"I do not think so," the man said with a sneer, and Cutter laughed.

"I think you're missing the point here, Mr. Tsaritsyn. I'm not asking, I'm tellin' you this is what you're gonna do."

The man's nostrils flared and his eyes sparked and ignited with rage, but he held his composure. Radar held up one finger and Cutter cocked his head to the side, waiting the man out, whose chest rose and fell with deep even breaths in an effort, I think, to calm down. I gritted my teeth, and hoped like hell our Pres knew what the fuck he was doing here.

"What d'you say, Mr. Tsaritsyn? We have a deal?"

"Niet!"

"Well, I thought you'd say that," Cutter said sitting up and readjusting his position, just as the door behind the man crashed inward, a blur of black leather, some rapid gunfire and when the smoke cleared and the laptop righted on the desk, Baby Ruth's face filled the screen.

"Well! Thank you kindly, Cutter, my friend. I do believe we have helped each other out tonight." I felt my shoulders sag with relief.

"No problem there, Ruth, sorry it took my guys so long to get through the fire walls, of course, the cheap bastard should have realized, if we could get through to call him, it meant we could get through to locate him. Nicely done, my friend, nicely done."

"Again, why thank you, kindly. Sorry you had to keep him talkin' so long."

"No worries, let us know when you boys want to head our way for that R&R, you hear?"

"Absolutely!" We could hear groaning behind Ruth and he turned and let off a few rounds at the floor. "Oo-we! These Russians can be tough bastards! We gotta go, talk soon."

"You have a good night, now, y'hear?"

"Oh, I'm bettin' it'll be one hell of a party!" Ruth declared and the call ended.

"Atlas, wipe all traces of us out of that system," Cutter ordered.

"Already on it, Captain."

"So that's it?" Hope asked, and she was just as poleaxed as me.

"I do believe that's it, yes. Grigori gave us what we needed; it was just buying Atlas and Radar the time to do it in. Unfortunately, that gave Tsaritsyn's men the time to rally for an assault, but like always, these dumb motherfuckers underestimate us," Cutter said and sighed.

"Oh, I am so gonna fuck your brains out," Hope said, dropping into the Captain's lap. Hell, I would never admit it out loud, but if he told me to drop and blow him in that moment, I was so grateful, I'd seriously consider it. I shook my head and scoffed a laugh.

"You did it again, you clever bastard," I muttered, and Cutter held up a fist, his mouth glued to his woman's. I knocked mine into it and went to find my own woman, heading up the stairs, two at a time.

I knocked twice on the door, and popped it open to find Charity sound asleep, her hands tucked beneath her cheek like some kind of angel. I wanted so badly to wake her up and tell her it was cool, that she was safe, that her sister was safe, but I just didn't have it in my heart to do it with how peaceful she looked.

Instead, I got undressed, tucking my clothes away neatly on top of my bag, and I got into bed with her, laying down so I could just stare at her, and stare at her I did, probably for an hour or more until she turned away from me in her sleep. I smiled then, and carefully pulled her back into the protective curve of my body, hers warm and soft where it fitted against mine.

CHAPTER 37
Charity

"Hi," he uttered, and I stretched luxuriously, like a cat, along the length of his warm, hard, body beneath the comforter.

"Hi," I muttered back and sighed, freshly awake, "How long have you been awake?" I asked.

"A couple hours."

"A couple of hours? What were you doing?"

"Watching you," he murmured and caressed the side of my face, leaning in for a kiss. I gave it to him, blushing, and a little self-conscious about any potential morning breath. He leaned back, and as they ever did, his soft gray eyes slayed me.

"What happened? I mean, is it over?" I asked quietly.

"I can't give you any details, but yeah, Baby. It's over," he said with enough certainty, I had to smile.

"Good, because I'd really like to get back to saving people rather than hurting them."

He rolled his eyes, "You and me both!"

I searched his face, "You mean that?" I asked and he tipped his head to the side, considering.

"Yeah, I do, but to be honest, painting houses pays me more… Speaking of which, I kind of need to get back to it today."

"So soon?" I pouted.

"Storm only bought me *some* time, not enough." He sighed, "Trust me, I'd rather be right here… with you."

"It's okay," I said, "I should really put in more applications and send out more resumes, I haven't gotten *anything* yet."

"Ah, well, it's the medical field, bureaucracy at its finest. It moves at the speed of light on the ground when you're understaffed and overworked, but you get up into the suits and talking heads of any hospital, it's all budgets and finding the right person for the job and they act like they got all the time in the world."

"You don't sound bitter at all," I said dryly, rolling my eyes again. He smiled and held me a little tighter.

"Saw a lot of really good nurses turn bitter and blow out when I was a medic, the only people that kind of bullshit hurts is the patients in the end... There's a rough and ugly side to medicine they don't teach you in school."

"Yeah, I know. I was in the advanced nursing program and did a rotation of hands-on training in one of the busiest emergency departments in the state. It was eye-opening, to say the least."

"Yeah, well down here, we've got Florida Man, too... so don't forget that."

"Florida Man? What is that, some kind of superhero?"

He laughed, a bitter barking sound, "More like a super villain, Florida Man is what the internet calls it, but it's a high instance of super bizarre and fucked up cases. Polk County is the worst offender. I think it has something to do with a lack of infrastructure in place to handle the mentally ill, and we definitely have a high rate of drug use down here. For sure *that* system is overloaded."

"Okay, so give me an example of Florida Man in action," I said and he thought for a second. I rested my chin on my hand across his chest, and relished the warm contact.

"Best main-stream media case was that bath-salts case a few years back where the guy on bath-salts chewed the homeless guy's face off."

I jerked back, and couldn't keep the horror off my face, "Ew!"

"I once had a case where this caregiver left this old woman to lie on a couch for so long, bedsores developed, and she ended up healing to the cushions, she was literally fused to the couch, we had to take cushions and all on the stretcher and take her to the hospital. Never did hear how they got her separated."

"Oh, my god!" I jerked back even further at that one.

"Florida Man in action," he said and sighed.

"Yay, just one more thing I get to look forward to," I uttered unhappily.

"Pretty much. Human beings do some seriously fucked up shit to each other. The good news? At least you get to come home to someone who gets it, and you don't have to censor yourself. Talking helps... I only got to talk to my partner. Corrine had a weak stomach for those things. Probably because she'd lived it."

"I saw the scars in the photographs, do you mind if I ask what happened?"

He was quiet for a moment and pulled me back down to lay on his chest. I closed my eyes to listen to his heartbeat while he mulled over whether he wanted to talk about it or not. I was surprised when he did...

"I met Corrine on a call, my partner and I were called to this shitty apartment in this shitty part of Portland."

"Maine?" I asked.

"Oregon, actually. Anyways, her boyfriend at the time had flown off the handle, had carved her up but good. Slashed the side of her neck, stabbed her multiple times in the upper left anterior of her chest, she was bleeding out and a total mess. We got her to the hospital, but I couldn't forget her, you know? Just something about her eyes..."

He paused for a really long time, and I thought he was done talking, but he picked up again, "She was staying in this battered women's place, about six months later, when another unit was dispatched to it for something or other. She asked the crew to take me a note, had remembered my name and everything. Invited me to come by the coffee place she was working at so she could buy me a cup and say thank you. The rest is history."

"Aw, that's sweet. Sounds like something out of a romance story you'd see on TV, or read in a book."

"Yeah, it does, doesn't it?" he gave me a squeeze and rubbed a hand up and down my arm in a firm caress. I snuggled into him knowing any minute we'd have to get up and face the day, and sure enough, a few minutes later, he heaved a giant sigh.

I groaned, and he chuckled, "Please don't make this any harder than it has to be," he said and with a grin that was purely devilish, I wrapped my fingers around his jutting cock.

"Mm, seems like it's a little late for that," I said playfully.

His eyes slipped shut and he dropped his head to the pillow. I loved that I could have such an effect, and it urged me to stroke him lightly with my hand, sadly he stopped me, wrapping his fingers around mine to still my motions.

"To be continued?" he queried and I smiled, leaning in to kiss him.

"Absolutely," I whispered against his mouth.

"Okay," he agreed and swallowed hard, and I relinquished my hold.

We got up, he got dressed and so did I, and neither one of us looked fancy. He went down the hall towards the kitchen and diverted at Marlin and Faith's room.

"Yo, Marlin. I need my cage back, bro," he called out, rapping his knuckles against the closed door. I slipped past him down the stairs, intent on getting coffee started, because let's face it, coffee is both the blood and the life, and my caffeine system had way too much blood in it, it was time to thin it out.

Nothing came down just as I was grinding the beans I'd found on the countertop, he sniffed the air and groaned, "God, yes please."

"It'll be a few minutes," I said and finished loading the coffee maker, hitting the switch.

"Mm, come here then," he said and I straddled his lap, kissing him until the coffee maker gurgled its last. Loving that I was with a man who wanted to make out like teenagers every chance he got. There was something seriously sexy about that.

"Let me fix your coffee," I whispered against his lips and he smirked.

"Just hook me up with an IV," he said.

"Good lord, the day they hook us up with an intravenous caffeine delivery system is the day we'd never sleep again." I got up and set about fixing two cups, holding up cream and sugar and fixing his to his liking with the requisite amounts he rattled off.

"Gotta sleep sometime," he said stretching.

"Like when you're dead?" Marlin asked, coming heavily down the stairs, my sister ghosting down right behind him.

"Like when I'm dead," Nothing said, nodding.

I fixed my sister a cup after handing Nothing his and taking my first sip, and asked Marlin how he took his.

"Black, thanks," he said and I made a face.

"Heathen," I uttered and he raised an eyebrow, on the unbattered side of his face.

"Actually, I'm the purist, you're the heathen for watering that shit down with your froo froo little creamers and sugar and shit. Give it to me straight, no frills; no gimmicks."

I laughed a little and handed him his coffee. It wasn't long before the whole house was up, and I was brewing another pot. Nothing, in the middle of all the hulabaloo of getting everyone situated, slipped up behind me and with a light kiss to the side of my neck, left with the quiet promise of "See you later."

Just about everyone scattered, going back to some day job or other sort of business, and before long it was just me and my two sisters at the dining room table. Hope and I with our laptops open and Faith sipping coffee and playing with the cord on a pair of headphones to a pink iPod.

I was staring at my laptop screen, contemplating the web based application I was staring at and I looked at Hope.

"Would you be mad at me if I took a job considered to be below my station?" I asked.

"What?" she asked confused, looking up from her email.

"Would you be mad at me if I took a job that didn't pay me as much as a job as, say, an RN would."

She frowned, and did something I hadn't ever really seen her do, she *thought* about it before saying anything... *Maybe these guys really were having a good effect on my sister.* I thought to myself. I exchanged a look with Faith, who gave me a bewildered look and a shrug.

"Let me ask you this," Hope said and I gave her my full attention. "Is the job a medical one? I mean, is it still technically using your degree?" she asked.

"Well, yeah, I don't want to *not help* people, it's just... I don't know, it's like to some people I wouldn't be living up to my full potential, and all of that."

Hope raised an eyebrow, "Just sayin', Blossom, you've never done *anything* out of the norm and almost always 'what's expected' of you. You've not once done anything out of character without having a damn good reason to do it, and I don't think this is any different. I mean, you would still be helping people, right?"

"Absolutely," I said.

"And you'd still be living your dream, right?"

"For sure," I said.

"So fuck what anyone thinks. Money just makes things easier, it can't buy happiness. It can't give you the warm fuzzies of coming home to people you love and it can't give you family. Just make sure you're doing what's right for you."

"Are you feeling okay?" Faith blurted out, and I laughed.

"Feeling just fine, Bubbles. Just had a serious adjustment in my priorities over the last few months," Hope said with a heavy sigh. She put her hand on the table and Faith covered it with hers, a sympathetic look on her face.

"What're you thinking about doing, anyways?" Hope asked.

"I'll let you know if it pans out," I said distantly, my focus on the keys as I pecked out my information into the little boxes.

"Okay," Hope said, drawing the word out with her sigh.

We spent a few hours at the computers, me filling out applications, Hope filtering through weeks of business emails until with a noise borne of frustration and boredom she slapped her laptop lid shut.

"Problem?" I asked.

"Let's just say you aren't the only one questioning their chosen career path lately."

"Ah."

"I'm gonna have to suck it up and do a few more jobs out of town," she sighed, "But all I really want to do is stay here."

"Mm, I feel you," I said, "So what're you going to do?" I asked.

"Seriously? Up my rates, until only the desperate are willing to pay me. It will cut down on my travel, for one, and for two, I'll be pulling in about the same amount of money. I just don't want to be doing this anymore, especially right now when I have so much more to stay put for."

"I'm surprised you can do it at all," Faith said unhappily.

"An arrest does not equal a conviction, Bubbles. I got off, so while I have an *arrest* record it's not like I have a *record*. Besides, there's no one that can do what I do with half so much the efficiency. I've created a pretty niche market for myself." Hope shrugged.

"Can we go for a swim?" I asked, staring out the back slider, longingly at the distant waves down the beach.

"That sounds like a *fine* idea," Hope said dryly and so that's exactly what we did.

CHAPTER 38
Nothing

"I don't want to call you Nothing anymore," she said.

It was late, I'd come back to the Captain's place after one seriously agonizing long day painting a house two towns over. I'd stopped at my house to grab some more clothes and had spent a long few minutes staring into my guest bathroom. At the stark walls, and empty shower curtain rod, leaning in the bathtub.

I didn't *really* have the money, but I needed to redo it. The bathroom, I mean. I didn't want to bring Charity back into my house until I did. I wanted to erase every aspect of the horror she'd had to endure in that bathroom and start fresh. My mind made up, I'd called a couple of the guys to see if they could help me out.

Now, Charity and I were stretched out in her bed, getting ready to sleep after yet another mind blowing round of sex. She had her chin propped on her hand, which was flat on my chest, her bright, inquisitive eyes, boring into my own.

"It's my name, Baby. I have to earn 'Galahad' back, and that's going to take some time."

I smoothed a hand over her golden hair and her eyes slipped shut in simple pleasure, "I know that," she said, "But, it's not who you *are* anymore. I get that you felt that way, and I get that you felt that way for a really long time and that you may be used to it, but it's not right." She opened her eyes and I could see something akin to hurt in them, as if she ached for me, and it was all over a stupid name... so I humored her.

"There's always Shepard, Shep, or Dominic," I murmured, "Corrine always used to call me Dominic, she hated Galahad," I said with a wry twist of lips. I'd hated it too for a while, but had eventually grown used to it.

Charity smirked, "Dom it is, then," she said and leave it to her to put her own twist to things. I smiled and gave a nod, once up and once down.

"Dom it is," I agreed and she leaned forward and kissed me.

I wondered vaguely if it would ever stop feeling brand new when she did it. Every time her lips met mine, I felt that pleasing little jolt in the center of my chest. Like when you're in a car and you crest a hill and go over the other side, that funny feeling you get in your stomach as gravity does its thing where it suspends and everything inside you feels like it lifts, going buoyant for that split second before gravity catches up to things. Usually you felt it in your stomach, but when Charity kissed me, it was higher up, around the center of my chest, like my heart fluttered or sprouted wings. It was a feeling I thoroughly enjoyed, and I secretly hoped that it never went away.

I slowed Charity down before she got too heated on me, I had another long day the next day in a bid to catch up on work, and the sultry, sexy as hell whimper she let out when I drew back damn near did me in for saying 'fuck it' and going in for a round two. My dick throbbed beneath the top sheet and let me know its opinion on the matter, and I sincerely hoped I wouldn't regret this act of adulting by way of a set of Smurf balls the next morning.

Charity cuddled into my side, and I held her close, a content and complete feeling overtaking me.

"Night, Baby," I whispered, kissing the top of her head and she sighed out, a contented happy noise that put me on cloud fuckin' nine.

"Good night, Dom," she murmured and I couldn't keep the smile off my face. I liked the sound of my name on her lips, even shortened as it was. Something, for the most part, that was uniquely hers.

***

The next morning was almost a new ritual, we got up, Charity made us coffee, we talked for a bit and I left for work. I finished up the edging and brushwork on that house, painting the trim around the windows and doorways, as well as up under the eaves, then headed home to meet up with Lightning and Gator to deal with demolition on the bathroom. Gator was waiting in my driveway with his pickup truck and I parked on the street, hitting the switch for the garage door.

"Aw, shit," I called out, coming up the drive, "I totally forgot that I was holding Charity's Jeep hostage over here."

"You got the key?" Gator asked.

"Nope, but if I'm lucky..." I went in and tried the handle, "Ha! Unlocked and it's a stick, we can push it."

"Sweet."

We got vehicles swapped, and Gator's Toyota pickup backed into the garage. The bathroom was across the hall and adjacent to the doorway leading into the garage, so that worked out for us.

"How far you thinking about tearing down?" Gator asked, standing in the doorway with me.

"All of it, man. I was thinking vanity, sink, shower wrap, floor... Toilet is meh, floor is just shitty linoleum from whoever owned the house before. I figure if I'm gonna do it, I might as well do it right."

"I hear that."

"Yo, Nothing!" Gator and I turned back towards the garage.

"Yeah, Lightning! In here."

"Hey, what're we doing," Gator saved me from having to repeat myself by repeating it for me. Lightning looked the bathroom over.

"You know this is all still in pretty good shape, man. Why you doing this?"

"Don't want to bring Charity back over here, you know? Want to fix it. I can't take the memories out of her head but I can change the whole room, you know? Make it so they aren't as biting."

"You're really gone on Hope's sister, ain't you?" Lightning asked, his wide grin taking most of the bite out of it.

"Shut up," I said, and he laughed.

"Alright, let's do it," he said and the three of us got to take some frustration out on ripping my bathroom to shreds.

We got the vanity out, the shower wrap, and ripped up the floor in short order, and I was kind of glad we did when Lightning let out a low whistle. I saw exactly what he meant.

"Fuck," I muttered.

"Blessing in disguise," Gator said bitterly.

"Yep, now we just need to find the leak," Lightning started looking and I started poking at the subflooring.

"Son of a bitch, this is all going to have to be replaced. Goddamnit!"

"Who's going under the house?" Gator asked.

"Since you volunteered, you are," Lightning said and Gator shrugged.

"I'll get a flashlight."

The good news was, the joists under the house were still sound, the bad news? All of the subflooring needed to be replaced. The leak was a pain in the ass to locate, but it was a relatively easy fix too. It was just going to have to be done another day, we were out of time and daylight for today.

"Same bat time, same bat channel?" Lightning asked.

"Yeah, but not tomorrow, day after tomorrow works though. I'm going to have to get some houses done if I'm gonna be able to afford this."

"Fifteen bucks an hour under the table and I'll come help you paint," Gator offered.

I considered it, and nodded, "You're on."

"Sweet! See you at the Captain's house."

"Six o'clock," I said and his face fell. I laughed, "You wanna work; you get your ass up." He gave me a salute and we went out to switch the cars around.

"Let me know how much I owe you for dumping this crap," I told Gator, giving Lightning a handshake.

"Don't worry about it, man. I got a guy at the transfer station, he lets me dump shit for free."

"Awesome! That's a big help."

"Yeah, my old man was good for something, who knew?" I raised an eyebrow.

"Trash collector, my guy might as well have been my uncle all growing up."

"Ah."

"Anyways, see you tomorrow, might want to get home to your little missus," he jibed.

"Yeah, fuck you. No wedding bells in our future yet, I need to make sure she can deal with me for real."

"Probably a good idea not rushing it this time," Lightning observed. I nodded, my mood crashing and smoldering a bit. "Hey, I didn't mean anything by that, honest," he grimaced, "Just put my foot in my mouth hard, didn't I?"

"It's okay, you're not exactly wrong, dude. It's just still a new truth for me and the truth's a bitch."

He nodded and we parted ways, I made a mental note to get Charity's keys from her so I could bring the Jeep back to her. I didn't want her over here until I finished the house. For some reason it was important that I keep this a surprise. I felt a little bad, almost like I was lying, but I think it had more to do with keeping anything from her after promising that we were done with that. Still, I convinced myself that this was different, and it was.

I left the bike and her Jeep in the garage, and locked everything up tight. It's was high past beer-thirty in the afternoon and I just wanted to kick my boots off and chill in the sand with a cold one. It was that kind of an evening. I was hoping Char was up for watching the sunset and having a drink. I was after low-key, and I think all of us could use it after all the ridiculous excitement of the last few weeks.

When I pulled up to the house, it was to an empty driveway, when I let myself into the place, it was full on empty; a rare occurrence as of late. I went to the fridge and pulled out a couple of beers, cracking one open, and saving the other in the event I ran across Charity. I started upstairs in the bedroom, but no dice, so my next logical stop was out back. I found her lounging in the sun down the beach a ways on a lounge chair covered by a towel. Not going to lie, I was kind of tickled at the empty one beside her but didn't want to get too excited. Faith might be out here, or Hope, and it might belong to one of them.

"Hey, stranger!" she called to me and she patted the towel on the lounge chair next to her, "Saved you a spot."

I handed her down the open beer I had yet to drink from and she smiled, "Brought you a drink." I cracked open the second one, using the hem of my shirt to twist off the cap, and dropped onto the towel and chair next to her, leaning over for a quick kiss.

"How was your day?" she asked and it warmed me from the inside even as the sun toasted my shoulders through my shirt.

"Same shit, different day," I said, taking a mouthful of beer. I picked at the laces on my work boots and toed them off, stripping off my socks and stuffing them down into them. Felt damn good to dig my toes into the sand to either side of my seat.

"Looks like it was pretty adventurous to me. What'd you do? Some interior painting today?" I looked down at myself and some of the plaster dust from my bathroom.

"Yeah, doesn't come along very often, but when it does, it's nice to be in out of the sun." I felt a pang about how easy the lie came, but I really, *really* wanted to do this for her.

"What about you? Anything on the job front?" I asked, changing the subject.

"Put in six more applications today, received a call back from a plastic surgeon's office but I *really* would rather help people who need it, you know? Somehow dealing with Muffy and Stuffy who just want bigger titties just doesn't seem like the right job for me." I laughed a little and she sighed, "I know! I'm being a judgy little bitch, and I probably can't afford to be too picky…"

"Hey, no, I get it, *trust me*, I get it. Still, why don't you go do the interview anyways, it'll be good practice for the ones that count, and if they offer you the job, you can always take it until something better shows up, or if something better shows up first, you can always turn it down."

"You are a wise master of adulting," she said and held out her bottle. I clicked the neck of my beer against hers and snorted.

"Yeah, I could argue that point and so, probably, would the

rest of the guys."

"Meh, fuck what they think, my opinion is the only one that matters," she said it so deadpan and she gave me a dazzling smile before taking a drink of her beer I had to laugh.

"So," she said after my laughter died down, "What do you want to do?"

"Actually, this right here. It was a long day, and I was really just looking forward to a chill evening on the beach, catching the sunset with you."

"Sounds good to me," she declared and we lounged, talking while the sun dipped lower in the sky.

"Where is everybody?" I asked and she looked back over her shoulder at the house.

"Hope had Cutter take her to the airport; she should be back the day after tomorrow. She headed out to do an assessment, or whatever it is she does, up north somewhere. Marlin took Faith with him on some kind of fishing trip, and everyone else; who knows?" She waved her hands in the air, "Cutter and Pyro are doing whatever their thing is, so I just came out here after my daily job search to relax and wait for you."

"Hope I didn't keep you waiting too long."

"Nope, you were right on time," she said and her smile made her glow. "You getting hungry?" she asked.

"Yeah, I could eat, what'd you have in mind?"

"I raided the fridge and freezer; the chicken should be done marinating soon, so no worries, I got this."

"You're making me dinner?" I asked, kind of surprised.

"You worked all day, I didn't, seems only fair."

"I think I love you," I said, spur of the moment, out of the blue, and immediately wished I could take it back, afraid it might weird her out, but not regretting it at the same time.

She held out her beer for another cheers, "That makes two of us, Dom. That makes two of us," she said and I could definitely drink to that, relief flooding my system.

CHAPTER 39

Charity

I could get used to this whole domesticated bliss thing. I mean seriously, it was nice to watch the sunset, talking over a couple of beers and it was even nicer that he brought in the chairs while I got to work in the kitchen fixing dinner. Still, it felt a little like we were just playing house with it, you know? With this place not being either one of our houses. Still, as much as I hated to admit it to myself, I wasn't exactly in a big hurry to go back to Dom's place. It seemed like whenever I went over there, it was something else. I was even reluctant to go back and get my Jeep, which was just downright silly. I mean, eventually I was going to need my car; I just didn't need it right now.

"What 'cha thinkin'?" he asked when I'd been quiet a little too long, moving around the kitchen.

"I was thinking I should pick up my Jeep at some point, I can't just leave it in your garage forever. I'll need it eventually, I just don't need it right now."

"That reminds me, I meant to grab your keys from you so I could bring it back. Perfect opportunity tomorrow, Gator's going to be helping me out the next couple of days."

I stilled and looked at him, "I don't want you to think that I don't want to come over ever again," I said softly.

"I don't, but I get it, seems like any time you come over shit goes sideways."

"Were you seriously just reading my mind?" I asked grinning.

"I was about to ask you the same thing out at the beach," he said, "That was exactly what I needed."

"Hmm, maybe we're meant for each other?" I ventured and he got up from his place at the table and came over to me, pulling me into his arms.

"Sorry I was being a stubborn asshole at the start," he said voice low, turning up the heat that was blooming in my bikini bottoms.

"You're making it up to me," I murmured, just as his lips descended onto mine. We kissed, long and slow and I was glad I hadn't gotten around to turning on the stove yet. I was the one who pulled back first to look him in the eyes.

"Somehow I doubt that Cutter would appreciate if I fucked you in his kitchen," he said and I laughed.

"Read my mind again," I said.

"Guess we're just on the same wavelength today," he lifted a shoulder in a shrug.

"I guess, maybe," I agreed.

I cooked dinner without any further interruptions from groping or making out, and I have to admit, that made me just a little bit sad.

Dom helped with the dishes, and it was pretty quickly evident why. As soon as the dishwasher was loaded, soap pack and all, and no sooner had I twisted the dial to start it, Dom had me yanked back into his arms. He twined them around my waist, standing behind me, his mouth playing along the side of my neck until he found that spot to make me shiver.

"Hmm, time for dessert," he murmured and I laughed lightly. I took a step forward to turn around but he pulled me back, nipping my shoulder. "C'mere," he said and I cuddled back into his arms.

"I'm right here," I said, "Not going anywhere."

"Good," he turned me in his arms and his lips found mine. I cupped his face in my hands and kissed him, long and deep until we both lost our sense of self and simply became 'us.' It was only a natural progression from there that led him to picking me up, one arm behind my back the other beneath my knees. I marveled at the sheer power of his body when he did things like this. He didn't strain much, and it almost felt effortless, the way he took the stairs and hall in long determined strides.

He set me down in my bedroom, his hands warm and careful where they caressed my skin, holding me close, pressing my body the length of his. He unraveled the tie at my neck, holding my bikini top on, and slipped the knot free at my back next, letting the lycra fall to the floor. I pulled off his paint and dust splattered tee off over his head, and admired the coil and bunch of his musculature beneath his tanned and golden skin.

He worked the knot of my sheer wrap free at my hip, while I went to work on his belt. For long moments it was the whisper of cloth and the soft sigh of breath when we each liked what the other was seeing. It was a feast for the senses, both sight and touch, and I was almost slightly disappointed when it ended, but not for long.

Dom pulled me tightly in to the warm shelter of his body, our mouths locked in a fierce kiss, even as the soft skin of his erection very nearly burned against my stomach with the intensity of its heat. I wrapped my arms around his neck and let him back me up against the bed, sitting when he urged me to do so, which put me at exactly the perfect vantage point to take him into my mouth, which I did, picking him up with gentle fingers and stroking him lightly.

His head tipped back and his eyes slipped shut, even as he ran his fingers softly through my hair, holding it back from my face so he could watch. When he looked, his eyes were filled with appreciation and heat, and I could tell, it was taking all of his self-control not to thrust into the back of my throat. I plunged my mouth over the top of him, taking him all the way back until my lips met his body and he cried out, head tipping back, voice reverberating back to us from the ceiling. I moaned around him, and the vibration caused him to gasp.

He pulled back, and gripped my upper arms, firmly but carefully, setting me back further on the bed, kneeling in front of me. I felt a little thrum of excitement in the center of my chest and realized this was still something we hadn't done much of, even as I lay back, and Dom parted my knees.

He slid a finger into my wet and waiting pussy, sealing his mouth over my clit, his tongue teasing, and I nearly shot off like a rocket. I arched, and gasped out his name, squeezing down around him. It was a relatively quick build up and explosion, sending me shuddering beneath him, small little shocks of pleasure coursing through my body. He didn't waste any time standing and drawing me back to the edge of the bed, wrapping his powerful arms around my thighs and pulling me, bodily, closer.

He pressed his hands into the backs of my thighs, nearly folding me in half, every movement he made powerful, deliberate and dominant. He checked with me with his gaze and when he still found me wanting and desiring, he slid inside of me and *oh my god*... The angle was deep, and it felt like he went on forever, touching the deepest parts of me. He carried on, with long and unforgiving strokes, seeking, adjusting his hips every time, until he found what he was looking for and when he did? He switched to short, deep strokes, torturing that spot over and over until I came, crying out, just by virtue of his cock inside me.

It was amazing, it was mind blowing, and it was quite literally the best sex I've ever had in my life, given how short the duration of it. It was the wildest, most intense few minutes I'd ever experienced with a man, I thought, but that was before I discovered that unlike when we usually had sex, Dom wasn't done with me.

"Get on your knees for me, Baby," he murmured and languidly, I turned to give him what he wanted. Hell, I would give him anything and then some if he kept it up like this.

I knelt for him, arching low to the mattress. He fitted himself at my entrance and said, "Warn me if this is too intense." He smoothed his hands over my hips, and started out slow, the warmth of his fingers trailing up my back and down my arms until he gripped me just above the elbows.

If I hadn't had two orgasms already, and if I weren't still riding the aftershocks of the one I'd just gone through, what he did next could very well have been too intense, bordering even, on painful. He gripped my arms, just above the elbow, and pulled back on my upper body, burying himself impossibly deep. He stilled and I panted, getting used to the intensity of it.

"Don't stop!" I cried and he chuckled low and dark.

"Okay, I'm going to go slow," he said and he was as good as his word, thrusting slow and deep at first, before picking up his pace.

I can't describe it, at least not completely. It was as if he reached my end and pushed farther. It rode that line between pleasure and pain, and went a little bit over, but not enough for me to want him to stop, at least not just yet. I think he could tell I was riding a similar line of indecision, because he let up on my arms, just a little bit, and kept adjusting according to the feral cries pouring from my throat.

While I couldn't describe him as a gentle lover, at least not this time, what he was, and always would be, was a considerate one. He was almost fucking me like he hated me one second, but the moment I voiced or jerked with displeasure or anything less than satisfaction, he stopped or eased up, back into my comfort zone. He also spoke encouragement and it was sexy encouragement at that.

"That's it, Baby, you can take me. Oh, god you feel so fucking good, you're amazing. Yes! Yes, yes, yes, yes, yes!"

He thrust into me one final time, bodies coming together with the sharp sound of skin on skin and that last thrust *did* hurt, pitching me forward as it shot through me, leaving an intense wave of pleasure in its wake. I collapsed onto the bed, and Dom let me, folding over the top of my sweating, but strangely cool body. Warming me, his hands stroking my skin wherever he could reach.

He pulled out of me and I felt warmth and wetness trickle down my thigh from the aftermath of one of the hottest rounds of sex I *know* I had ever had. Dom rested his forehead between my shoulder blades and we both panted, trying valiantly to catch our breaths. He laughed a little and said to me, "I think a shower's in order before bed."

"Just give me a minute; I don't think I can walk."

I yipped when he flipped me over and pulled me to the edge of the bed, he scooped me up and stood fluidly, saying, "You don't have to. I'm happy to carry you."

Sweetest. Man. Ever.

"Hmm, then sally forth! Or whatever they say."

"As you wish," he said raising an eyebrow and I grinned.

"Bonus points for The Princess Bride reference."

"Didn't think you were old enough to get that one," he said making for the hall.

"Are you kidding me? Death before dishonor buddy, Hope

would cave your nuts in for even suggesting she lacked in sisterly duty to pass that one down to us."

"I stand corrected!" he cried laughing and it felt so good to hear him do it. He set me lightly to my feet inside the bathroom door and asked me, "You good?" before letting go. I tipped my face up to his and kissed him.

"Always when I'm with you," I said smiling.

"Not *always*, but I'm trying to make up for it," he said softly.

"You're doing a damn fine job," I confided.

He smiled and started the water, helping me into the shower.

"Lock the door?" I asked and he paused, nodding and humoring me, locking the door, turning on the heat lamp and fan.

He got into the shower with me and pulled me into a long kiss, his earlier, almost frenzied and possessive love making forgotten. Dominic was all tenderness and soft wonder now, and I loved the contrast. I didn't mind the occasional rough sex, I found it a nice change of pace and thrilling, but it was nice and almost perfect to be cared for after. It made me feel like a woman, and that I was loved and cherished, not just an object to be used for sexual gratification. Dominic had the right amalgamation and I loved that about him.

He washed my body carefully, smoothing gentle soapy fingertips over every sensitive bit, and massaging where he'd gripped and between my shoulders. I took the care and time to show him the same consideration and we stayed in the water until we were both prunes and it'd started to run cold on us.

It was perfect; *he* was perfect, and most of all, we were perfect for each other.

We got ready for bed, which mostly consisted of drying off and going back to the bedroom. I sat on the edge of the bed and picked up my phone which was charging to check it while Dom ran the towel over my hair. I'd missed a call earlier in the afternoon, while I'd been on the beach, but that was okay. I couldn't do anything about it right now, it was too late; so I left the voicemail until morning, preferring to cuddle with my man instead.

"Hold still," he said, turning my head with the towel to face back forward.

"Why?" I asked and he chuckled.

"You're so damn nosey," he said.

"Hey, I prefer 'inquisitive', what are you do – oh!" He stroked my brush through my hair, careful of any knots, holding it so it wouldn't pull against my scalp as he detangled it, and I think I very nearly melted.

"You can do this any time you want," I assured him, voice soft and a touch deeper with my relaxed pleasure. I *loved* having my hair played with, and come to think of it, I didn't know many women who didn't.

"I used to love doing this for my wife," he said gently, "I hadn't realized how much I missed it, so thanks for being cool with it."

"Oh, my pleasure, and I mean that quite literally."

I could hear him smile and it made me smile too, it really was the perfect, low key evening and I found myself hoping and wishing for many, many more like it.

CHAPTER 40

Nothing

I woke up just before the alarm went off and I secretly found myself glad for it. Just because *I* had to get up, didn't mean that Charity did. She slept like an angel, and I didn't have the heart to wake her, so I slipped out of the bed, hijacked her keys off the nightstand and took some clothes with me down the hall and into the bathroom to change.

I did miss her making my coffee for me, like she had the last couple of mornings, but I could seriously get that going on my own, which I did. I'd just poured myself a travel mug of the stuff when Gator came through the front door. I craned my neck back to see through the living room to the front of the house and put my finger to my lips in the classic sign for 'shut up.' He tiptoed back into the kitchen and made a longing face toward the coffee pot and I flipped open the cupboard full of 'Ander's Maritime Salvage' travel mugs the Captain kept on hand.

"Fucking-A man, you rock," he said low and quiet.

"Need you to run me over to my house so I can bring Char's Jeep back over here first. She should start getting calls for interviews and shit with as many applications as she's got out there."

"Cool deal, yeah. Let's get that done first," he agreed.

Footfalls on the back stairs had us turning, Marlin lumbering into view, I sighed in a bit of relief and said, "Well, that answers that question."

"What question?" he asked and went for the coffee that Gator was setting back on the burner.

"Whether or not anyone but Char and I were in the house."

"Ah, yeah, we got in late last night."

"I must have been out," I said.

"Yeah, Faith looked in on you two and she said you both were passed *out*." I grinned and he grinned and he said, "I figured. Why you wondering if we was home?"

"Gonna run and get Char's Jeep, just wanted to make sure she was taken care of."

"I know what you mean," Marlin said, sipping from his freshly poured mug, "Threat's over, but without benefit of bein' there handling business first hand, it don't feel like it, does it?"

"Not exactly," I admitted.

"Go on an' do your thing, Bro. I got this. Johnny and I ain't got shit goin' for the next couple of days so Faith and I figured we'd chill here, she's got some damn show she wants me to watch," he made a face and I chuckled. Marlin had never been much for TV. Still, he looked like he could use the R&R, his face still resembled hamburger with eggplant chunks thrown in for good measure.

"Cool, thanks, we'll be back in a couple of minutes."

We made the drive to my place, picked up Charity's Jeep and drove back to the Captain's. When I went through the door it was to spy Charity in the kitchen.

"There you are!" I went to her and kissed her and she wrapped her arms around me giving me a squeeze. "You trying to sneak out on me?"

"Thought you could use a little extra sleep," I handed her the keys to her ride, "Brought you your car, thought you might be starting to miss it."

"Not yet, and you didn't have to do that, go out of your way, I mean."

"Weren't no thing," I said with a wink. She hugged me tight and leaned up for another kiss which I gave without hesitation.

"Have a good day at work," she said, voice husky.

"Gonna miss me?" I asked.

"Already do," she said with a charmed little smile.

"Oh, please! You're gonna make me puke," Gator complained.

"Don't look at me for help," Marlin said, bouncing Faith in his lap. She giggled and held onto his shoulders.

"Can we please just go?" Gator asked.

"Alright, alright, you pussy, let's move," I rolled my eyes and Charity let me go.

"See you tonight?" she asked.

"It's a promise," I told her and away Gator and I went for another thrilling day sweating our asses off in the sun laying paint on a house neither one of us could afford in our lifetimes.

CHAPTER 41

Charity

"This is Charity Dobbins, returning Watch Commander Figaro's call," I said into the phone. The lady proclaiming to be a dispatcher on the other end of the line, told me she'd put me right through. The line crackled for a second and started ringing.

"Figaro," the gruff voice on the other end of the line said by way of greeting.

"Yes Sir, this is Charity Dobbins returning your call, you left a message for me on my voicemail yesterday afternoon."

"Oh, yes! Hi, I was wondering if you could come in for an interview," he said.

"Absolutely," I told him, "When would be good?"

"Can you be here in an hour?" he asked and I was taken a bit aback. I cued up Google maps on my laptop.

"I'm still new to the area, can you tell me where 'here' is?" I asked.

He rattled off an address and I punched it in, "Says you're forty-five minutes from me, and that's with no traffic, so an hour is pushing it."

"Great, see you in two then," he said and hung up. I sat up straighter and looked at my phone, a little stunned.

"Holy shit," I uttered and busted my ass to get upstairs, presentable and into the Jeep in record time. I was betting this was my first test and when I arrived in an hour and a half flat, to see a man standing in the parking lot, lit cigarette in his mouth checking his watch as I pulled into the parking space in front of him, I felt like I'd hit the nail on the head.

"You Dobbins?" he asked.

"Yes, Sir."

"Great," he stubbed out his cigarette in the ashtray at his hip,

"Come this way, step into my office."

I dutifully followed him into a small office in what looked like an industrial warehouse. He had windows looking out onto the garage floor where there were several ambulances in various states of being washed, stocked or repaired.

"Now when I saw your application and résumé, I thought to myself, 'why is a girl with an education like hers, going for a job like this?' Care to shed some light on that for me?"

I pursed my lips and gave the Watch Commander a good once-over, "I'm going to do us both a favor and cut the bullshit," I said and he crossed his arms, mouth drawing down at the corners, his head bobbing up and down, impressed by all outward appearances.

"That'd be nice," he said.

"My first choice, when it comes to medicine, was to be an ER nurse," I said.

"And you figured Paramedic would be a good place to start until you could score that position?" he asked.

"No, not exactly," I said, and he cocked his head to the side like I'd done something interesting.

"We both know I'm over qualified for this job, and I happen to know, you're understaffed, but what if I told you, if you hired me, that I could bring Dominic Shepard back?" He sat up as if I'd finally really said something interesting.

"What makes you think you can get Shep back in here?" he asked.

"He's my boyfriend for one," I said laying it all out on the line, "For two, he's not meant to be painting houses for a living. He's meant to be out here saving lives. It's in his DNA."

"Won't argue that, girly. Shep was one of the best guys I ever got and it was a damn shame losing him." He looked me over, mulling it over, judgment all over his craggy face, like the older white guy in *Men in Black*, Tommy Lee Jones or whatever.

"It might take me a few days, but I'm fairly convinced that I could convince *him*," I said.

"Tell you what, I'll give you a week. If you come walking through those doors with Shep this time next week, I'll not only give him his job back; I'll give *you* a job and start you *both* out at the top of the pay scale."

"Doesn't sound like you think I can do it," I said with a feral grin.

"I don't," he conceded.

Game on. I thought to myself, out loud I said: "Well Sir, you don't know *me* very well, so I'll give you the benefit of that doubt." I stood up and held out my hand for him to shake, which he did, and I said, "We'll see you next week."

"Yeah, we'll see about that," he shot back and sounded as dubious as they came.

He followed me out and the paramedic who'd spoken to me the day Dom and I had saved the boy on the beach asked the Watch Commander, "What is she doing here?"

"Says she can bring Shep back."

The paramedic scoffed, "Yeah, good luck with that," he said, disbelieving.

"I don't need luck," I called back to them, getting up into the Jeep; I winked at them and with a false bravado said over the top of my windshield, "I got this."

They both shook their heads and I put it in reverse and pulled out of the lot, heading back to Ft. Royal.

* * *

"How was your day?" Dom asked me back as I set a plate of food in front of him.

"Had an interview, actually," I said and he looked interested.

"Oh, yeah? How'd it go?"

"I'm not sure, we'll see," I answered and hoped it sounded non-committal while at the same time, I tried not to feel awful for lying. I quickly changed the subject, "What about you? Have anything else lined up?" I asked, and he nodded, chewing through a bite of his food and swallowing before answering.

"Yeah, a few things," he said.

"Aw, yeah? Maybe I can come help out, I've kind of exhausted the current application pool," he shifted in his seat and hedged.

"Ah, yeah, sorry about it, Baby, but you can't. I would have to buy additional insurance and sign you on as an employee and all that garbage. I'm really only covered to have one assistant and right now that's Gator. He needs the money, and I'm always one to help a brother out."

I smiled, understanding completely, "Hey, it's no worries, but maybe come the weekend I can stay with you at your place. I'm getting tired of the scenery around here."

He smiled and shifted in his seat again, and said, "Sounds good to me."

We ended up spending a fabulous, low key evening, laying in each other's arms in the hammock out back, watching the sun set, and the stars come out, talking in low and even tones, finding out multitudes of little small things about one another.

I found myself wondering what it would be like to live with this man for real, and let myself daydream about the possibility of working with one another, too. He held me close as if I were his anchor to the Earth and he were afraid to let go, and I liked that about him. I also liked that he held true to his promise, and was open with me, talking about what was, and what is, freely; without any fear of reprisal. I mean, he wasn't going to get any from me.

Evening wore into night, and we retired up to my room, tucked into each other's embrace. We skipped sex in favor of domesticity tonight, and I was okay with that. So, apparently was he. I fell asleep in his arms, his hand lightly tracing random patterns on my back. It was bliss.

CHAPTER 42

Nothing

"Fuck, man. I don't know how I'm gonna do this," I said and Lightning was laughing at me.

"Bit off a little more than you can chew, eh?"

"Yeah, just a bit," I said frowning. The plumbing was fixed and the subflooring in, but that was seriously as far as we'd gotten today. Plumbing was always a bitch, and the simplest fixes always came with ridiculous problems one after the other, and this one had been no exception. Add like seven trips to the hardware store and I was as agitated and just generally as fucked off over the whole damn thing as one man could get.

"Look, I'm willing to stay late if you are," Gator said and I sighed out, grateful.

"Thanks, man. I'd better call Char and tell her I'm not coming tonight, just easier to stay here if I've only got two days to finish this."

"Pfft, two days, that's easy. We got this," Lightning said.

"Hell we work through the night that should give it all of tomorrow to dry. You can stay at the Captains tomorrow night, and Saturday, if you both go out and do stuff, that'll give it another day... it's tight, but doable." Gator mused aloud.

"Thanks, guys. I owe you big for this."

"Hell fucking yeah, you do," Lightning agreed.

I called Charity. She was disappointed that I wouldn't be there tonight, and that my job was running late, but Hope was home, so she assured me the girls would have a night and that everything would be fine. I loved her for that, I really did. The fact that she was independent enough to *not* freak out on me was kind of refreshing. I'd loved Corrine with my all, but sometimes her anxiety had made life difficult. It was still a struggle coming to grips with what she'd done; a struggle that, for now, I could keep conveniently shoving to the back burner with how busy I was, but eventually it was going to catch up with me and I was going to have to deal with it.

"Dude, Nothing, where you at, bro?"

I looked up at Lightning, "Sorry, man. Old ghosts for a second."

He nodded, "That part of why you're doing this?" he asked.

"What do you mean?"

"Look, I get what happened to Charity in here was a good excuse, but you sure this doesn't have more to do with erasing Corrine starting with this room?" he asked.

I thought about it, and nodded eventually, "Hadn't thought of it that way, but yeah, I guess it could be."

"Dude, that's cold," Gator said and Lightning swung blindly behind him hoping to connect, he did and Gator jerked back. "Hey!"

"Shut up, noob!" Lightning declared, "You don't have the full 4-1-1, it was before your time." Which was true, Gator was only around two and a half years involved with the club while we were coming up on four for my girls leaving me. *Except they didn't leave you. They died.* That inner voice chastised me, and I sighed, relieved, that the reality bit, but not quite as hard as it used to.

"Come on man, let's do this," Lightning said, and I nodded.

"Yeah, let's get this done," I agreed and we attacked the monumental project in front of us with renewed zeal.

I installed a new, white shower wrap with a different, more user-friendly shelving configuration. I wish I had the time for tile, but at the same time, I was glad I didn't because tile was an ever loving bitch when it came to getting the grout clean whereas the shower wrap wiped clean with minimal effort.

We worked on through the night, bringing in a flood light on a stand to paint the walls and ceiling, taking a break with a beer or two while the paint dried before we put in the fixtures.

We installed a new toilet; we had to with the new plumbing hookup we had to put in. The old one wasn't as water efficient as the newer model anyways, and with luck, it should pay for its self in the form of a lower water bill every month now that the leak had been found and resolved.

Next, the lights above the vanity went in, a nice fixture, not one of those ugly round bulb things, but three tulip fluted glass ones coming out of an old fashioned metal plate backing. Classy, and way nicer than what'd been in here before. I'd gotten it on the cheap from the clearance section to boot, still, I was gonna hate my credit card bill come next month.

By the time the vanity went in, it was after midnight; by the time we got the sink hooked up and the water uncrossed so the cold flowed cold and the hot flowed hot, it was almost two in the morning. Still, by the time we'd finished laying in the floor, it was three. Thank fuck we'd had the forethought to cut the tile for the floor before the noise ordinances went into effect for the evening. We tried to be good neighbors and keep it cool with the rest of the town. We realized the importance of a symbiotic relationship between The Kraken and Ft. Royal. It was how any of the shit we got away with was going to work.

"Are we fucking done?" Gator asked.

"I think we're fucking done," Lightning affirmed.

"Cool, Nothing, I'm crashing on your fucking couch," Gator moaned and dragged himself down the hall to my living room.

"Be my guest," I said absently, casting a critical eye on the bathroom. None of the fixtures had *moved*; the bathtub, toilet, and vanity all chillin' in the same spots as before, but the room was totally different just the same. It looked good. It looked real good. It just needed a shower curtain and the towel bars installed, but I could do that myself tomorrow – well, later today.

"Dumbass," Lightning muttered after Gator had gone, "I'm taking your guest room," he said to me.

"Use my bathroom, grab a shower first," I said, and he saluted and went into my bedroom.

I leaned against the doorframe and stared into the bathroom for a real long time, pleased with how we'd banged it out. It'd felt impossible, but with the help of your brothers, the impossible was totally doable, as was evidenced by my rockin' new bathroom. I still never wanted to do it again, though. This shit was rough.

I went into my room and dropped heavily onto the foot of my

bed, staring at all the photos of Corrine and Katy around my mirror, old ghosts and betrayal stared back at me and I allowed the grim weight of what my wife had done to sink in.

I bowed my head and gripped the back of my neck, pulling to ease the tension there as Lightning stepped out of the bathroom.

"You okay, man?"

"Yeah, just fucking *tired*."

"Well get some sleep, see you later." He went out into the hall and swung my door shut behind him. I stood up and went to my dresser, palms flat to its wooden surface and let my eyes roam over the photos and little mementos around the mirror.

It was all bullshit; every last bit of it. Bullshit and lies. With an angry sigh I started pulling it all down, stacking it in a neat pile; I looked at the stack in my hands and with no little amount of pain, dropped it into the wastebasket between the dresser and the door.

It was time to start fresh, start new, and put the old ghosts to bed, and speaking of bed, it's where I needed my ass to be. I got in it, and picked up my phone. No messages, but I hadn't expected any. I opened up a text screen to Charity.

Me: Good morning, Baby. I hope you have a great day, I'm thinking about you and my bed is kind of lonely. See you after the club meeting tonight.

I put the phone down, feeling marginally better, and dropped off into an exhausted, dreamless, sleep.

CHAPTER 43

Charity

I woke up to the sun streaming through my blinds and sucked in a deep breath, stretching luxuriously. I picked up my phone to check the time and had a waiting message.

Nothing: Good morning, Baby. I hope you have a great day, I'm thinking about you and my bed is kind of lonely. See you after the club meeting tonight.

Aww! God, he was awesome, I stared at the text for a long time before going into my contacts and erasing 'Nothing' and replacing it with 'Dom.'

Me: I miss you, too. Didn't know there was a club meeting tonight, but yes, definitely I will see you after. I hope you have a good day, too. Call me if you get the chance, I know you get busy. – XoXo

I hit 'send' and lay back down, staring at my ceiling, worry gnawing at my gut. What the absolute fuck did I get myself into with Figaro yesterday, and how the hell was I going to convince Dom to go back with me?

"Ugh, god!" I said to myself and covered my face with my hands, huffing out a big sigh.

"Uh, oh! What'd you do?" Hope asked, barging through the cracked door with a cup of coffee in each hand, Faith coming in right behind her with a cup in hers.

"Oh, god. The lord bless you and keep you," I said taking the proffered cup of coffee off my sister.

"Dude, that catholic university perverted your brain," Hope said, making a face.

"Shut up, I'm pretty sure it being a *catholic* uni, it did just the opposite," I said taking a sip. Ah, perfect temp, screw sipping, I gulped.

"Still doesn't answer my question," Hope said, flopping down on the edge of the bed, "What'd you do?"

Faith sat cross legged in the middle of the floor and looked like she was, for once, glad she wasn't the one being grilled. I shot her a dirty look and she looked well pleased. She was becoming more like the sister I remembered every day, and I was grateful for that. More of her fire was showing.

"I may have applied to the ambulance company Nothing used to work for and I *may* have gone for an interview yesterday."

"Annnd?" Dammit, Hope was like a dog with a bone.

"And I may have told them I could get Dom to go back to work for them in exchange for securing me my own job." I wrinkled my nose and Hope busted up laughing.

"Oh! Oh, that's good!" she cried.

"Shut up! I'm trying to figure out how to convince him, any ideas?"

"Oh no, oh hell no! All those times lecturing me about letting Faithy here make her own decisions and then you go and pull this? I'm going to *enjoy* watching you squirm, you are so on your own for this one." Hope cackled and got up, "Good luck!" She called over her shoulder and went back downstairs, just howling with laughter.

Faith just sat on the floor and smiled while I probably looked like I'd sucked on a lemon. I looked to my middle sister and raised an eyebrow; she raised both in return and said, "Don't look at me! But if it's one thing I know, if you want something bad enough, you'll figure out the words. I think it's a great idea personally."

"Yeah?" I asked.

"Oh yeah," she said nodding, "Nothing was great when he took care of me, you know, when I was sick. He's wasted painting houses. I bet you all of the guys would agree with you, too."

"Agree with her about what?" Marlin asked from the doorway and I felt my eyes roll. *Was there no fucking privacy at all in this house?* I wondered, and honestly I chastised myself right on the heels of that thought for it having been a rhetorical question. Of course there wasn't. It seemed to be a way of life when it came to these guys, one big happy family, and by family I meant everyone all up in each other's business. I was beginning to miss the autonomy of my college years where the only person I had to worry about was my dorm room roomy.

"That Nothing needs to go back to being a paramedic," Faith said.

"Hell yeah, he does. He's wasted on painting houses, being a medic is that man's calling."

"Yeah, well, I have a little less than a week to figure it out," I groused and Marlin raised an eyebrow over the battered side of his face. "Don't ask," I told him and he nodded.

"Say no more, I was just coming to collect my girl, see if you wanted to go out on the boat with me and Johnny.

"Can Charity come?" Faith asked.

"Sure can," he said.

"Thanks, I actually think I would like that," I said.

"You got around ten minutes to get ready and meet us at the marina."

"I'll ride with Charity; show her which boat it is, we'll be right there." Faith jumped up and gave her man a kiss and he ducked back out into the hall. I swallowed the rest of my coffee at light speed and got up.

Faith handed me a swim suit and wrap and said; "Bring something to work on or read, you're going to *love* this."

We piled downstairs, me with my laptop bag over my shoulder, loaded with stuff for me to do, and went out to the Jeep. Hope was already gone, probably with Cutter. My butthurt was still strong enough I didn't care but I'd be over it soon enough. We drove out to the Marina and I don't think I remember Faith ever being so excited.

"Hey!" she called out to a man on a rather expensive looking fishing boat.

"Hey you! Who you got with you? That Charity?"

"I'm Charity," I confirmed. He pulled Faith up onto the boat and reached down for me, I let him haul me up.

"I'm Johnny, Jimmy, er, Marlin's brother."

"Nice to meet you, Johnny."

Marlin appeared on deck and said without preamble, "Don't get your hopes up, Johnny, she belongs to Nothing."

I raised an eyebrow about to smart off on a feminist rant, but Faith caught my eye and shook her head. Curious, I let it go for now.

"Come on, Charity, let's get situated and let the guys work."

I followed my sister to a couple of lounge chairs at the front of the boat and once we were well clear, I asked her, "What was *that* all about? I '*belong* to Nothing,' like some piece of cattle?"

"It's not like that," Faith said and I gave her a look.

"You got some explainin' to do, Bubbles."

"Okay, it's like this..."

Faith had *a lot* to say and by the time she was through, I was a little misty eyed and honored that Marlin would think I belonged to Dom, and I found myself wondering if Dom felt the same way, because, I've got to tell you, the thought was really nice.

"So you and Hope seriously wear vests like theirs that read 'Property of Marlin' and 'Property of Cutter?'" I asked.

"Want me to go get mine?" she asked.

"Yes, yes I do."

She got up and went below decks, and I waited for her. She came back with a fitted, black leather riding vest, the front reading 'Firefly' on the nametag. She turned it around and sure enough, it read 'Property of' at the top, and down below, where the guys' vests read 'Ft. Royal,' hers read 'Marlin.'

"Wow, it's beautiful." And it was, a blue and silver marlin fish, leaping out of the water was embroidered where The Kraken men wore their club patch.

"Hope is sort of an honorary member, so hers is the club colors in the middle. Most Ol' Ladies from other clubs don't have anything in the middle, just the 'property of' and their Ol' Man's name."

"I kind of like this better," I confided.

"Me, too." She got up and went and put it back, returning to the lounge chair next to mine.

It was a great day spent on the water, bonding with my sister after that. I loved every minute of it.

CHAPTER 44

Nothing

"Am I late?" I asked, pulling my phone out of my cut and checking the time. I frowned, I was on time, but the guys were already gathered around the table, Hope leaning against the Captain's throne and it looked like they'd all been here a minute.

"No man, you're not late," Cutter said, "We just had to put something to a vote."

I started to sweat a little, "Yeah, what's that?" I asked.

"C'mere," Cutter said, standing and I swallowed hard, and did what I was told.

"What's up, Captain?" I asked nervously.

He put an arm around my shoulders and flicked open one of his knives. In fact, the one he opened up was that fancy switchblade Reaver, the guy from up north, had given him.

"We've decided, this has got to go," he said and he started to slice one of the flash patches off the front of my cut. I held still, my heart dropping that he was taking my treasurer's flash but when I looked he'd taken my name flash. Relief flooded my system.

"Pyro, do your thing, Man." Cutter tossed the flash that read 'Nothing' to our Road Captain who pulled a bottle of lighter fluid from somewhere and his zippo out of his cut. He dropped the flash into an ashtray and soaked it, flicked his zippo and torched it. I watched it burn.

"Get this on your cut before we conclude this meeting," he said, handing me a name flash slightly less worn than the one burning. I took it, and looked down at it, 'Galahad' emblazoned across it.

"Why?" I asked and it was Hope that answered.

"Because my sister is gonna look dumb as hell wearing this if you don't make the change," she said tossing a shopping bag at me. I caught it against my chest and opened it up, pulling out a leather vest, fitted for Charity's slim form.

'Property of Galahad' was emblazoned on the back, and where there was supposed to be nothing, a white knight on a white horse, lance and all was embroidered. It was what was on the shield that caught my attention though. The caduceus, the widely known symbol of medical knowledge, the staff wrapped with snakes, bold and in red on the shield's gray background.

"Holy shit," I uttered.

"Yeah, that was me," Radar said, grinning.

"You designed this?" I asked.

"Yup, and you better get busy," he said sliding a sewing kit down the table at me. I took my seat, setting my rag for Charity aside and slipped out of my cut, making good on my Captain's order.

"I don't know what to say, guys, except thank you," I said, choking up with emotion.

"It's cool, bro," Cutter said, retaking his seat, "Next order of business," he said and it was business as usual while I hand sewed my name flash onto my cut. I glanced down into the bag, and had to smile. On the front of Charity's vest, the name flash read 'Trouble' and I wasn't sure the Captain was ready to fully reap the benefits of that name, although I was feeling pretty blessed that I had.

I tuned back into the conversation, "I say we all just go for a fuckin' ride tomorrow man, I mean fuck, when was the last time we went anywhere for the sake of the ride, versus having a destination in mind?" Stoker was saying.

"I say that's a fine, idea. I second that motion," Beast said.

"Not that it needs it, but I third," I put in. A ride with my brothers just for the sake of it sounded fantastic.

"What say you? A ride down to Roy's Crab Shack, lunch and ride back?" Cutter said.

"Sounds good to me," Pyro put in.

"All in favor?"

A round of rowdy yeah's went up and it passed, good thing, too. I think we all could use some wind therapy.

"You're riding with me tomorrow," Cutter told Hope.

"No argument here," she murmured.

"Good deal, anything else?"

"Yeah, what're we doing tonight?"

"Barbecue at my place?"

"Shit, yeah!" Radar said, there were more noises of agreement.

Cutter looked over at me, "How you doing over there? Looks like this is wrapping up sooner than expected."

"Man will you stop busting my balls like I'm some kind of fuckin' prospect?" I demanded.

"Depends, you gonna stop *actin'* like a fuckin' prospect?" Marlin shot back, teasing.

I paused in my work long enough to give him the finger, "Keep it up I'm gonna rush and sew this thing on crooked, plus when was the last time any of you fuckers sewed anything on to one of your cuts by hand?" Silence. "Yeah, that's what I thought."

Guys started laughing, and Pyro called me a pussy. He got the finger next and Hope called out, "Girls, girls, girls! I think you're both pretty, now let the man do his thing so I can get out of this sweatbox? The beach is callin' my name."

A round of cheers went up at that, and I think all of us were ready to relax and party. I know I was looking forward to seeing Char. I missed her. I'd woken up to a text back from her that afternoon and it'd changed my whole outlook for the day. Energized me in a way I couldn't really begin to describe and allowed me to get those towel racks up and the rest of the bathroom odds and ends wrapped up. It'd felt good to have it finished and looking solid, and it was ready to use as early as tonight if need be.

I finished sewing on my name flash and shrugged back into my cut to a round of cheers. Cutter called the meeting and everyone started to filter out. I pulled the property cut meant for Charity out of the bag and looked it over again.

"You don't have to give it to her unless you're sure, but we all see the way she's changed you, and I guess it's just our way of telling you that not only do we approve, that you'd be stupid to let her go." Cutter said. I looked up and over at him and Hope.

"I'm not letting her go," I said and looked to Hope, "I'm going to work on being the best thing that's ever happened to her, same as she's been for me. I really do regret how I treated her at first."

"I know," Hope said and sighed.

"Now if you don't mind, I gotta run home and make myself presentable before tonight's shindig," Hope and Cutter mock groaned and laughed and I took my leave. I really did need to run home, but not to shine myself up any. I wanted to swing by the store and grab a couple bottles of wine, a white and a red, because I didn't know what Charity liked. I also wanted to stash the cut my brothers had given me for her. I honestly didn't know if I was ready to ask for such a monumental commitment, but I had to admit, it was nice having the option at the ready. I mean, I was going to have one made, had every intention of asking her at some point, but my brothers' had saved me the trouble of figuring out sizes and what to put in the middle so she'd look as rockin' as her other two sisters. It was nice to have my brothers' know me almost better than I knew myself sometimes, and this was definitely one of those times.

I left The Plank and did my thing; stopping at the store and heading home. I put the wine in the fridge, taking a quick second to stash Charity's property cut. When I went to leave the house, I paused in front of the refinished bathroom. I stared into it for a long time and sighed, scrubbing my face with my hands. Who was I fucking kidding? I loved this woman enough to completely rip out and redo a bathroom just so she could be more comfortable being in my house. How could I then hesitate to make her my Ol' Lady? What did I want her to do? Find someone else? *Fuck no.* I thought. The real question was, *how* was I going to ask her?

I shut the door to the bathroom and left the house, riding over to Cutter's and thought about it the whole way there. I wanted it to be just me and Charity tonight, so that meant bringing her to my place. I figured a fire out back in the fire pit, a cold glass of wine and then if things went right, I could ask her.

When I got to the Captain's place, I backed my bike into line, I was a little nervous, my palms sweating. I wiped them off on my jeans and took a deep breath to steady myself. I went into the house and found Charity in the kitchen, making salad.

"Hey, Baby," I said going up to her. The smile she turned on me liked to have my heart doing somersaults in my chest. She lit up, from the inside out, and immediately raised her lips to mine, standing on tiptoe to kiss me enthusiastically.

How could I be so lucky?

"Hi! I missed you," she said and a bunch of the guys all went "Aww!"

"Shut it, you ass goblins!" I barked, and was met by a bunch of laughter.

"Why is it when you get a group of men together they always revert to a bunch of thirteen year old boys?" Hope asked. Charity rolled her eyes and went back to her salad prep.

"Is this a rhetorical question, or do you really want to know?" Marlin asked.

"Totally rhetorical," Hope confirmed. It set the tone for the rest of the meal and light hearted antagonistic banter just kept on rolling out.

I was helping Charity with the dishes when I brought up the rest of my evening plans.

"How about you and I get out of here?" I asked. "I figure we can go back to my place, lounge in the backyard, maybe a fire and a glass of wine... what do you say?" Charity stopped, drying her hands and wrapped her arms around my neck. My hands found her waist and we simply stood together, soaking in each other's presence for the time being.

"I thought you'd never ask," she said rolling her eyes at a couple of the guys getting rowdy out on the back patio. Her fingers slipped down to my chest, the tips caressing my name flash. She smiled and said, "I like this," and I kissed her.

"I'm glad on both counts; I'll be right back," I spun her back to the sink and I kissed the back of her shoulder, heading off to find Faith.

"Hey," I said and she looked up, shading her eyes in the sunset. "Do you have a spare set of riding gear here at the house that Charity can borrow for tomorrow?" I asked.

"Might be a little bit tight on her, but yeah," she answered.

"Can you grab it for me? We're going to head on over to my place."

Faith smiled and nodded and got up from Marlin's lap, she went upstairs, still wraithlike, moving through the crowd out here and up the stairs as unobtrusive as possible. The girl, for as beautiful as she was, did invisible well. It was a damn shame how she'd acquired the skills.

"You gonna ask her?" Marlin asked me.

"Gonna try," I affirmed.

"I think it's a good move. You two are made for each other."

"You think so?" I asked.

"I know so, brother, I know so."

I smiled and we knocked fists, Faith came back downstairs with a bundle of leather, and I took it from her, "Thanks, Babes."

"You're welcome."

I slipped around the house and stashed the bundle in my saddlebags, then went and found Charity. She was up in her room, packing an overnight bag.

"Ready to go?" I asked.

"Almost," she smiled and sighed, a happy sound.

"What was that for?"

"Honestly? I feel like I get zero privacy around here, it'll be nice having it be just you and me tonight."

I smiled, "Yeah it will," I agreed.

We rode to my place, and I have to say every time she got on the bike in just denim, I got nervous, hence why I'd asked Faith for some tougher leather for the long ride the next day. *Dress for the slide, not for the ride,* played out in my head for like the thousandth time as I pulled us into the garage when we got to the house. I breathed a sigh of relief when Charity got off the bike, whole and in one piece. I shut it down and heeled down the kickstand. I needed to get her into her own gear so I could stop worrying and enjoy the ride more.

I told her, "Go ahead and stash your bag in the bedroom, I'll get the fire going out back. There's a couple bottles of wine in the fridge, pick which one you'd like and meet me out there?"

"Absolutely," she said and we went into the house. She hesitated outside the bathroom door, but didn't open it, I smiled to myself secretly. She was going to have to eventually. I had the lid off the back of the toilet in the half bath off my bedroom, in a bid to make it look like it was out of order.

She slipped into the bedroom, and that's where we parted ways. I headed straight out back to the fire pit, which sat in the grass at the foot of the two lounge chairs. I picked up some wood from the stack along the house by the back slider and set to work, glancing back and watching Charity move through the kitchen.

This was going to be nice.

CHAPTER 45
Charity

I slipped into Dom's room as he had suggested to set my bag down and the first thing I saw was the pile of photos and mementos sitting on top of the contents of his wastebasket. It made my heart hurt a little and I quickly salvaged the pictures and EKG readout strips, tucking them into one of the end pockets of my gym bag. I felt like I was sparing him from a horrible mistake. That he might have been hurting when he'd tossed these things, but some day there would be regret. This way, he could be rid of them, but when the day came that he regretted throwing these things out, I would have them for him.

I tucked my bag on the floor on my side of the bed and slipped out into the kitchen, giving the bathroom door a wider than necessary berth. I'd use it eventually, but figured it would be *after* a glass or three of wine to loosen up. I found two bottles, a white and a red, chilling in his refrigerator. I selected the white and after some cursory hunting in the cabinets and drawers, came up with a couple of glasses and a cork screw.

"Need a hand?" he asked, coming through the back slider. I smiled and nodded. He took the bottle of wine and the corkscrew from me, and got it open. I poured us a couple of generous glasses and followed him out into the twilight.

We settled into our respective seats and set our glasses on the little table between the wooden lounge chairs. He'd brought the bottle out and I sighed with utter contentment.

"What is that?" I asked, over the crackle of fire and the emerging sounds of frogs and insects.

"What is what?" he asked.

"Can't you see it?"

"See what?" he asked laughing, looking around.

"The little sparkles in the air," I said.

"Are you serious?" he asked.

"Of course I'm serious! What are they?"

"Haven't you ever seen lightning bugs before?"

"What, like fireflies?"

"Yeah."

I sat back in my chair, and my hand naturally drifted to find his between our seats, "No," I said, "I'm a California girl; they aren't that far west and the university I went to was too far north. I've never seen them before."

"Well, now you have," he said and brought the back of my hand to his lips, planting a soft kiss against my knuckles.

We sipped wine, and alternately watched the fire and fireflies, listening to the night come alive. It was beautiful, and soothing, and I wouldn't trade these moments for the world, but eventually the wine worked its magic and I had to go break the proverbial seal. *Damn alcohol and its diuretic effects*, I thought with a sigh.

"Bathroom," I murmured and hauled myself to my feet.

"Toilet's broken in the one in my room; sorry, Baby," he murmured back. I nodded and slipped back into the house. I went to the bathroom, steeled myself and opened the door, flipping on the light and gasped.

It was completely different. The walls were now a light grey with light blue undertones, like a mist settled on a lake on a rainy day. The floor was slate tile rather than the cheap linoleum it used to be. The vanity had a granite sink and an old fashioned fixture. Even the lights above the oval, silver framed, antique looking mirror bespoke a classic era. The delicate, frosted glass of the shades casting a muted glow into the room.

He'd bought lighter gray bath mats and the shower curtain was beautiful too. A magnolia tree depicted on the light gray cloth, the trunk a darker gray with white and pink blossoms. A white little bird perched in the branches.

I heard the scrape of Dom's boot on the hard wood of the hall and turned to look at him, tears in my eyes.

"You did this for me?" I asked.

He took me into his arms and nodded carefully, "I want you to feel comfortable here, I want you to feel safe," he uttered.

"So you tear out your *entire* bathroom and redo it, rather than just getting a new shower curtain and maybe some new rugs?" I asked, the first tears from the overwhelming, just *love* and gratitude began to fall.

"Does it make you happy?" he asked.

"Oh my *god*, you have no idea!" I wrapped my arms around his neck, and buried my face in his chest and felt so incredibly *guilty* about going behind his back with the Watch Commander.

"Shh, hey, it's okay, Baby," he said laughing a little.

"No, it's not!" I cried. "I've done something incredibly stupid and I feel so bad about it but you have to understand, *you are so wasted* painting houses! Just promise when I tell you, that you won't be mad at me."

"Charity, Baby, what's wrong? What did you do?"

I spilled it. The whole thing, and the look on his face was surprised, but he gave absolutely nothing else away.

"Please say something," I begged and his face broke into a wide grin.

"Go to the bathroom and come back outside, we'll talk about it." He smoothed his thumbs through the wetness on my face and the smile on his was beatific. "I promise, I'm not mad."

"Okay," I said, apprehensive.

"Go to the bathroom, Charity, and meet me back outside," he said and I nodded.

I used the brand new, beautiful restroom. Even the *towel* bars were ornamental, a decorative brushed steel with old fashioned end caps. The towels that hung on them gray, white and pink, matching the shower curtain. He really had thought of everything.

I quickly washed up, and splashed some cold water on my face in hopes of diminishing the blotchiness. I ugly cried any time I cried, which is why I didn't make a habit of doing it often.

I went back outside and retook my seat. Dom looked over at me and handed me my wine. I took a fortifying sip and set the glass back down and he took my hand in his.

"Better?" he asked, and I nodded. He looked thoughtful for a second and said, "You're right. I'm not meant to paint houses, I'm meant to be out there helping people and I know your heart's in the right place, Baby, because you're just like me in that regard."

I nodded again, sensing he wasn't done speaking, and I was right. He drew a deep breath, let it out slowly and said, "I want to ask you something, and you can say 'no,' or 'not right now' but..." he pulled a shopping bag up from the other side of his chair and held it out to me. I took it and looked inside.

"No, way!" I said stunned. He smiled and hung his head, and I pulled the leather vest out of the bag. "Are you sure?" I asked quietly, "I mean, are you *really* sure?"

"Babe, you're taking care of me, as much as I'm trying to take care of you... and yeah, I'm sure. I want this, but only if *you* want it, and if what you're saying is true and Figaro is offering the top of the pay scale for both of us, then yeah. I'm in, let's do it."

I stood up, and crossed in front of the fire, straddling his lap in his chair, kissing him fiercely, the shopping bag getting crushed between us. He put his arms around me and held me tight.

When we finally came up for air he said, "Figaro is a fucking budget Nazi, if he's hurting bad enough to offer the top of the pay scale right off the bat, then we need to get our boots on the ground and do some good; he just doesn't do that."

"I don't care about him right now, I care about you and me and *us*," I told him.

"God, Charity, I love you," he groaned and his mouth crashed down over the top of mine again. I kissed him back soundly, glad for the six foot privacy fence ringing in the back yard. I should have known better that he wouldn't leave us out here. Instead he stood, with me clinging to him, like I hardly weighed anything at all. He carried me into the house but we didn't make it to the bedroom. Instead, he laid me on the couch, covering my body with his.

It was a frenzy of blind groping to get our clothing off as we didn't want to stop kissing and when we finally did manage to get it far enough removed to make sex possible, neither one of us wanted to slow down long enough to make it last. Instead, we crashed together in an explosion of passion, love, and ecstasy.

I wrapped my legs around his hips and held on as he thrust into me hard and harder, that golden weight of orgasm building at a phenomenal rate until I came, crying out, and holding on as my world disappeared completely only to fade back into existence. Dom kissed me, and I kissed him, and we lay crammed on the couch which was too small to accommodate us both, panting and breathless, but *complete*.

* * *

"You nervous?" I asked, five days later.

Dom's fingers tapped out some unknown pattern on his jeans clad knee, belying his answer of "No, I'm cool."

I smiled to myself and pulled us off the interstate, the sun shining down, and the world golden and new and full of such promise. We'd gone for an extended ride with the rest of the club on Saturday. On Sunday, the club had helped move my things into Dom's house. On Monday, Dom and I had spent the day in varying stages of undress, putting everything away and having sex something like two or nine times.

Yesterday, he and Gator had gone to paint the exterior of a house and today, now, we were headed back to the warehouse full of ambulances to make good on my promise to Watch Commander Figaro and to see if he would make good on *his*.

When we pulled up in front of the building, Figaro was outside smoking a cigarette, standing with another medic whose face split into a wide grin. Figaro said, "Well, I'll be damned," and the other medic started laughing and clapping. I shut off the Jeep and Dom and I got out.

"She really talk you into coming back, boy?" Figaro asked.

"She did indeed," Dom said and went to him, holding out a hand. They shook, heartily and Figaro looked at me. I raised an eyebrow.

"Okay, Princess. You got me; I didn't think you could do it."

"Never, ever, doubt a Virtue," I told him, "We'll surprise you every time."

"Virtue?" he asked.

"There are three of them, Sir. Charity is the youngest, Hope's the oldest and you have Faith in the middle."

"That right? They medically trained too?"

"Hope's a defense contractor, Faith's between jobs. I'm the only medically trained one of the bunch, sorry."

"Well, come on in, let's get some of this paperwork filled out and talk salary."

Dom and I traded a look and I raised my eyebrows, "Don't believe there's anything *to* talk about salary wise. You said 'top of the pay scale' and that's exactly what we mean to collect." I said, following him to the office.

"Ballsy, ain't she?" Figaro asked Dom and Dom laughed.

"You have no idea, and you should meet Hope."

"Eh, I think I can do without, and she's right. You know me, Shep, I stick to my word."

"That you do, Sir. That you do."

"You want anything else?" Figaro asked and I smiled with the devil's own grin...

"Actually, there is *one* thing..." And *that* is how Dom and I ended up in the back of one of the ambulances, giggling and trying not to grope each other as we took each other's EKG readings and printed them out. I had something specific in mind for his, and an offer to make him when it came to Corrine's and Katy's but that was for another day. For right now, I just needed to get the print outs.

"*Why* do you want to do this?" he asked me, and kissed me gently.

"Because reasons!" I said playfully.

"Because reasons... that is *so* helpful, Baby. Really, no seriously... don't quit your day job."

"Hey, thanks to me we both *have* day jobs," I said and tore off the strip of his readout writing 'Galahad' in the corner.

"This is true," he said, clipping the leads to the stickers covering my torso.

I wriggled and he laughed, "Will you hold still?" he demanded.

"I can't! It tickles," I said and we both dissolved into a fit of happy laughter.

"You know, I can't thank you enough," he said and he was so very serious it gave me pause.

"For what?"

"For bringing my smile back, and for breathing life back into me."

"It was there all along, you just needed a little bit more of a guide wire out of the dark."

"Yeah, and that lifeline was *you*, silly girl, and when I get us home, I'm going to have to thank you proper, over," he kissed me, "And over," he kissed me again, "And over again."

BOOM! BOOM! BOOM! BOOM! BOOM!

I jumped and let out a shriek, and both Dom and I dissolved into fits and peals of laughter.

Figaro called out, "All right you two! That's enough shenanigans for one day, get on out of there, it's time for this bus to get out on the street."

"Sir, yes, sir!" I called out and Dom tore my EKG readout strip off the machine.

He jumped down out of the back of the ambulance first and lifted me down after him. Figaro chuckled.

"We'll be seein' you day after next; you're on the night watch."

"That'll do for now," Dom said, "But eventually, I'd like to get us on a day shift."

"Noted," Figaro said, "Now get on out of here."

We left, and I drove us home…

EPILOGUE
Galahad

The first week of the night watch was rough on *both* of us. Figaro had bent the rules and let us ride together, with me as Charity's training officer. She'd had the creds to do it with her nursing degree, but she still needed to pass the certs; which she did, the day before work, with flying fucking colors. My girl was smart as hell.

We'd just gotten our first paychecks and were a couple of weeks into the job and happy when she stopped me in the hall coming out of the bathroom with a hand on my chest.

"What I do?" I asked.

"It's not what you did; it's what I'm going to do. I have a rule; when you first start a new job, you have to buy something for yourself with part of your first paycheck."

"I'm listening," I said.

"I want a tattoo and I want you to take me to the best shop you know around here," she said.

"That'd be 'No Regrets' on the boulevard," I said without missing a beat, "That's where all the guys get their ink done, but what are you going to get and where?" I asked.

She pulled out my EKG strip and held it up, "I'm getting your heartbeat, and I'm getting it right here," she said, drawing a line with her finger from wrist to elbow along the outside edge of her left arm.

I blinked, "You serious?"

She smiled impishly, "As a heart attack, Baby."

I thought about it, "Then I want to get yours done, too."

"I actually had a better idea," she said softly, and went and got into the bottom drawer of the dresser. I stood in the doorway to our room and watched her extract a book.

"I saved these for you," she said, "And I thought you might want to get Katy and Corrine's around your forearm, like this..." she pulled both of their EKG strips out and lined them up, bottom to bottom, wrapping them around my forearm above my wrist. I did some quick mental calculation and nodded.

"I actually really like this idea, with some adjustments," I said.

"Yeah?"

"Yeah," let's go.

We rode into town and down to *No Regrets* and as soon as I walked through the door we were greeted by Alex, the shop's owner.

"Howdy folks, what can I do for you?" he asked.

Charity bounced to the counter excitedly and showed Alex what she wanted done. Alex talked with her and asked, "What if I ended the line with a little heart, like yeah?" he said, tracing my EKG line onto a piece of tracing paper and embellishing a tiny little heart at the end. "Fill it in red, you know, add a tiny splash of color?"

"I really like that!" Charity agreed, "Dom, what do you think?" she asked.

"I think, are you really sure you want to do this?"

"Absolutely!" She nodded emphatically.

"Then I think it'll be great, Baby."

"Shouldn't take me longer than ten minutes, let's say forty bucks? Most of that is the cost of materials," he said and Charity nodded.

"Sounds good," she said.

"Alright then, fill these out, and let me get a copy of your ID."

She handed over her license and Alex turned to me, "What about you, bro?"

I detailed what I wanted and he nodded along, "Pink and purple, huh?" he asked.

"Lavender, but yeah, on the right here, and where the lines flatten out I want 'Katy' on the pink line, with the dates..." Charity kept looking at me, and I smiled, Alex nodding and drawing out what I asked.

"And you want this on the left arm, like hers?" he asked.

"No, I want it on the right, on my left arm," I dug out Charity's EKG readout from my wallet, "This one and I want 'Charity-Forever.'" She stilled and watched me, and Alex asked me what color I wanted that line to be. I answered, "Blue, like my lady's eyes."

I pulled her into my arms and we kissed, and I sighed, a happy man. Charity. Forever. It sounded like a plan to me.

The End

ANNOUNCING THE RETURN OF
SACRED HEARTS MC

Melody Beswick thought she was bringing herself and her thirteen month old son home to his father. It was her last ditch effort to make a better life for her and her boy. One in which Noah had a father to look up to and guide him. While she knew Grinder wasn't perfect, she believed in him, and love always found a way, right?

Melody never thought her dreams for herself and her son could twist into such nightmares, and that it was so true, the old adage, that the road to hell is paved with good intentions. She's about to find out that another adage is true, that *sometimes it's better the devil you know* when instead of finding Grinder, it's his cold and critical brother Archer at the end of her long drive that she must contend with.

With no other options, and no place else to go, Melody is about to make a deal with *this* devil that she can't refuse. Who knew it could, quite possibly, be the best decision she's ever made?

THE SACRED BROTHERHOOD #1:
BROTHER TO BROTHER

OTHER BOOKS BY A.J. DOWNEY

THE SACRED HEARTS MC

1. Shattered & Scarred
2. Broken & Burned
3. Cracked & Crushed
3.5. Masked & Miserable (a novella)
4. Tattered & Torn
5. Fractured & Formidable
6. Damaged & Dangerous

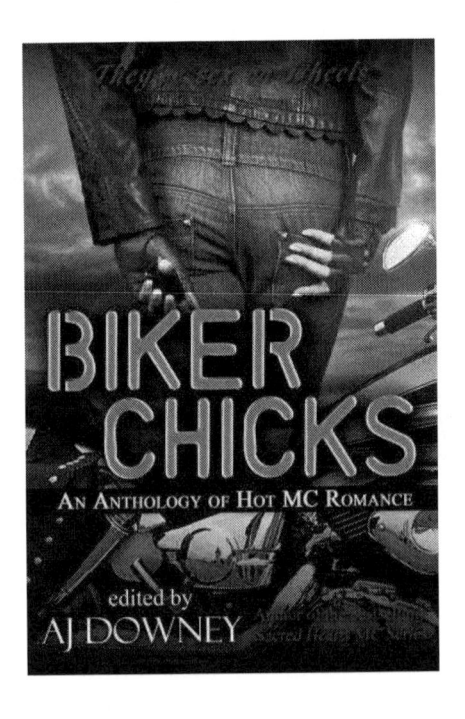

Paranormal Romance
I Am The Alpha (with Ryan Kells)
Omega's Run (with Ryan Kells)

About the Author

A.J. Downey is the internationally bestselling author of The Sacred Hearts Motorcycle Club romance series. She is a born and raised Seattle, WA Native. She finds inspiration from her surroundings, through the people she meets, and likely as a byproduct of way too much caffeine.

She has lived many places and done many things, though mostly through her own imagination… An avid reader all of her life, it's now her turn to try and give back a little, entertaining as she has been entertained. She lives in a small house in a small neighborhood with a larger than life fiancé and one cat.

She blogs regularly at *www.ajdowney.com*. If you want the easy button digest, as well as a bunch of exclusive content you can't get anywhere else, sign up for her mailing list right here:

http://eepurl.com/blLsyb

Made in the USA
Middletown, DE
28 January 2018